# UNSTOPPABLE MOSES

# UNSTOPPABLE MOSES

TYLER JAMES SMITH

FLATIRON
BOOKS
NEW YORK

UNSTOPPABLE MOSES. Copyright © 2018 by Tyler James Smith. All rights reserved. Printed in the United States of America. For information, address Flatiron Books, 175 Fifth Avenue, New York, N.Y. 10010.

www.flatironbooks.com

Designed by Steven Seighman

The Library of Congress Cataloging-in-Publication Data is available upon request.

ISBN 978-1-250-13854-5 (hardcover)
ISBN 978-1-250-13853-8 (ebook)

Our books may be purchased in bulk for promotional, educational, or business use. Please contact your local bookseller or the Macmillan Corporate and Premium Sales Department at 1-800-221-7945, extension 5442, or by email at MacmillanSpecialMarkets@macmillan.com.

First Edition: September 2018

10  9  8  7  6  5  4  3  2  1

*For Jim and Jane and Jesse. Always.*

UNSTOPPABLE
MOSES

# ONE: MY HATE CRIME

CHARLIE BALTIMORE MURDERED ME when we were eight years old.

We had broken into his dad's—my uncle's—home office because we'd watched *Raiders of the Lost Ark* and because his dad had recently bought a handgun. It was a walnut-handled .38 with a snub nose that his dad bought because he was nervous living so close to Chicago, and Charlie wanted to show me the *click* noise that guns make in the movies when the heroes or villains run out of bullets. I stood in the earth-toned office with a yardstick in my hand, doing the best sword moves my arms could muster, complete with the most menacing face anyone had surely ever seen. Charlie smiled and pointed what was supposed to be an empty gun at me and pulled the trigger.

The gun kicked in his hand and put a bullet[1] in the wall eight inches behind my chest, tearing a hole in my lung, nicking a ventricle of my heart, and spattering the wall behind me a deep

---

1 A Smith and Wesson Model 642 weighs fifteen ounces and has a five-shot capacity. The sound of a gunshot is loudest when you are seven feet away, eight years old, and directly in front of it.

shade of suburban tragedy. I don't remember it hurting; mostly I just remember Charlie screaming the gender-neutral scream that only an eight-year-old can make, followed by everything going dim and weightless.

The rest of the evening was fuzzy. I remember a lot of jostling: my brain being jostled as my Aunt Mar put my head on a pillow on her lap while we waited for the ambulance, muttering, "Ah Jesus. Ah Christ Jesus, just breathe, Moses"; jostling as Charlie buried his sobbing face into his mother's arm, holding my sleeve; jostling as a large Ambu bag was fitted over my face before two very big men wheeled me out of the house.

The ambulance smelled like electronics and plastic and rubbing alcohol.

At some point, between snapshots of consciousness, we got to the hospital where the jostling stopped because gunshot wounds are nasty business, and for three minutes Charlie Baltimore was a murderer.

I know what happened because I've heard the story a hundred times:

*They lost you for those three minutes until they found you again. It was bleak.*

*Grim. Darkest—pardon the language—but the darkest fucking hours of my life.*

*You were lying there, and then the EKG started monotoning. At least that's what the doctor says.*

*We were hysterical. We didn't even know about the flatline until after.*

*Both just sobbing in the hall.*

*No, that's only something they do in the movies—they only use shock pads to fix a heart that isn't beating right.*

*I just—I'd rather just skip to the part where—*

*They were about to call it when you came back.*

*You sucked this great big gulp of air in.*

*Tension pneumothorax. Had to put the chest tube between the lung and the chest wall.*

*It was a mess. The bullet broke apart.*

*Then the machine—right, the EKG—started beeping again.*

Not that I remember any of that, obviously. I just remember the jostling and then all of a sudden being very thirsty because it had become three days later. The doctors had brought me around and I was lying in a bed that was much too big for me with tubes running out of my arms and my parents were sitting on the edge of the hospital mattress.

Sometime before I woke up, my parents had put a huge Superman shirt on me, like it was something I'd grow into—since death had apparently lost its sway over me.

I don't know if I dreamt it, and I never asked, but I seem to remember my mom twirling my hair through her fingers before I woke up. She was sitting with me, running her hand through my hair, and I remember starting to hear her words midway through her sentence.

". . . thought that all the beams that held me up inside were going to freeze and fall apart if you didn't wake up, sweetie."

I blinked and they were all standing around my bed.

My father looked like someone who'd been told that his son had been shot in the chest and had spent the whole night picking out which clothes to bury his kid in. My mother looked more like a person who'd come back from the dead than I probably did—like she kept disappearing, if only just inside herself and only until she snapped back to the raw and focused world.

They were holding hands, which was something I hadn't seen them do since Dad had moved out the year before.

When Charlie came to visit the next day, he brought me his Nintendo DS to christen this new, post-trauma version of us. It was the first time I saw the unstoppable look in his eyes. There had been lessons on both sides of that barrel: one that said, "You can put a bullet through my heart and I will rise again," and one that said, "I can pull the trigger and it will not keep you down."

Like so many evenings for high school juniors that begin with the perfect storm of boredom, teenage hormones, and a wild abundance of free time, this one began with the disposal of a body. We barreled down the empty main drag in town, spiraling up tails of December snow in our wake.

"Shit Moses, *go!* Go go go go go!"

"Stop yelling!" I yelled. "Freddie's fucking dying on us. He's gonna fucking die," I said more to myself than to Charlie.

"Don't you fucking doubt Freddie!"

I risked a look over my shoulder to see if we were being followed. There was a very good chance that we'd been spotted and the police had since been called. But in the frantic sideways glance over my shoulder, I didn't yet see flashing sirens; I saw the large, human-shaped pile under the blanket in the back seat that was banging back and forth with each unsteady turn we made.

"Do you think Harper saw us?" I asked Charlie, my eyes beaming down each side street that we passed. We were headed for the unincorporated patch of woods at the edge of town— the closest thing to no-man's-land that stood between our sleepy little town of Guthrie and the much more awake Greenfield, which paled wildly next to Chicago, just seven miles north of *that* town line. I turned down the radio so that I could focus better.

"He's a *priest,* of course he did! Guy has the eyes of God!"

"Minister," I said, still half-looking at the rearview mirror.

*"What?"*

"Harper's a minister, not a priest—" I cut the wheel left, hard, sending the car fishtailing around the corner, bouncing the wheels off the snowdrift and making the ABS whir. "He's a minister of a Protestant church."

Charlie grunted and twisted in his seat, checking behind us. A hand fell out from beneath the blanket in the back, pointing toward our destination: Pinz!, the bowling alley that was only a mile away, *still* only a mile away.

*"Regardless* of his official title—"

Then, red and blue flashing lights erupted into the dark night behind us, maybe two blocks away, because of course we *had* been seen. "Cops," Charlie said over the seat. "Floor this motherfucker! Freddie, don't you even *think* about dying on us."

But Freddie didn't answer.

Even though the heater didn't work, I felt my body going hot and my ears turning red, matching the red and blue lights flash-flooding into the car. Flooring it is exactly what I did not do. The squad car was blazing up behind us and I slowed down enough to make the sharp right turn on the dirt road that would wind us through unincorporated land, right to the bowling alley. We went skidding onto the icy road as the cops blazed past us, the sirens changing quality as the squad car spun uncontrollably.

"Holy shit," I said to the rearview mirror.

"Holy shit is right," Charlie agreed. Then, hammering the dash with his open palm, "Come on Miracle Boy, go! Go go go!" He was smiling while he said it, while the small-town cops were pirouetting on the ice behind us, because we thought that we were juggernauts.

When you've come back from the dead, it's hard to imagine any other rules applying to you. Even when the police have been called, even when the minister witnesses the first of your numerous crimes that night . . . when your cousin calls you Miracle Boy, you remember how unstoppable you are. I flipped the headlights off so we'd blend into the night as we wound down the dirt road before being dumped into the lefts and rights of the moonlit industrial street behind Pinz!. We peeled into the lot, lit by one streetlamp whose bulb cast a circle of yellow light filled with dreamy snowflakes.

The streetlamp flickered out as we careened past it, sliding to a stop near the dumpsters in the back. The sirens were bouncing off the buildings just a few blocks away, the police still looking for us as we threw the doors open and ejected ourselves from the car.

"Grab the rope!" I said as I clicked the trunk button for him and flung open the back door.

He didn't need to be told; he was already headed for it. We were running on two hundred percent—an already well-oiled machine, power-injected with a cocktail of adrenaline and a fresh batch of Brain Evulsion. The sheet had loosed itself from the body in the back and its lifeless eyes found mine in the harsh light. I tucked the white sheet under and around it while Charlie pulled the neatly coiled rope through a hole in an old crate in the trunk marked Live Snakes.

The body was stiff but didn't weigh enough to stop us. I pulled it onto the lot and Charlie looped the rope under its arms. Its ankles in hand, we headed for the rusty ladder leading to the roof of the bowling alley.

Just like all of the other—albeit cop-less—nights, this was going to be the hard part.

Charlie jumped onto the ladder, trailing the rope with one gloved hand and climbing with the other. He popped his head over the edge of the roof, said, "Ready. Go!" and then started hoisting the rope, pulling the shape under the sheets toward the roof. From below, I supported the weight as best I could, balancing the cold, stiff feet on my shoulders until finally, grunting and cursing, we made it to the roof.

The sirens had gone silent and dark.

"We're doing this, man. We're doing it!" Charlie said, stage whispering.

We stood the body up on the stage made of wooden pallets we'd lashed together. This was not the first night powered by Brain Evulsion; we'd spent the last month getting everything together, making sure it was all as perfect as we could possibly make it. The other shapes, huddled under dark sheets, sat silent in the night.

"You ready?" I asked as I secured the feet of the last body.

He didn't answer; he just smiled and ripped the sheet off like a lounge act pulling the cloth from beneath the crystal glasses full of brilliantly clear water.

We'd seen the man with the beard thousands of times. The

most famous carpenter in the world. The Wine Maker. The Fish Giver. But we'd never seen him like this.

Jesus stood before us, his plastic electric guitar slung by his side and his finger pointed at the ground. The minister, Harper, had gotten Rock 'n' Roll Jesus on special order with the hope of getting the kids excited about religion.

I aimed his arm up, pointing it toward the clouds and the city and past all of the innumerable onlookers that would drive by in the morning. Behind me, Charlie started taking the other sheets off.

He tore the bulbous low-to-the-ground sheet off of Plastic Buddha, who sat with his bass guitar comfortably in his lap. (Only Jesus had brought his own instrument. The rest we'd bought at garage sales or garbage-picked.) On drums—which were way harder to bring up a ladder than plastic religious deities—Vishnu sat with four drumsticks, poised for the best drum solo the universe had ever seen. Behind the mic, the Lou Reed cutout was on lead vocals with his hands taped to the microphone and a yarmulke rubber-banded to his head. When we couldn't easily find a figure to stand in for Muhammad, we settled on hanging an enormous Pakistani flag behind the band.

"Cops?" he called over to me, the sheets draped over his arms.

I skirted the edge of the building and, when I didn't see anything, I gave him two very enthusiastic thumbs-up. He nodded and went back to working on the cords. We ran hot with Brain Evulsion—an unholy combination of No-Snooz trucker pills, black coffee, hot sauce, and Mountain Dew—and we were unbeatable for it.

"Does it smell funny up here?" he called over his shoulder.

"What?" I didn't smell anything, and I didn't think to realize that maybe him asking a question like that was a red flag. In all of the night's torrential adrenaline, I forgot who I was dealing with; I forgot I was with Charlie Baltimore.

"You don't think it smells funn—nothing, never mind."

"It's a bowling alley, of course it smells funny. Probably the dumpsters."

"Okay, let's do it!" he said. He had managed to shuffle his cigarettes out of his pocket and was contorting around the armful of sheets to light a Winchester.

"Wait!" I said. "I almost forgot." I started patting my pockets, looking for the Glo-Paint Sakura marker I'd brought. And even though for a second I'd thought I'd forgotten it, of course I found it because we were unstoppable.

Across Buddha's big loving belly I wrote, *And the Lords said, "Let there be jams."* The words showed up green and lurid in the night, and lo, they were perfect.

I dropped to my heels, connected the orange extension cord under the pallets, and jabbed the play button down on the old paint-stained and sticker-covered radio at the foot of the stage—a cheaper and more dramatic alternative to leaving an iPhone behind. We waited in heavy and humid silence to see if it would work: if, just this once, all of the elements would work together in perfect harmony for us.

Radio static through the boom box.

Hissing nothingness from the speakers that were supposed to be playing the mix CD we'd made.

The band looked through us, their instruments ready to go, unity through rock and roll crackling beneath their sacred fingers.

Lolling siren lights scanned for us with red swooping eyes.

Nothing.

I stayed crouched in front of the boom box, willing it to sing. Praying to all the gods before me to make the damned thing work.

Nothing.

And then everything.

The opening chords to Guns 'n' Roses's "Sweet Child o' Mine" were like a holy javelin of rock and roll that exploded into the night. It was the only song we'd put on the CD: all twenty-three tracks were the very same, and they were set to repeat.

"*Yes.* Okay, go! Go go!" I shouted back to Charlie, who was waiting at the edge of the roof.

Charlie was already sliding down the icy ladder, his coat flying out behind him in a cloud of nicotine. I didn't turn into a pillar of salt when I looked back; I watched the gods of rock play under a banner of white icicle lights. They were the greatest band in the history of time and culture, equalized under the gospel of rock and roll.

And in the morning, when all of the bleary-eyed people found the ladder locked, they would have to see it. They'd have to see all of their gods that they couldn't agree on, all playing the same song, and they'd have to stop and stand still and listen.

An act of love and unity as absurd as hate and destruction.

Something big and bawdy and beautiful.

Something only a superhero could pull off.

I shot down the ladder and closed the gate around it, latching it shut with a padlock that we'd brought ourselves, as Charlie dove into the driver's seat. There were only so many roads for the cops to check before they found their way to Pinz! and the music was loud enough that we wouldn't have been able to hear their sirens if they were right on top of us. I jumped into the car next to him.

"Hey," he said, turning to me, pulling the world to a stop. Even in the dark of the car—a darkness made more complete by the overcast winter night and the shadow of the old bowling alley—I could see his face. He was staring straight out over the steering wheel, his eyebrows pinched together, the muscle in the side of his jaw clenched tight. He pulled his hat off and scruffled his short brown hair.

"What?"

"It's two days until Christmas."

After a beat, I said, "Merry Christmas."

He looked at me, then broke into a big, stupid smile. I held my hand over, palm up, and he slapped it just as he slammed his foot down on the gas. The wheels spun before catching the pavement and launching us forward; we made it twenty feet before the engine made a dropping, thrashing noise and we rolled to a clunky stop.

"Freddie!" Charlie said, banging his fists down at ten and two, before attempting to seduce the engine into working again, saying, "Come on baby," and trying to get it to turn over. Freddie, the 2002 Mercury, was dead. Smoke bled from beneath the hood and drifted toward the sky.

I splayed my hands out in front of me and closed my eyes, running all of the options we had against all of the options we didn't. Across the expanse of snow-covered cars and lamps, I saw a single headlight sweep into the lot; it was attached to a cruiser that looked freshly beat up. I knew the cop had seen our car when the red and blue lights came to life and the vehicle started rushing toward us.

My guts turned into a tight, heavy fist. "Charlie. Charlie! Shut up, man, I'm trying to think." I squeezed my eyes shut harder, focusing on an imaginary dot in my mind; a nexus, a laser point, the middle of a whirlpool. "Okay. I got it: We panic."

"Way ahead of you, man."

"No, no, we act like we just got here and found the car because someone stole—just get out and look panicked and out of breath."

He gave me a dull "That's it?" look before dropping his shoulders and screaming as he whipped the door open, yelling about goddamned thieves.

"Not hysterical! Do *not* act hysterical!" I said, grunting, as I climbed out of the car.

We stood next to Freddie while "Sweet Child o' Mine" started up again. The divine band was framed by two enormous, unlit bowling pins. From the parking lot, the music sounded crisper than it had from the roof as it expanded above us.

The encroaching red and blue strobe lights from the cop car turned our shadows into giant black cutouts against the doors and windows of Pinz! Our negatives flashed, growing and framed by red, then blue, then red, as the cops came careening to a stop in front of us, and I swear that for just a second, in the epileptic chaos of the lights, it looked like the music and lights lined up. For one perfect moment the gods and the world and us played together, all lit by the same uneven glow, and when the music swelled and the lights went brighter, we were looking at a miracle.

When the music started warping and the lights we'd strung up started popping, sending sparks raining down on the flag and the pallets, I realized we weren't only being busted for stealing Rock 'n' Roll Jesus—we were also looking at arson charges. The green flag had ignited and dropped, draping around the band. It brought Buddha and Vishnu together in a warm embrace before the flaming polyester melted through and through, igniting the deities and the pallets we'd bolted them to.

The music around us became police sirens and wheels grinding deep into snow.

Somewhere Charlie was yelling, and in that somewhere, my heart was pumping hot pulses of clean and utterly genuine panic in my throat and ears.

And I remembered Charlie asking about the smell.

And I remembered who was standing next to me.

And I thought, *No fucking way did you just get me to burn a building down.*

The flames licked up from the wooden base, growing with each violent gust of December wind. The heat circled Jesus and Lou Reed, intense enough to light the end of Jesus's guitar and droop his pointing arm until it addressed me and me alone. Lou Reed toppled, sending tendrils of smoke rising past the yarmulke that was singeing and lighting.

I felt my gloves reach up and grab two fistfuls of hat. I clicked over to autopilot as the officer spilled out of the squad car and demanded we turn around and get on our knees. Hands already on my head, a gun pointed at me for the second time in my life, and my body trembling from the Brain Evulsion, I turned. And out of the corner of my eye, I saw that Charlie was smiling.

Even after all the shit Charlie had pulled over the years— even after the many, many times I'd seen that smile—my first thought was that he was smiling because he knew, somehow, that it was going to be okay. But as we dropped to our knees, I realized what that smile really meant.

"You fucking didn't," I said.

"I did," he said, awestruck, like even he didn't believe what he was seeing.

He'd finally pulled off the special kind of stupid and reckless stunt he'd always talked about.

In front of us, I could hear the cop barking into his radio that he needed emergency response vehicles. He cut himself off and yelled at us to get on our stomachs. I watched, twisted around with my hands still on my head, as Jesus sank into the flames. Jesus sank how you'd imagine a ship sinking: straight down, permanent, and hugely silent, vertically into the pool of nothingness beneath. In the paradoxically sped-up and sloweddown moment, he eventually melted into an amorphous, bubbling pool of smoldering plastic where all the gods we had thought to steal swirled together into one holy and indefinable mass.

My blood was molten lead and every movement was a heavy gesture through air that had gone thick. The heat from the building was starting to find us; it caressed our faces and made our kneeling shadows shudder in fiery prayer.

Sometimes, when you've just inadvertently lit a bowling alley, a handful of gods, and a boom box on fire just a couple days before Christmas, and a police officer is pointing a loaded weapon at you just like your cousin did nearly ten years prior, you can't help laughing.

You laugh because you're a miracle and bullets don't slow you down and because the more you try not to laugh the more you can't stop. You laugh especially hard because you fell for your cousin's shit the way you've always fallen for it. You laugh because you realize you're laughing when you should be crying or screaming.

I heard my voice stumbling over words, trying to articulate to the officer that it wasn't what it looked like, and felt my legs slowly insisting themselves to a standing position since standing had to look less criminal than lying prone in a bowling alley parking lot. The officer pointed his service weapon at me and demanded I get down.

If the fire had been part of Charlie's stupid, reckless plan, then what the cop did next was something my cousin had failed to imagine: the officer took a step forward, tensed his shoulders, and readjusted his grip on his gun, moving like he was a half second away from pulling the trigger.

And then Charlie's voice, which, even through the roaring flames, wasn't filled with the absurd laughter I'd expected. It was the tone of someone who'd expected to watch the fire on the news, not in person, and not with a gun trained on us. It wasn't the tone of someone who expected a gun pointed at his best friend and cousin.

The tone was rattled. The kind of tone I hadn't heard from him since we were eight and I was all but dead.

Charlie's voice cut through the heat as he stood up too, taking a step toward the officer with his own hands up. I didn't hear what he was saying because the officer was faster and louder than him: Guns 'n' Roses warbled and drowned in the fire as peaceful, loving Buddha expanded and burst and the startled officer shot Charlie in the head.

# TWO: MIDWEST TRAJECTORY

"WHY?" THE KID ASKED AGAIN. He wasn't older than eleven or younger than eight, since the kids on the bus were exclusively between third and fifth grade.

"Because I have to be," I said back to him mechanically while I stared, stagnant and cramped, out the window.

"Why?"

"Because the judge said so."

"Why?" he said, musically and shittily.

"Because she said I was lucky enough to be a minor and she determined I wasn't dangerous and because if I don't prove I'm a responsible member of society, then my scholarships will be shot down and I'll end up at GCC and working in Guthrie for the rest of my life," I monotoned to the window, past my thin reflection, using the exact words the judge had used. I decided not to mention the irony of punishing me for acting dangerously by putting me around a bunch of innocent children.

The other little kids on the bus were mostly talking with each other, sleeping, or being aggressively ignored by the teenage Camp Buddies. Except for the kid sitting next to me. Behind us, there were two more busloads of kids and Buddies[2]—a bus-load for one of each of the counties making up the tri-county combo: Lake, Cook, and DuPage County.

"Why?"

"Because if there's a school that can reject you based on a criminal record, it's Duke. And Duke is a place you want to go."

"Why?"

"Because they're picky. Like really, really picky. And because now I'm not necessarily someone they would still want," I said, not explaining that I didn't care whether or not it was Duke anymore, which is where I'd always thought I'd go, as long as it was Anywhere but Here. That I would take The University of There in an instant, even if it meant pulling myself apart to get it. That it could be a crap college in some small town, in another state, hours from a city I'd never heard of, so long as it wasn't in Guthrie.

"Wh—"

"Because my cousin and I made some bad decisions."

"Why—"

"Because they didn't seem like bad decisions at the time."

"Why?" the kid asked, steeling himself. He had gotten tired of the Why game thirty miles back, and had stopped until we'd pulled over at a travel center, where he'd bought a Red Bull from a vending machine. At some point it had stopped being a game to him and had transformed into a battle of wits.

It was a battle I wasn't going to lose.

---

2 They insisted that we refer to ourselves as "Buddies" instead of "Counselors" since "Buddy/ies" felt more approachable. Like we were supposed to be more to the kids than just authority figures. The vast majority of Buddies were not there on any sort of court mandate.

"Because we were over-caffeinated and spent too much time watching adventure movies and because we didn't plan for things going balls-up." In the window, I saw his face crinkle up a little, like he wasn't used to people saying things like "balls-up" around his baby ears. "Just balls to the fucking sky," I said, watching him to see if he'd go running to the front of the bus to tell the hulking driver about me.

The driver looked like an aging bodybuilder who'd fallen on hard times and had to supplement his allowance for bronzing creams and Heavy Things to Pick Up by driving children to and from museums and camps. Exactly the kind of person who had enough misplaced frustration to pick me up and bend me in half over his head when Why Kid inevitably went screaming up the bus aisle to tell on me.

And who knows, maybe getting theatrically murdered by an angry bus driver was a fitting end for someone who was supposed to be smart and supposed to be a superhero but who wasn't smart enough or heroic enough to stop his cousin from getting shot.

When Why Kid didn't, I yawned and stretched the hand that was supporting my head against the window.

"Why?" he said, recovering.

"Because we were unstoppable," I said. Outside, the Midwest ticked by like a scale model on treads: barn, barn, field, field, field, field, corn, cows, barn, billboard about God, field, field, field. We'd driven out of Illinois, skirted the top of Indiana's industrial corridor, and hooked up into Michigan, due north. "We had plans."

"Why?"

"What."

"What?"

"Exactly."

"*What?*"

"You meant 'what.' "

"Why?" Why Kid asked, visibly becoming frustrated and tangled up in his own stupid game.

"Because *why* isn't the question you really want to ask me. '*Why* did you have plans?' is probably more nihilistic than you meant it to be," I said against my palm.

"*What,* then?" he asked, exasperated.

I looked over at him. "What were our plans?"

"Yeah, *what plans?*" he said, exactly like someone not old enough to add, "Jesus fucking Christ, just answer the question."

I almost said, "We wanted to give our miserable little town a jolt, something new for them to care about besides politics. To get them to look up from their fucking phones. We just happened to have different ideas about how to do it. I wanted a town full of people to see all of our gods playing Guns 'n' Roses together. We'd bring people together through something absurd and beautiful. Charlie wanted everything to burn though, and I guess it all kind of backfired," and when I'd pause to let him think I was done and when he took a breath to ask me "Why?" again, I'd say, "Because it turns out you can't ever really know someone. Even your best fucking friend, who is also your cousin. We just wanted to do something big, and funny, and ridiculous; instead, a bunch of bad shit happened, and I've spent almost a year wondering how fucking dead I have to be, given the fact that I haven't cried even one time."

I almost said, "You're not talking to a bad person, kid, you're talking to a goddamn robot."

Instead I said, "It involved a bowling alley and Guns 'n' Roses."

Twenty minutes later he'd given up or forgotten about asking "Why?" and had moved onto the real, burning questions locked away in his fourth-grader brain. "But why aren't there seat belts? My mom says I always have to wear my seat belt," the kid said to me.

Talking to him wasn't half as bad as having to listen to the Buddy sitting a few rows behind us. He'd loudly introduced himself as Jeffrey to the kids sitting around him before narrating every Podunk landmark we passed. This kid was ten times better than hearing another word from the sentient travel magazine behind us. The worst part was that he didn't need to be everything that he was so loudly being. There were plenty of students and Buddies alike sleeping or talking quietly. Jeffrey was just making it known that he was the type of person whose own mother always wanted to tell him, *Goddamn, dude, just shut up for like five minutes.*

"Right, I get that. What I'm saying is that your mom is wrong." His forehead scrunched up and he looked like a person who'd gazed into the abyss and found the single most terrifying secret that the universe had to offer. "No, I mean, she's *mistaken*. About *this*. Yes, you should wear your seat belt. But it's different on a bus."

"But *why*?" he asked, more legitimately than before.

"Okay, do you actually want to know? I can give you a grown-up answer, but . . ." I raised my eyebrows at him, eyebrows that said, "It's going to be full of big words that you aren't going to understand and then you're just going to ask 'why' again but I'm not going to explain it all over just because you were dumb and didn't listen." The kid's face went deadly serious and he nodded, ready to receive whatever extremely confidential and adult information I was about to give him. "All right. Seat belts wouldn't do much of anything on a bus, so they rely on compartmental-ization. It—see? Huge words. Compartmentalization is the seats being so close together and with high backs that absorb impact. Specifically—"

"Do you ever have to pee so bad it makes you mad? Like just absolutely livid?" one of the other Camp Buddies, four or five rows up and within earshot of the bus driver, said. He was not-quite-yelling to his friends who were sitting on the other side of the aisle. They were some of the few Buddies that didn't have their Buddy shirts on. I looked down at the brightly colored Buddy Shirt that hugged me like claustrophobia and tried to imagine what kind of jokes Charlie would have made about it.

The Buddy who had to pee was wearing a shirt that said, "WWJD" with a picture of John Denver giving a thumbs-up.

The immense bus driver's eyes flicked up in the rearview mirror, just long enough to betray that he was, unfortunately, listening. The abundantly hydrated Buddy went on with his pee spiel, much to the rolling laughter of the little kid sitting in the window seat next to him. The kid had a hatchet-job haircut—like it had been done in the dark, in the kitchen, by a mother with a grudge.

"It's actually beginning to boil inside of my body, that's how mad it's making me. It's just going to come out as yellow steam. It's infur—Furinate! I'm going to *furinate* as soon as this bus slows under fifty. Like *Speed*, but with pee. *Peed*." I recognized the John Denver Buddy as the one who'd bought three Red Bulls immedi-ately before I got to talking with the Why Kid. The empty cans were a pyramid of bad decisions at his feet. He combed his dark hair out of his face with his hand, then looked over at the kid sitting next to him, making sure he was still smiling.

The bus driver was shaking his head, but not in a "Man, do

I love my job and these wacky kids" kind of way. I was going to continue explaining compartmentalization to the kid next to me, but my physics lesson couldn't compare to this.

"Toilet's in the back," the driver said to the mirror.

"*That?*" the Buddy said, pointing back without turning around. "I'm not falling for that. I'm not going into your execution tube. One press of a button and I get launched out of the bottom of the bus with my pants around my ankles."

The bus driver didn't say anything, but his bleary, jaundiced eyes told the Buddy to go endlessly fuck himself.

Pee Guy had black hair and dark skin, and was handsome in that unintentional "Yes, this is legitimately bedhead" kind of way.

"Just go pee in the thing, Faisal!" said the Girl Buddy sitting across the aisle from Pee Guy, turning and motioning toward the bathroom in the back of the bus. She was wearing an oversize Evanston Panthers Class of '18 hoodie that didn't quite manage to hide her frenzy of brown hair. When she turned and her eyes landed on mine, they lingered in a flash of recognition. She spun back around and leaned over on her knee to Faisal, who nodded for a second and slipped back into the forward and upright position. After a beat, he dramatically stretched and looked back at me. The girl slapped him in the ribs and his hands shot out in a "What?" gesture. The Buddy sleeping next to her against the window shuffled around a bit, somehow managing to tune out all of the bus noise—I could only see the back of his head from where I was sitting, but he'd slept through the last pit stop we'd made and I'd gotten a look at him. He slept like the kind of person who could fall asleep without a second thought on a bus full of wolf-children. His surprisingly crisp button-down shirt and side-parted haircut made him look Wall Street, even while sleeping.

I knew they recognized me because it had been ten months since the bowling alley, and when it turned out that the community didn't take kindly to their gods being publicly burned, we'd hit the news and the town had hit us back. The first leg of the ordeal had been heavily televised because the facts weren't all in and everyone was outraged and demanding to know why we'd done it.

I cleared my throat and tried to figure out how to best hide behind the hand I was leaning on. It was still technically possible that the camp admins would decide my best and most effective job over the next week would be doing the camp's dirty work, somewhere tucked away where nobody could see. Something that didn't involve me talking to people any more than I needed to.

But I knew it was too late. They had already seen me, picked up my scent, and they'd be the same as everyone else I'd dealt with since Charlie.

They, the good God-fearing people of Guthrie, had insisted that what we did was a hate crime, even when I'd told the police and reporters and the lawyers and the judge and my parents and anyone who would listen that we were trying to be funny, and maybe even do something good. Stupidly.

Mr. Coleman, one of two barbers in Guthrie, and someone who gives free haircuts to police officers and veterans, said, "That's what they all say. Allah, Islam, whatever."

Hollie Bridge, a girl I'd gone to school with since I was in kindergarten, started a local charity called WARMTH which raised funds for the bowling alley and stood for We ARe More Than Hate.

Stirring testimonies from prominent members of Guthrie— and, to a lesser extent, Greenfield—ranged from outrage and contempt to a terrible, rattled melancholy. That was the worst part: the slow pain. Footage that would've broken your heart and then glued it shakily back together. The news story juxtaposed our high school portraits over the burning remains of the bowling alley, to really emphasize how far we'd fallen. Then they showed the community holding vigils and praying together: solemn masses of people wearing WARMTH shirts holding hands regardless of card-carrying religion, Christian hands holding Muslim hands holding Jewish hands holding the hands of every shade of faith in between. We were an example of what happened when the privileged youth got restless.

All of the stations shared variations of the same footage. It always started with a shot of the reporter standing in front of Pinz!, the screen undercut with some tired version of the superimposed smear campaign "Local Arson, Possible Hate Crime" before the camera panned up to the half-destroyed, still-smoldering bowling alley. Depending on which network was airing the piece, it would either cut back to the anchors, looking as upset as reporters are allowed to look, or to footage taken the previous summer of a very happy barbecue that Pinz! had hosted in its parking lot.

They always rolled the "after" shot next: it was B-roll taken when the sun had finally come up and the fire had been put out. The focus of the shot was on the gods-blob. It was a cloud-shaped heap of blackened, bruise-colored plastic with bits of fabric and hardened bubbles dotting its surface. The camera always lingered on the smoking Holy Blob while the booming newscaster solemnly narrated in omniscient voice-over.

Then the public reactions.

The angriest reaction we saw, the one lined with the most

wrath and resentment, was Reverend Harper's. Harper on camera with the church behind him, which was notably lacking a Jesus with a Gibson guitar. Harper, who had seen us take his Jesus with a Gibson guitar. Harper, who was a minister and not a priest.

Most of the other religious leaders just looked confused.

Eventually it would cut to the courtroom, when I got to talk. By this point it was spring; when most of the facts had lost their mystique and most of the outright fiction had been sheared away—when the hateful dust settled and it became clear that our crime was being idiots, not bigots—we were slowly but inevitably becoming nothing more than a footnote in small-town folklore.

Living that close to Chicago, there were always bigger stories to pay attention to.

Still, some people persisted—like the lady in line at the coffee shop, who'd had the same flash of recognition in her eyes before tugging at my sleeve and saying, "Jesus still loves you, even if you hate Him."[3]

Or the kids at school who would lower their volume whenever I walked by, who would watch me like they were waiting for me to start screaming and crying and confessing that the news reports had all been right. They looked at me the way doctors look at benign tumors. Unsettling and unwelcome, but not life-threatening. Probably.

And each time they pointedly did or didn't talk to me, every

---

3 More examples: every week during the trial, someone, at some point in the middle of the night, would leave a candle burning on our front porch like a vigil for the dead or dying, while on Sunday mornings a gaggle of old women would drive by our house, slowing down like they were trying to work up the nerve to come talk to me but ultimately deciding to drive on and say a prayer.

time they made sad, lingering eye contact before looking down and shaking their heads just the slightest bit, I'd feel the cold exhaustion dig itself deeper into my bones; I'd feel my undercurrent freeze just a little bit more. But I kept moving and I kept going to coffee shops and kept on showing up for class because I was Moses the Machine; I was the one who always got back up, the one who came back.

One of the advantages of growing up in a small town and being privileged is that sometimes the judge who decides your fate happens to also have been your soccer coach from third grade, not some daytime-television asshole who doles out theatrical Old-Testament punishments for crimes of every nature. The disadvantage of living in a small town is that sometimes third-grade-soccer-coaching judges also decide that your best course of action is a second chance surrounded by a bunch of screaming children in the woods for a week.[4]

The bus's hydraulic brakes hissed as the driver pulled us off the highway past signs promising Camp Jaye'k, just three miles down the road. Ten more minutes of kids and Buddies alike staring out the windows of the huge yellow bus that relied on compartmentalization rather than seat belts to keep us safe. The three Buddies ahead of me settled back into their own worlds. Girl Buddy was trying to type something on her phone as No Longer Sleeping Buddy leaned across her lap to talk to Pee Buddy, who nodded, said something while gesturing with his hands, then started laughing.

---

4 A second chance that, the soccer-judge made very clear, would not be followed by a third. A second chance that, if I took it, meant paying back the damages to the bowling alley for the rest of my life—instead of being tried as an adult, going to jail, and paying back the damages to the bowling alley for the rest of my life.

Even this close to our destination—a time generally reserved for mild panic attacks and escape plans—the bus was a frenzy of individual ecosystems. From the Buddies in front of me talking with the hatchet-haired boy, to the Travel Show Host behind me pointing out native trees, to the clutch of angry-looking little kids in the back of the bus who were swearing loud enough for the bus driver to hear and then acting like it wasn't them, to the little girl in the aviator hat sitting next to a student wearing noise-canceling headphones, the bus was a geopolitical map of life and hormones and stories, and up until just a few minutes ago, none of them had involved me.

A quarter mile down the country road, a small shape was trundling along the center line with its spiny back turned toward us. As we closed in on it and the bus driver made it clear that he had no intention of swerving around the porcupine, the girl with the brown hair next to Faisal spoke up, pulling her hood off, as if that would make her voice more clearly heard.

"Hey— There's a—"

The front half of the bus let loose a collective squeal when the bus ran the porcupine over. Every ecosystem on the bus synced up as it banged under the front of the chassis, smacked up against the floor under my feet, and got tossed out behind the vehicle.

The curious kid next to me spun around and looked out the back window. His fingers dug into the back of the seat and he kept scraping his shoes against my leg, trying to get a better view. Behind us, the tiny broken shape lay motionless on the shoulder, upright but facedown, and it was impossible to tell if the other buses hit the broken-apart little animal.

"He hit it! Why didn't he move?" he asked, and I didn't have the heart to tell him that the bus hadn't moved because that's life: the bus does not swerve.

"Yeah, why didn't you try to move?" It was the brown-haired girl who'd recognized me; she had a voice like classic rock, like power chords. She had a voice you paid attention to.

"Didn't have room," the driver said without looking back.

"It was moving *with* the bus; you didn't have to *swerve*," she said.

The driver didn't say anything back.

"You aren't supposed to swerve if you see an animal in the road. Especially if you're driving a bus full of students," I said to the kid as my phone buzzed in my pocket. Neither the kid nor the Buddies toward the front of the bus seemed to think the driver was anything less than an asshole though. General road precautions aside, they didn't seem wrong about him either.

The kid had his face mushed against the window to try to get a look at the animal behind us when I pulled my phone out to check it. It was a text from my mother that said,

Hey SB![5] Have a great (court-ordered) time! You'll do great.
Love u lots.—Mom

---

5 Mom Shorthand for "Super Boy." Ever since I woke up after Charlie put me down, even after the bowling alley and trial and Charlie, my parents had talked to/ about me like I was their constant miracle. Like it wasn't okay for them to hurt or be fucked up about everything and the best way to show how not-fucked-up they were was to stomp through the eggshells everyone else insisted on tiptoeing around.

# THREE: A MOM AND DAD MEET THEIR SON

A WEEK AFTER CHARLIE and the bowling alley, I still can't sleep. I lie there wide awake, hoping the whole goddamned thing is a nightmare, until I fall asleep and have actual nightmares that are really just my memories. And it fucking sucks.

We're in the middle of Christmas break so I don't have to deal with seeing all of my classmates and teachers yet, but life has taken a weird turn where break kind of resembles school: I wake up early, I don't see my parents, and I go to bed earlier than normal. There's weight attached to every conversation that I have with my parents, like we all know that there's this massive, jagged canyon forming between us, and nobody knows how to address it.

Somewhere around one in the morning, I decide I want coffee in the middle of the night because I don't want to sleep and deal with dreaming and if I'm going to be awake, then I want to be *awake*. But when I go downstairs, Mom and Dad are still up.

They don't see me because the front of the couch faces away from the entrance to the living room and because our old wooden stairs are somehow almost entirely non-creaky, but I see them.

They're sitting on the couch, and he's lying sideways with his head in her lap while she stares straight ahead and absently runs her fingers through his hair.

Dad clears his throat, and his breath comes out stuttered, and I realize he's crying and Mom's been crying, and the TV isn't even on. They're not pretending. They're just sitting there together being wrecked.

I back up to the stairs, quiet, climbing up two or three steps, and fake a cough as I come back down, stepping on one of the creaky parts of the stairs, letting them hear me.

This time, when I go to cross the living room entrance, Mom is thumbing away any trace of tears under her eyes and Dad is already halfway across the other side of the room, headed for the bathroom.

"Hey, sweets," she says, trying to smile. "What are you doing up?"

Lately, I don't bother asking either one of them why they look like they've been crying.

"Can't sleep. Gonna make some coffee."

"Coffee," she says, smirking. "Why are you such an old man?" She holds her hand out as she says it, an open-palmed gesture that says, "Come here. Come sit with me."

So I do.

And I don't expect to feel so far away.

I don't expect to be so nebulously mad. I want to say, "You can cry around me. I know what happened. I was fucking there. You trying to hide it makes me feel like you're crying because you're ashamed of me. Which you probably should be." But of course I don't say anything.

And I know she senses something, because I know everything

inside of me is tensed up and moms can read that sort of thing. Then Dad flushes the toilet to uphold the illusion that he was just in there peeing and steps into the room, and he looks just as tired and frustrated as I feel.

When I sit up, ready to just go and make coffee and be by myself, I see Mom's eyes go hard and resolute. I see the moment where it clicks in her head that she's figured out how to approach the situation and how to approach me.

Dad sees it too, because he's staring at her and they're having a silent conversation that amounts to him asking her if she's sure this is what she wants to do.

Right there on the couch, my mother starts in on putting our pieces back together. "Our little firebug is up making coffee." She looks at me and there's love and thunder in her eyes. Eyes that dare the pain to even fucking try.

Dad's shoulders drop just a little, and he swallows, and he says, "You are such an old man."

And then we watch TV.

# FOUR: CAMP STOP THIS FEELING

I DECIDED TO PUT THE PHONE away without replying, and ten minutes later we pulled into Camp Jaye'k.

After we gathered our carry-ons, we clamored out of the bus and loitered around until we were told what to do. Across one of the fields, other buses had already arrived, bringing their own loads of kids and Buddies from other districts to have their own educational adventures.

The camp was every camp Charlie and I had seen in all of the movies we'd watched growing up. The buildings were faux Lincoln-log and nestled into lush green woods by a small lake with a tangle of brightly colored canoes on the shore. There were bull's-eye targets attached to hay bales, and there was a battered old speaker mounted to a flagpole that proudly waved both the American *and* state of Michigan flag. The only things missing were wood-paneled station wagons and a killer in a hockey mask.

Jeffrey the Travel Guide stood with his hands cupped around his mouth and announced, very officially, where the students were to go and where the Buddies were headed. His Buddy shirt even said TEAM LEADER on it—written, I noticed, by hand. We divided into two groups as per our gleaming leader's order: Buddies and non-Buddies. The roughly sixty non-Buddies ran screaming and flailing to their assigned cabins, kinetic after three hours of built-up energy and eager to meet with their friends and classmates that had already arrived, while some of the roughly twenty Buddies[6]—eager to move themselves—called after them half-heartedly not to run. "Remember, Buddies. Head to the den for your assignment! We've got young minds to nurture!" Jeffrey said, unironically.

The little girl in an oversized aviator's hat elbowed past him, not slowing down or looking back. A stern look flashed over Jeffrey's face like he was going to act like the adult and tell her to apologize, but she was moving with too much purpose; by the time he'd readjusted his hair, she was already halfway to the other kids piling up around the flagpole.

We made our way to a squat log cabin that looked like it went on forever, and looked like something Thomas Kinkade would have painted—warm-toned and sincere, Lincoln-log walls with antlers that adorned the doorway, the word "Nakwatuk" carved deeply into the cedar log above the entrance.

A life-size fiberglass Buddy stood next to the doorway, thumbs up, grinning like an asshole, with a sign shackled around his neck that said, "Be someone's better half!"

I vividly imagined trying to pull the fiberglass Buddy's head off.

---

6 There were no teachers. The whole idea of the tri-county Buddy program was to give everyone a certain opportunity: high schoolers got a chance to experience and demonstrate leadership/responsibility while the teachers and students got to take a break from one another for a week. The adults on-site were all camp staff, and the kids were our shared responsibility.

The roughly twenty of us tri-county high schoolers shuffled into the building, while a middle-aged man standing in the center of the room directed us to the folding chairs stacked against the wall. We arranged the chairs in a loose circle around him.

"Okay. So, welcome, Buddies, to Camp Jaye'k." He was not a tall man and his face was hidden away behind his glasses and mustache; he was the kind of person that wore shorts in pants weather. "I see some familiar faces and I see some new ones. That's great." He paused his speech for effect, but he never really stopped moving—his hands were constantly gesticulating or his feet were tapping back and forth. "For those new faces, I'm *Mister* Test. You can call me Coach. Or *Mister* Test." His eyes were set firmly on the three Buddies who had recognized me—and his gaze told stories. The girl, the one who'd recognized me first, raised her hand. "Matty, yes."

Faisal and the Sleeping Buddy both went aggressively quiet and straight-faced when their friend was called on. All of a sudden, they were the picture of model student leaders. They operated like they were a single organism—there was a fluid, silent communication between them, even when it just meant fucking with a camp counselor. The Buddy who'd been sleeping was biting both of his lips, forming a tight straight line like he was trying not to laugh. Matty, though—her face was entirely composed.

"Just wanted to say hi, Coach." There was the slightest beat before she said "Coach" and her face was so entirely void of laughter and so entirely full of "I am the kind of person who calls a random adult 'Coach'" that the Buddy sitting next to her, the one who'd been sleeping on the bus, immediately fake-yawned in order to hide his smile into his sleeve.

A suspicious pause.

"Hello," he returned. Faisal, who had sat down late to the circle after using the bathroom, raised his hand next, and Test squinted, even more suspicious. "Yes, Mr. Al-Aziz?"

"Hi, Coach. Just . . . wanted to say hi too. Coach."

Sleepy Buddy buried his face in his hands, almost to the point of tears but doubling down on his "I'm just tired and this is how I yawn" act.

Test twitched his mustache before saying, "What about you? You want to just say hi?" He was looking at the Buddy who was struggling to draw out his fake yawn.

"No, sir," the kid said, clearing any laughter off of his face. "I'm just looking forward to a productive week of camp activities and team building." Mr. Test—Coach—wasn't buying it.

Somebody cleared their throat.

"Right. We need to get started. I hope you all brought warm clothes; you should know by now that Lady Nature plays by her own rules up here. For those of you that are new: expect everything from the weather. It's going to be Halloween in a few days, which, if you've been here before, you know doesn't mean S-H-I-T. It doesn't mean jeans and sweaters. This is the other side of the lake and we have a little thing called Lake Effect. It can mean winter coats and boots, it can mean T-shirts and jean shorts, it can mean anything in between," he said, speaking like a man who's seen some real shit. "We've got plenty of work to do this morning, so I need you in groups." He spoke with his hands out, his arms like ramps leading down to his fingers where the words could launch off, directly to us. "Count off from one to three," he said, starting with Faisal.

Faisal shot his friends a look that said, "Oh shit, we always forget to sit the appropriate number of seats apart in order to be put in the same group for activities!"

It was a complicated look. It also meant that I was guaranteed to be grouped in with at least one of them—one of the people who was part of the group that recognized me. It meant that I couldn't just blend in. Couldn't be just a face in the crowd.

# FIVE: MOSES THE IMPOSTER

I'M IN CHICAGO, STANDING in line at the convenience store on the corner of Clark and Addison, across from Wrigley, on lunch from another day of sitting in front of a panel of youth counselors. It's springtime, and this is all part of my evaluation process. If all goes according to the judge's plan, I'll pass the eval, stay in school and maintain my grades, head off to camp in the fall, and maybe go to college, where no one will have heard of two fuckup kids named Charlie Baltimore and Moses Hill.

The news frenzy has died down, especially in Chicago, but every now and again there's a blip about us on the news.

And of course, it happens today while I'm trying to buy a coffee and a banana. For a few seconds, my face is on the screen and the lady standing in line right behind me makes a *tsk* noise and I reflexively look back at her.

And I think:

*You idiot, don't look back at her!*

And: *Now she's going to recognize you, asshole.*

The lady—an anonymous, middle-aged woman with short hair and a big coat—sees the screen, then looks at me and says,

"See, more kids need to be like you. Nice shoes, a tie, not like the—pardon my language—*shit* we see on TV."

She doesn't recognize me; she just sees a nicely dressed young person trying to buy a reasonably healthy snack.

I say, "Guess my parents just raised me right," and give her the most disgustingly sweet smile in the world.

I think: *You goddamn machine.* I think: *Charlie wouldn't have pretended. Must be nice knowing you can blend in.* I think: *That's not how people with beating hearts respond.*

After I pay and step outside, I give my lunch to the homeless person on the corner. I feel like I'm about to throw up, I hate myself so much.

# SIX: THE IMPOSTER
# IN THE WILD

A WALL OF RANK SHIT-STINK wafted over my group as we rounded the barn's corner. Group three, it turned out, got to help set up the petting farm.

A hundred or so yards away, Aviator Hat Girl was staring at her feet as one of the angry kids from the back of the bus said something and pointed at her head. Hatchet-Haired Kid looked like he was trying to moderate, and to persuade Angry Kid to apologize.

My job was mostly just clearing out the pen area of leaves and old manure left un-pitchforked and un-shoveled by the last group of campers and Buddies, while a couple of the other Buddies worked on repairing a fence that had blown over in a storm. I was busy pitchforking at a pile of frosty leaves and frozen turds when I heard someone walking up behind me.

I turned around and saw the third Buddy from the bus—the banker-looking one whose name I still didn't know. He had that "I should approach this person I've never met and talk to them" look about him. And like all the other ones I'd spent the last year dealing with, there was a moment of fake surprise and literal finger-pointing with the nodding head before he started talking. "You're familiar. You look familiar from something."

He had a garden rake, and I imagined him saying something like, "I've been *raking* my mind, but now I remember your face: you hate Jesus," and then taking a swing at me with the rake, which I would dodge by roll-diving out of the way, and then we'd pitchfork–rake fight for a while before one of us died violently: me with a metal rake sticking out of my head, or the other Buddy with a pitchfork through his chest.

"Just one of those faces, I guess," I said, bunching up my shoulders, trying to ignore that familiar sting in the back of my gut. I went back to poking around at the frozen farm shit. The guy waited a beat and then tried again.

"No, I swear—from TV? Right? Something on TV?"

"Must be somebody else," I said, as pleasantly as possible. I leaned on the pitchfork like a casual farmer, but the tool was tactically positioned just right for me to go flying into farm combat if necessary. We would fly off the goddamn rails into a mortal farm battle because he and his friends were missing the fucking point just like everyone had missed the fucking point. The same way everyone who'd recognized me for the last ten months, young and old, all had something to say: some advice or prayer or warning, some piece of wisdom, to give to me, the poor lost idiot.

Or worse, he'd be like all of the other kids at my school. The ones who side-eyed me when I walked by, the ones who would pull out their phones and start texting the person sitting right next to them when I took my seat in class. Even down to the way that Mr. Stone—the sweetheart of a janitor at our school who gave every passing student a high five when they saw him in the mornings—pretended like I didn't exist.

All the kids I used to know and be friends with.

The ones I felt like I'd let down, because why else would they all have stopped talking to me?

The Buddy tried again with, "You sure? There was a thing. On TV."

I took a slow breath. "Look, man, it's not me." I just wanted to be left alone, to not have to pretend; and, after ten months, it had seemed like I'd actually have an opportunity to do just that. But instead this teenager, with his salt-of-the-earth farmboy–banker face, just couldn't leave it be.

"All right," he said, nodding. "All right, hang on."

I couldn't tell if he actually meant I should hang on or if it was just a filler statement as he walked away. He was headed toward the barn and, just as he walked inside, he pulled his phone out. The idea of him meaning "hang on" rhetorically didn't seem half as likely as him coming out of the barn with a torch, leading an entire mob of people with rakes.

Either way, I put my back to the barn and went back to shoveling until I heard his footsteps five minutes later.

"Listen," I said, spinning around. "I don't fucki—"

He was holding two baby teacup pigs, one in each hand. The pigs just hung there, draped over his hands with their legs pointed at the ground, which for them might as well have been a mile down. He waggled one of the pigs at me.

"Let me try again. Here, have a pig.[7] You're Moses, right? Moses something?"

---

7 It is statistically impossible to have any sort of defenses up against someone with an armful of teacup pigs. Even when you feel like you need to have all of your defenses up.

Powerless in the face of the tiny, pink, muddy animal, I scooped it into my hands. It snorted at my thumbs.

"I . . . yeah." I held out my hand and he shuffled the pig around, resting it on his left forearm so we could shake.

"Nice to meet you. I'm Michael." He pointed at the pig in my hand with the pig in his hand, and said, "And *that* is Kevin Bacon. I named him like three minutes ago."

I didn't want to let the Kevin Bacon joke make me smile. "What about that one?"

"Hamibal Lecter. It was either Hamibal Lecter or Magnum P.I.G. but he bit me, so I stuck with Hamibal. I would have brought Jurassic Pork, but he was too big to carry. So hey, full disclosure: I don't recognize you. But my girlfriend does." My brain insisted that this was where the big rake showdown would ensue, because sometimes my brain is an asshole. Kevin Bacon kept squirming around in the nook of my arm and trying to nuzzle his face into my coat; Kevin Bacon would most definitely lose the pig battle with Hamibal Lecter and the pig overlord, Jurassic Pork. "She thought she recognized you on the bus earlier and she wanted me to find out if it was you. Something about national . . . chemistry . . . or something."

From his point of view, it had to have looked like I'd simply powered down for a second, because I had absolutely no goddamn idea what he was talking about and I just had to stare at him to try to make sense of it.

Then my brain powered back up from Idiot Mode and it fell into place.

When I was in eleventh grade—while we were still planning on how to get a drum set to the roof of a bowling alley—I had competed in the US National Chemistry Olympiad and won gold. I had caught their attention with a paper I'd written for AP Chem about a theoretical solvent that could break down any organic matter a thousand times faster than hydrochloric acid. The actual Olympiad was a five-hour laboratory practical and a five-hour written theoretical exam, with the award ceremony televised to dozens upon dozens of viewers worldwide.

Neither one of us expected me to start laughing. Being recognized for anything except alleged arson felt dumb and out of place, like hearing pop music on the radio at the police station an hour after your cousin has been shot in the brain. Dumb enough and out-of-place enough that you can't *not* laugh.

"Yeah, that's me. It was the Chemistry Olympiad."

"Oh," he said, trying really hard to sound enthusiastic about competitive junior science. "Well, hey. We wanted to know if you'd be interested in hanging out with us some night. There isn't a lot to do around here, but there's a town a couple miles away. You kind of have to trespass. And hop some fences. But there's some cool stuff to do in town," he said, and shrugged.

"Um," I said. "Maybe." The laughter had died out by then and left this uncomfortable, exposed raw spot.

"Fantastic." He ignored my ambiguity, opting to focus on the small pig in his hand while the Buddies around us worked in their small factions, picking away at bits of animal refuse to make the petting farm safe and habitable for everyone else. We stood in silence for a moment before he said, "So I kind of I have to go deal with this pig situation."

The tiny pink animal was desperately wiggling around, trying to mash its poorly designed face into Michael's palm, while mine was snoring, apparently asleep with its eyes open.

"I meant to ask about that."

"I stole them. Or, well, *borrowed* them. Without explicit permission. There's a whole litter of them just kind of bumming around in the barn, so I snagged a couple. Figured they needed some acclimating anyway. Plus, come on: baby teacup pigs."

I handed Kevin Bacon back to him. I had more questions, but it's tricky asking someone if they're quite sure they don't recognize you from a nationally televised courtroom shit storm.

"We're meeting up tonight. Just come out to the rope wall. You'll have to sneak out of your cabin, but it's pretty easy to appoint one of the kids as Cabin Guardian or Cabin Defender. They love that kind of thing. Just come over when the kids head to the bonfire." When I looked confused, he said, "They're having the big welcome bonfire thing tonight and the Buddies pretty much get a night off on our own for icebreakers and team games in the den. Won't be hard to get out for a while."

I nodded. "Also: rope wall?" It felt like the kind of semi-illegal, endearingly stupid thing that Charlie would have suggested.

"Yeah, that . . ." He gestured toward the trees. "Okay. You can't see it from here. There's a big fenced-in rope wall. The kind you see in movies about army basic training. But we made keys to the padlock a couple years back so we can climb it whenever we damn well please."

"Why?"

"Why do we climb it?"

"Yeah."

He didn't need to think about his answer. "Because it's there."

I blinked, and in the millionth of a second where my eyes were closing it wasn't Michael standing in front of me but Charlie. Because climbing something for the sake of climbing it was the kind of thing Charlie would have proposed. Michael made like he was about to say something but noise broke from the barn behind us and he spun, hiding the pigs behind his back in a fluid whirl of tiny oinks and squeals. Somebody was yelling to "get the gate" right as three young deer came charging out, all bounding in the same general direction: straight for the broken fence. Test came blasting out behind them, bent at the waist with his arms straight out. He managed to grab one of the deer by its back hooves as he went crashing down.

The other two kept going—legs kicking and pumping in a fevered cloud of panic toward wild freedom. One of the Buddies jumped in front of the miniature stampede with his hands and feet out in proper goalie formation. The fawn in front decided that the best way out was through, and went straight into the kid's gut. That Buddy went down with the air rushing loudly out of his lungs, the deer clasped firmly in his hands.

But not the other one.

The last deer was already a thousand miles outside of anybody's reach. It bounced away through the dry and yellowing grass, dipping up and down, just a hint of ears and white dots on a small brown body. Mr. Test bumbled his way back up and, having passed the first fawn back to a sorry-looking Buddy, came storming over to us.

"Oh! What a coincidence!" he said, barking the words at Michael. "You do this? *Hm?* Somehow? You leave that gate open? What do you have behind your back?"

"What—"

"*Behind your back making teacup-pig noises.* What's back there? Is it teacup pigs?"

"He picked them up when the deer ran out," I said.

I was thrown headfirst onto his shit list.[8]

"I'm sorry, did I ask you, Mr. Hill?" He knew who I was too, and not because of chemistry competitions. "You're already on thin ice, buster. You think I don't know all about you?"

I looked over at Michael like, "Buster?" while Test stared me down.

"Wow. I am out of the loop with this chemistry thing," Michael radioed in from another world.

"You screw the pooch once—*even once*—and I'll have your ass. You see this ground?" He pointed at my feet. "Thin ice. *This* thin." He pinched his thumb and forefinger together and, to his credit, it was a very thin space indeed.

"Mr. Test?" somebody called from the group of Buddies, who were still wrestling with the fawn, thwarting its adorable attempts to skitter past them.

"Both of you," he said, pointing at each of us, one hand apiece. He took a couple steps backward before turning and jogging pastily over to the Buddies, who definitely didn't know what to do with jumpy, tiny farm animals. "And put those pigs back, Bachman. Now," he called to Michael over his shoulder.

We watched him usher the kids away and grab onto the deer.

My face said, "Well. That guy's a dick," and the Charlie part of me wanted to call out after him that he could go fuck himself.

---

8 I was thrown headfirst onto my own shit list as well because it's so much easier, all the time, to not say something like that. If I'd learned anything from being an infamous local celebrity, it was that you just shut up and ignore the world until it goes away.

Michael looked from Test to me and said, "Test isn't so bad. I mean, he's kind of shitty almost all of the time. And clearly, the shorts thing is an issue. Plus—and this is new—he wants people to call him Coach." When I didn't say anything right away he added, "Last year he tried to give out Halloween candy and he only brought Mary Janes and pennies."

I cracked and said, "His mustache freaks me out."

"I've heard him say 'co-winkee-dink.'" He glanced over at me out of the corner of his eyes and I could tell he was gauging how funny I thought he was being.

Without thinking, I sucked air in through my teeth, hamming it up right along with him, and immediately thought that I was an asshole for doing it, since who the fuck was I to be making friends right now.

"But: he is who he is. Seems to have a hard-on for you already, which I wouldn't take too seriously. You should have seen him a bunch of years ago when Faisal shot him with an arrow."

I raised my eyebrows. "The John-Denver-shirt guy on the bus?"

"Yeah," he said, laughing.

"*Shot him? With an arrow?*"

"I mean, 'shot him' is kind of harsh. It was back when we were campers here in fifth grade and the arrow went a little . . . wayward . . . when the wind caught it and sent it grazing off a hay bale into the general exact vicinity of Test's hauntingly sculpted calf. Delicately. Barely broke the skin. But Test flipped out for a while and made Faisal write an essay about camp safety and archery range etiquette."

"That had to have either been the best or the worst essay ever written."

"Oh, it was definitely amazing. You ever read a camp safety essay with the phrase 'barbaric arrow-related violence' worked seamlessly in?"

I had not.

# SEVEN: OF BRUISES . . .

IT'S ONLY BEEN A few days since the bowling alley, and only a few minutes after a Christmas dinner where nobody seemed to have anything to say.

I'm sprawled on my ass, propped up on one arm, wondering what it was that hit me so goddamn hard—blindsided me hard enough that I don't remember falling, just standing in the rec room one minute talking to Charlie's brother, Jordan, and then staring up at him the next.

I remembered Jordan's face going hard—steeling himself, and making sure nobody was watching.

I'm trying to clear my eyes and I know that the faraway throb of dull, screaming pain in my jaw is only going to get closer and closer. I can't think straight and the impact has me confused and for a fraction of a second I think I see Charlie standing in the corner, watching.

And then the fuzzy sensation of dreams shifting to reality as my head starts to clear, and Charlie disappears as Jordan leans over and says, "He was my brother, you motherfucker," and hits me again. He has a mean smile on his face but there are tears in his eyes. "You were always getting into dangerous shit with him, you fuck."

Then he puts his hands on my throat. Jordan's a freshman in college—he's a year older than us, he used to help us collect rocks. He had a bike with pegs and knew how to get illegal fireworks and when he squeezes down on my throat, my head starts to swim.

And I look over to the corner where I swear Charlie had been standing, but he's still completely and utterly gone and I can't even bring myself to try to pry Jordan's hands off my windpipe.

My vision is getting red and fuzzy and the only thing I can think of while my cousin is choking me is, *What song would we have picked for this shit?*

Because there's no music playing.

Nobody bothered to put on Christmas music.

There's no one in the room with us. Just me and Jordan and the ghost of Charlie Baltimore. He's crying and his hands tighten, then relax, then tighten, like he can't decide whether or not this family can take another lifeless body.

And I think, *"All Apologies" by Nirvana.*

Jordan's hands go slack and he slumps off of me, crying hard and ugly like a little kid, and I want to cry like him but there's still nothing. I swear to all of the gods that we burned that I really am all apologies.

But I also can't figure out if some important part of me burned up in that fire, or worse, if I never had that important part in the first place.

When I come upstairs, everybody is sitting in the living room talking quietly. It's a quiet that goes silent when I walk in, which is something that I haven't gotten used to yet. I have my hoodie on so that nobody can see my neck, and Jordan is nowhere to be seen.

God fucking bless us, every one.

# EIGHT: . . . AND BUDDIES.

THAT NIGHT, WHILE THE RESPONSIBLE Buddies were rallied in the den, breaking ice and building teams, and the kids were huddled around the fire, I walked into the forest. Despite the voice in my head saying that they were just people my own age looking to be friendly, I imagined Michael, Faisal, and Matty smiling when they saw me walk up, right before beating me to death and feeding my body to a bunch of starving teacup pigs— vividly enough that every twenty feet or so I would stop, shake my head, and ask myself what the fuck I was doing because there was no chance anybody had watched the Olympiad and even less of a chance that those improbable people wanted anything positive to do with me.

I told my stupid brain to shut up.

The camp was nestled far enough into the woods that the darkness had, outside of the cabins and the bonfires, a primeval depth to it. The kind of darkness that presses in on you, where each rattle of bare branches reminds you that there is a whole world of claws and teeth just beyond the firelight. The kind of darkness that stares back. The kind that makes you remember all of your worst memories and convinces you that snarling people in WARMTH shirts are waiting just beyond your sight line.

I crunched through the autumn leaves, crisp and frozen under a sky that was the same, toward the distant voices below the rope wall. I couldn't hear the words but I could make out the pitch and cadence, and they were the kind of sounds you only hear from close friends—words swirling safely together and drifting in warm tandem. As I got closer, the words fell into fragmented focus.

"—*Coach?*"

Laughter, faint and trailing in the wind.

"—the end of—"

"—kidding me?"

I looked back the way I came. All I had to do was turn around and walk back. I'd see them later and shrug and offer some half-assed excuse and that would be it.

But they weren't talking about me. They weren't cackling. It was becoming more and more likely that they were just normal, decent people looking to do normal, decent things. Still, even if I knew they weren't going to go berserk on me, just turning around was the easier choice.

Right as I thought about leaving—about turning around and heading back toward the cabins, where I could just put my hours in until it was time to go home and then get out—I heard something pop. It was either a stick underfoot or a knot bursting in a log roasting on the bonfire behind me, but to me, it sounded like a gunshot.

Like a .38 fired at a child or a .45 slug put into the head of a teenager.

Either way, I was tired of hearing gunfire every time somebody clapped their hands or slammed a door.

"Fuck it," I said. I said the words; I made the words come out of my mouth and put them into the air where they were real.

I swam through the low-hanging spruce branches and past the skeletal birch fingers reaching out of the ground, just barely breaching the barrier between me and them. The taller shadow outline was nodding while inhaling from behind a cherry-red ember, listening to a smaller, girl-shaped outline while the third stood huddled close by. The air around them smelled heavy and sweet, and they stood in the shadow of a giant; the monolithic rope wall watched over them, fifty feet high, fenced with drooping barbed wire and surrounded by sand.

"Hey, guys," I said, louder than I meant to.

They jolted and the cherry-red ember disappeared, followed by a fit of coughing.

"Shit, hey, sorry. It's just me. It's Moses."

They stood hesitantly and quietly before all exhaling in relief at the same time. Stepping out from the shadows of the tower and into the puddled moonlight, Faisal started spitting and raking at his tongue.

"I swallowed it," he said to his friends.

"You did *what*? Wait, what?" Matty answered. Their attention shifted, easy and seamless, away from me.

"The joint. I swallowed the joint."

They asked him, silently, without words, *What the fuck, man?*

"The marijuana," he added helpfully, as if his friends didn't know what he'd meant.

*"We know what you mean!"* Matty said, arms out in theatrical outrage.

"How was I supposed to know it wasn't Test?"

"Faisal!" Matty said, swatting at him.

"I *know*! I didn—" He cut himself off by exhaling through his nose. "I've got another one somewhere. But I'm about to be pretty high because this shit's potent as shit."

"Hey, Moses," Michael said, and suddenly their attention was back on me. "You have any trouble sneaking out?" he asked me, shaking my hand in a very formal, fatherly way.

"I don't think they noticed. They were doing icebreakers. Something about pantomiming Two Truths and a Lie."

He smiled and said, "Sounds about right. Guys, this is Moses."

"I knew it was him!" Matty said as she walked over to me with her mittened hand jutted enthusiastically out. "I'm Matty."

I shook her hand. "Michael said he thought you recognized me on the bus. From the Olympiad?"

"I did! I told you it was him, *Faisal*."

"Pretty blown away that somebody actually watched the Olympiad," I said, completely honestly.

"My AP Chem teacher made our whole class watch it. Some of us kind of got into it though," she said, more generously than I'd ever heard anyone talk about chemistry. "Oh! This is Faisal," she said, dragging him away from digging a joint out of a hidden pocket in his coat.

"Hey, sorry about the whole—you know." I gestured at the spit-up chunks of weed and rolling paper around his feet.

"If I hadn't smoked half of it already and if I didn't have a lot more, I'd probably be more upset. Faisal," he said, shaking my hand.

"Yeah, you're the guy who had to pee furiously."

He lit the joint and laughed through a mouthful of rolling smoke. "I . . . yeah. Yeah, that's a pretty accurate first impression. Here: second first impression," he said, holding the joint out to me, a complete stranger.

Less than five minutes later we were tens of thousands of feet up on the old ROTC equipment. I inhaled, the air sucking in through the joint and making the weed crackle just a little bit. I held it. And I held it. And when my lungs started to itch, I sent a cloud the size of the moon out of my mouth. I closed my eyes and the smoke kept falling through the hundreds of teeth in my mouth, cascading up and seeping through the silver pinholes in the night sky, circling the quarter-moon drain in the middle.

"You sound like an asshole," I either thought or said out loud.

Faisal was not kidding about just how potent-as-shit the weed was.

Everything was soft, and we formed a circle on the top of the rope wall, staring into the deep sky.

"Okay. Matty. Your turn," Michael said. The group went quiet with contemplation.

"All right," she said, after thinking for a few seconds. Then, like a starting pistol, "James Bond: Brown Finger!"

"Glad-he-ate-her," Faisal yelled, ratcheting the air up to a new level of urgency.

"Dong With the Wind," Michael called.

"Twin Peaks!" I yelled, positioning my hands in front of my chest. There were bonus points for finding one that was already a porn title.

*"The Punisher but with butts!"* Matty said. We looked at her. "The Butt Punisher! Starring Clit Eatswood. Bonus points!"

Faisal started laughing but managed to say, "The Never Ending Erotica!"

"Quigly Going Down Under," Michael said.

"V for Vengina!" I said.

"Beauty and the Beef!" Matty nearly screamed.

"JFK!" Faisal said. He sat up and said, deadpanning, "Stands for John Fuck-Master Kennedy. Historical biopic. Bonus points."

There were also bonus points for historic films.

We all looked at Michael, who scrunched his face and said, "Shit!"

Faisal shot up and roared with his fists clenched.

Faisal claimed that no one could beat him at Porns. In the distance we could hear the camp coming alive with the night, and Faisal lay back down, completing the circle.

"They took the tower down. The one with the spinny bit," Faisal said after rejoining the circle and getting comfortable, gesturing awkwardly behind himself into the rolling waves of silhouetted trees.

I propped myself up on my elbows and stared at him, then at the darkness beyond, trying to make sense of his nonsense. Sure enough, there was a shape separate from the endless trees. Through a break in the branches there was a thin outline with a heavy top.

Something in my incredibly blitzed brain knew it was called an aerodrome beacon.

It was something my incredibly blitzed cotton-filled mouth couldn't articulate.

"They did that last year," Michael said, picking at the old

wooden rope wall and tossing the pieces straight up, watching them land on his coat. Every time he moved his arm, the key he'd used to unlock the gate around the rope wall would knock against the wood.

"No they didn't; it was still up last year, they just didn't have the spinny part on. Now there's no lights on it at all."

"Maybe they just turned it off," Matty said, while looking up at the stars.

"None of this. None of it makes any sense," I said. I was thoroughly impressed with how high I felt while also being able to make words that weren't slow-motion gibberish come out of my mouth.

"There's an old airstrip about a mile and a half into the woods," Michael explained to me. "It used to have a spinny light. Now . . . it doesn't. Apparently. I think they're in the process of decommissioning it," he said, tossing more splinters of wood up.

I started to say "aerodrome beacon" but only got through the first two syllables before I started swallowing too much and being too aware of how much I blink and then being positive that they knew I was swallowing and blinking too much.

Being with them felt comfortable. It was funny. And it was weird. And it was terrifying. It was an old feeling and it was a new feeling.

I laid back and it felt like I was looking down instead of staring up. Like something was holding me gently to the world's ceiling and was about to let me plummet down and down forever; like I'd been tossed up to the very top of everything and was only lingering in the moment before the fall.

"New game," Matty said. "Moses, what's your life story?" If we'd been sitting up or looking at each other, for just one moment eye contact would've been completely impossible, because my knee-jerk reaction to the question was to flinch away from it.

Because she knew. She had to know. Why else would they have gotten me away from everyone else and in the dark and now they wanted to know why we hated so many people and just who we thought we were? Yeah, okay, realistically there wouldn't be any violence, probably, but this was the real reason they'd wanted me to come out with them, and instead of just getting to be a stranger for one night, I'd get to be Moses Hill: Asshole from the News, Known Forever for the Stupid Shit He and His Cousin Did. The same as always.

Then Faisal said, "Oh, shit."

"What?" Michael asked, sitting up fast like he thought Faisal had spotted Test zigzagging through the woods with a flashlight. A pile of shredded splinters fell off of his chest.

"Two things. First: oh shit, that's a good question. But also, second oh shit, we have to go to the bonfire. High. We have to go to the bonfire high. And I'm pretty sure we're going to have to go soon."

Michael looked worried before saying, "Shit. This is going to be *amazing*!" His face broke into a grin and he and Faisal pointed at each other like it was something they had always talked about doing.

"Wait, you guys!" Matty said. "We need to hear Moses's life story!"

I started mumbling and the weed didn't help the outrageous paranoia that whispered how, if they heard my story, they would all suddenly remember me exactly like everyone else remembered me: as just one more douchebag that the legal system had let loose upon the world. One more fuckup kid who was guilty or who was innocent depending on who you talked to. The fear was compounded by the fact that I hadn't realized that we were going to have to be around a bunch of other people while I was bafflingly high. Still, if it meant avoiding questions about my life, I'd take it.

Through the dark we could hear the excited squealing of little kids around a roaring campfire.

"There's no time, Matty!" Faisal yelled. "We have a *blaze* to attend."

# NINE: WHEEL SPIN

"IF YOU LIKE HER, just talk to her," Charlie says to me.

We're standing outside of Econ, just before lunch, trying to see how many pennies we can slip into the slot of Mitchell Marrington's locker since Mitchell Marrington bought Charlie cigarettes and decided that he wanted payment with interest and Charlie decided to oblige. "This isn't the 1950s, you don't have to ask her to a fucking sock hop. Plus she's like the nicest person in a school that is otherwise made up of douchebags and assholes."

I pull a fistful of coins out of the paper bag in my hand and *plink* four pennies into Mitch's locker and say, "She's dating Langston Dilford."

"Shit, I thought they broke up."

"Got back together."

"But that guy's a fuck," he says, dropping more coins in one at a time. Mitchell Marrington is, at last count, around six hundred pennies richer. After demanding interest, he went to California for a week with his family because Mitchell Marrington is not the smartest extortionist in the world. "How can someone like Lana Mills date someone with a name like 'Dilford?' Even his last name is fucking stupid."

I shrug and plug some more coins into Mitch's locker. I never actually told Charlie that I liked Lana Mills, but he'd picked up on it—whatever there was to pick up on—and decided to make it his mission.

"Talk to her," he says, his eyes landing somewhere past my shoulder.

"No," I say, smiling, calling him an asshole without actually calling him an asshole.

"Talk to her," he says again, smirking and moving his eyes to mine.

"No," I say.

"Then pick a song."

"No."

"Yep."

"Charlie."

"I'm serious."

"So am I."

"Okay," he says, using the same "You're an asshole" grin I'd just given him. He pulls his Sharpie out of his pocket and scribbles "Wheel in the Sky" on the bag, then shows it to me.

I know Charlie thinks the song is about God or the universe conspiring against us—after binge-watching *Supernatural*, he developed a Sam-and-Dean complex where Journey's lyrics "the wheel in the sky keeps on turning" translated to, "Our teachers or our parents or God, et al, are being dicks and we need to show them what we can do." If he's picking this song for whatever stupid thing he's about to do, it's to show the powers that be that we have a say in the matter.

If the movies we watched growing up have taught us anything, it's that life demands a soundtrack. Especially when shit is about to jump off.

He takes the half-full bag of pennies and gives me a handful as Langston Dilford walks by from behind me, holding an armful of lunch. When his back is to us, Charlie says, "Dilford!" and whips the bag of pennies at him.

The copper fist explodes against the small of Dilford's back and he arches forward, dropping his three-high stack of pizza slices and large fountain soda. Pennies rain down around us as his lunch explodes against the floor, and when he turns, I'm the asshole holding a heaping pile of them.

And Dilford, fuck that he is, kicks my ass until Charlie heroically jumps in and pulls him off. That afternoon, as we head to my car, we walk by Langston and Lana—Lana, who is eviscerating Langston about his temper and his impulse control, and Langston, whose face is so red I swear I can feel heat radiating off of it as he stares into the ground, taking it—and Charlie winks at me.

They break up a few days later, and even though there's this weird clenched-up ball in my stomach—knowing that I was involved in their breakup, even if I didn't ask for it—there's also a sweet little sense of righteousness.

# TEN: SMOKE IN OUR JACKETS

"THEY FOUND HIM ON the fifty-yard line?" Why Kid asked, his voice barely audible above the crackling fire.

"That's right." The Buddy telling the story nodded solemnly, like he couldn't help seeing the grisly story playing out in his head. Our campfire was big—as big as the other ones that mottled the woods around us from the other campers and their Buddies from the other counties. The flames painted him in dancing shadows. "Found him chopped up in a neat little pile. And what's more? The *really* nasty and terrible part?"

The kids were enthralled and, on account of the marijuana, so was I. If the weed hadn't been military grade, I would have recognized the Buddy's smug-coiffed hair sooner as belonging to the annoying guy, Jeffrey, from the bus. Test was shaking his head and fumbling with a chintzy can opener and a giant can of beans that was supposed to complement the hot dogs roasting on sticks.

Under the campfire and wilderness smells, Michael, Matty, Faisal, and I reeked overwhelmingly of mouthwash and body spray.

"They say that it happens every ten years on the anniversary of the murder," the Buddy said grimly to the firelit ring of children. "That when the moon is just right and the town has forgotten about what happened to him, he comes back to possess a new victim and exact his brutal revenge by gutt—"

"Jeffrey!" Test barked, making Faisal yell "No!" and grab onto Michael. Test was rubbing the bridge of his nose. He adjusted his glasses before looking up at Jeffrey, whose face was still a caricature of agony and whose hands still formed rigid claws. Test put the still-unopened can of beans in the shallow cast-iron skillet and wiped his hands on his shorts. "They have to spend the next *week* out here—just because it's going to be Halloween in a few days doesn't mean they should go home with PTSD. Tone it down."

Test reached behind the log he was sitting on and pulled out a white plastic bottle with a red tip and squirted a stream of lighter fluid into the fire. The flames swelled with a *fwoomp!* noise, and for a second you could see everyone. Some of the kids were nervous and some of them were homesick, but Test was wrong—they weren't all terrified. You could hear them giggling and you could feel the nervous excitement in the air.

"But what happens next?" one of the little girls asked. She had on an oversized aviator-style winter hat—the kind with big earflaps that made it so her face was all bangs and mouth. "Did he gut him with his hook hand?"

She was smaller than the other kids, and while the other campers sat tightly packed together, she had a small vacant perimeter. She didn't seem to notice or care about the wide berth the other kids were giving her.

Faisal was sweating while Matty and Michael were trying not

to laugh themselves apart and I was lost, staring into the incinerator-heart of the fire. Not into the flames or even the embers that kept climbing up and away, but far into the center of the fire where the sparks hissed to life and crackled and glowed a deep orange.[9] Beneath the thick teepee of flaming logs, all of the original wood and newspapers had burned down to coals.

*What's your life story, Moses?* Matty asked, deep in my head. Her voice sounded like flames.

*What's your life story, Moses? Do you pray to the Holy Molten Blob that no one asks who you really are? They know you aren't like them; they can tell you don't feel things like they do. You're all knobs and dials, Robo-Boy. Tell them what happens to friends of yours. Tell them that you shouldn't be allowed here. Tell them what happened to Charlie. Tell them what Charlie's family went through because of you.*

*Go ahead and tell them.*

The coals burned; they hissed. The more I looked at them the harder they seemed to glow, feeding on oxygen and burning brighter with every question asked and avoided.

I moved my eyes from the coals to the fire to the kids to the coals and it all melted together. I lost myself in the dense and immeasurable blur.

The fire was stories high. It smelled like Charlie's side of the story because it turns out that flaming pallets on the roof of a bowling alley smell almost identical to campfires made of sticks and dropped marshmallows.

"Mr. Hill?"

---

9 Like really fucking orange. Orange-orange. Orange like burning gods except for Mohammed. Mohammed hadn't burned because we couldn't find one. Which is something I already said.

A thousand degrees of complexity. A million different interpretations of noise and memory.

"Are you listening, Mr. Hill?"

My attention jerked from the fire to Test, who, along with everyone else, was staring at me.

"Sorry," I said, with a mouth made of burlap. "What?"

Five seconds of silence, in which I was positive everyone could smell the cheap weed and panic-sweat coating my back. I opened my eyes extra wide to counter any marijuana-induced squinting.

"I said it's your turn, Mr. Hill." When my face showed no trace of understanding, Test gestured grandly while saying, "A campfire story, Mr. Hill. It's your turn. Preferably one without gratuitous violence or terror." He looked at Jeffrey. "Maybe something lighthearted. Something with a moral. Or elves."

At the mention of morals and elves, the girl in the aviator hat rolled her eyes so hard that my drug-addled mind legitimately worried she would sever her optical nerves.

But the night was determined to have a story from me and, at best, my mind was blank. At worst it was a fog-covered precipice that looked over an ocean of autobiography threatening to overflow and drown the world around me.

"Okay. Okay, a story. Once . . . upon a time . . . there were pigs. There were three pigs—"

"Are you about to tell us about the Three Little Pigs?" Test said, not at all trying to hide the frustrated boredom in his voice.

"No?"

"If you don't have a story, we can move on to someone more prepared, Mr. Hill." He twitched his mustache a little, and I hated that I had a story locked inside of me that didn't involve pigs or elves but one hell of a fucking moral about family and friends, and my lungs threatened to unleash my life story without flinching or blinking or holding anything back. To tell the true story. The one that happened. The one about Charlie Baltimore.

I cleared my throat, but Faisal spoke up, loud.

"Once upon a time!" he said, adjusting his volume, stifling the laughter threatening to churn out of his mouth. "Once upon a time there was a house . . ." He spoke slowly and deliberately, not completely succeeding at keeping the smile from his face.

"It was an old house nestled deep, deep, deep in a dead forest where nothing ever grew and blackbirds always filled the sky—blackbirds that would rest their tired feet and large wings on the naked branches and warm chimneys of all the dead houses in the forest."

The children's voices tapered off and even Test's attention was caught in the strange authority of Faisal's voice.

"But the birds never landed on the old, creaky house—for the old, creaky house had old, weathered shutters that always caught the smallest wind and would whine and slap against the siding, loud enough to send the forest animals scattering away every time."

Someone tossed a log onto the slowly dwindling fire, sending sparks crashing up and swirling into the night. The smoke from the smoldering wood hit us in waves; there was a kid who effectively looked like a banana since his hair was dark and his coat and pants were yellow, and when the smoke hit him he squinted his eyes and started waving the smoke away, saying, "I hate rabbits, I hate rabbits, I hate rabbits" to ward the cloud off. Banana Kid fending off the smoke was something Sober Moses wouldn't think was that funny but something that Incredibly High Moses found to be hilarious. Incredibly Paranoid Moses immediately worried he was laughing too loudly. The incantation sent the smoke swimming around the fire, tangling itself deep into our hair and jackets. Matty squeezed her smiling eyes shut and didn't take Michael's hand but rubbed her shoulder against his, just enough of a gesture to let him know she was there and he was there, but not enough to let Test know they were there together.

"It was a house older than the dead trees, and the other houses knew it. They would say to it, 'Old House, your crooked tin chimney is no good,' and 'Old House, your raggedy old picket fence isn't pretty enough, not one bit.'" Faisal punctuated the night with his story. "And the old house heard every hurtful word they said. It would hear them and look at its cracked windows and it couldn't help but feel all wrong. The old house would look at the tiny fire it had flickering in its belly and wonder what the other houses burned to make so much heat and smoke. It would look at its dusty stairs and creaky chairs. At its paint that peeled in teardrops. At its rusty nails, too bent and hammered to hold any paintings."

I blinked and in the coals, I could see Charlie and me, years and years ago watching TV, the news telling us over and over how terrible the world was and how broken we all were. Some newscast about a disaster's death toll and its mile-long vigil. When they cut to the footage of the aftermath—since there were no villains to show, no blame to place—they showed the people of this rural town working together to pull rubble away from the heaps, looking for survivors. One image they kept coming back to was of a kid about our age, wearing an Iron Man mask and carrying jugs of clean water. Everyone went crazy for Iron Kid, and Charlie and I weren't any different.

"But sometimes the house didn't listen," Faisal said, bringing me back.

"Sometimes the house's attention was somewhere else altogether, because inside, through the house's dusty living room and past the old mismatched trinkets, through the kitchen with warped floors, and down the crooked stairs to the cellar, there was a door." Faisal stopped and waved in front of his face to clear the smoke away.

"What was behind the door?" one of the boys asked.

Faisal looked at him and smiled a storyteller's smile. He couldn't hear me asking the same question. Aviator Girl shushed us, loudly, while keeping her eyes on Faisal.

"Behind the door, deep under the house, safely away from where the other houses could see, there was a lush and living forest that ran for miles upon innumerable miles." The way he hit the vivid points in the story, you knew it was one he'd known for lifetimes. "The old house would tend to its hidden forest, singing to its trees that were as green as its hidden nights were black and full of stars, and it would watch its secret birds fly spirals in its clearings. And if the old house listened real close, so close and quiet that even its creaking weathervane above couldn't be heard, it could hear drums somewhere deep inside its forest—"

The can of beans exploded with a shattering and metallic *THUNGH* noise.

Unbelievably Stoned Moses almost shit his Unbelievably Stoned Pants.

The can sent sparks and steam and maple-flavored syrup geysering up with fist-sized wads of beans blasting in every direction. The bean bomb was loud enough to jar a couple of the kids off their logs and powerful enough to send the can's lid slicing through the air.

The girl in the aviator hat yelped and fell back as Test shot to his feet, hands out and eyes wide, managing to yell "Jesus!" before the last of the beans rained down.

I reeled back, suddenly mostly sober and on my feet.

"Is everyone okay?" Test asked. "Is anyone hurt?" He was looking everywhere at once.

Matty and Michael poked their heads up from behind a log, Michael's shoulder covered in beans but the rest of them clean. They looked at Faisal, who was still standing with his hands out, covered in soot and food.

Faisal gave himself a once-over before saying, "What the *fu*—"

"Faisal! Language!" Test said, cutting him off while still checking on the kids.

"Excuse me?" the little girl in the aviator hat said. Nobody heard her but me. She raised her hand up in the air and said it again, but still nobody paid her any attention: Test was muttering and checking all of the wrong kids, Buddies were checking on other campers, Faisal was helping Matty and Michael, covered in beans, get up, but the little girl raised her bloody hand; she was surrounded by people and light and she was invisible. I saw her ask the world to see her, one more time.

And nobody did. And my THC-racked brain thought that that was fucking terrible. And that it sucks when the world doesn't see you. And how we're all functionally invisible to the majority of the world because we're so small. And how blood looks weird in firelight.

And then I was the furthest thing from stoned. Then I was just me.

I climbed through whatever high was left in my head and moved on legs made of wet rope toward the small, bloody hand flagging anyone down. I ignored the voice nestled in the fuming heart of the fire that told me I could try to help all I wanted, but it wouldn't amount to shit. That my scales were tipped permanently, that I could do no right.

Her eyes were wide and her face was pale.

"Hey. Hey. Let me see," I said. I moved her head to the side and lifted the earflap of her hat. The exploded lid had sliced up and under, leaving a diagonal cut across her cheek and along her ear. *"Test!"*

"Is she okay?" Faisal asked, already next to me and kneeling down.

"The lid got her."

Test was helping one of the students who had fallen backward off their log.

"Is my ear still there?" the girl asked as Faisal tilted her head back to check.

"Nope. Ear's gone. See?" He spoke on her undamaged left side before sidestepping and going silent mid-sentence, mouthing words on her right. He snapped his fingers on the left side of her head before moving his hand over and pantomiming a snapping motion on her right. He moved back to her left. "—ically you'll have to forget about a career in air traffic control. Or being a bat. Can't be a bat with only one good ear."

She smiled, and some of the color came back to her face.

"Faisal, we have to get her some bandages. Hey," I said, making myself smile at her. "What's your name?"

"Lump."

"*Lump?*" Faisal asked.

"Everyone calls me Lump."

"Your mother named you Lump?" he asked.

"No, but she calls me Lump too. She says we're *repurposing* it. I looked up what repurpose—"

"Jesus!" Test said again. "How bad is it? Is she okay?" He shouldered his way between us.

"She's fine," I said, "but she needs to get pat—"

"Then take her to the lodge and get her taken care of. Both of you." He stopped and smelled the air in front of us, staring us down. "Why do you smell so fresh?"

"What?" I said.

"It smells like you took a bath in Listerine."

"I'm still bleeding. My head is still bleeding," Lump said.

We turned to leave but Test grabbed my arm and said, "I'll be there in a few minutes to make sure everything is all right. I'm looking at you, Mr. Hill."

Faisal went to respond before he realized that he wasn't the one bring grilled.

Test craned his attention away from me and looked at her. "It's okay, kiddo. They're going to take care of you."

He didn't trust us, but he needed us to save the day.

We broke for the cabins like we were incapable of fucking things up.

# ELEVEN: TREASURE HUNTERS

CHARLIE HAS THE PICKAXE and I have a backpack full of rocks.

The plan, which makes perfect sense in our ten-year-old brains, is to dig until we find Underground.

Underground is exactly what it sounds like and everything else we can imagine: somewhere, right beneath our feet, is Underground, and if it's a place then surely it has tunnels and lights and danger and adventure. Treasure, in Underground, surely abounds.

So we strap my dad's pickaxe to Charlie's back with red bungee cords, load my backpack with stones small enough to throw but big enough to fend off any Underground monsters, and carry shovels deep into my parents' backyard. Our dig site—our entry point—is already littered with provisions: unopened Gatorade bottles, a kiddie pool where the things we find will go, a souped-up metal detector, and a wheelbarrow, full of tools we pulled off the garage wall.

"What are you going to do with your *booty*?" I ask, half out of breath from the homemade anchor on my back but still wrecked by how funny the word "booty" is.

Charlie's face is red from lugging tools back and forth and he keeps reaching back to adjust the pickaxe that's digging into his hip. "With my *booty*, first thing I'm going to do is buy a pool to put all my *booty* in."

Charlie is equally infected by booty.

"A booty pool!"

"Booty pool!" Charlie yells.

We dump our tools to the side as we get to the site. The location isn't arbitrary, on account of the military-grade metal detector I've cobbled together.

Forty minutes later there's a minor canyon dug in my parents' lawn. It's Charlie's turn to tear up the ground to make digging easier.

He brings the pick down and we hear exactly what we've been waiting for: the metallic *pang* of iron hitting fame and/or fortune.

"The shit was that?" he says, the tool still sunk into the ground, his eyes locked on mine.

"Keep digging keep digging keep digging!" He tears the pickaxe out of the ground, heaves it above his head, and brings it down. Again and again, trying to loosen the earth. "Wait!" I say, throwing my hands out. "Wait, stop!"

"What, why?" he asks, pickaxe hovering above his head for a minute before falling backward. "What is it?" The energy in his voice has a heroic edge to it, like he's expecting me to say that I hear someone coming, or see one of the monsters we're prepared for.

"What if the treasure isn't in a trunk?"

"What?" The heroic edge is gone.

"What if the treasure isn't in a big metal box?"

"I don—"

*"We need to stop hitting it with a pickaxe."*

The realization that he is potentially littering our priceless heirloom with puncture wounds sweeps across his face. "Aw shit, you're right. We've gotta dig. Gotta dig dig dig dig!"

We trade out and I dig.

Four feet in the ground, I work the best I can to uncover the shape that is becoming less and less boxlike with each shovelful of dirt I pull out.

The thing in the dirt starts to take shape and it definitely doesn't seem big enough to be worth a booty pool. But it's solid; no matter how hard we hit it, no matter how much we dig around it, it remains where it was planted.

Eventually we have a length of it uncovered, however caked in black earth it may be.

We've dug enough of a crater that we can sit with our backs against the cool earth. Charlie wipes at the dirt coating his arm and says, "You think it's, like, part of a ship? Or like a whole ship?"

Then I say a word I've only ever heard in movies and have never yet said myself:

"Fuck."

I scramble to my knees, grab the Gatorade that's sitting next to me, and dump some on the hopefully-a-treasure still trapped in the earth.

"What are you doing!" he yells, mostly in disbelief that I'd pour Gatorade on our artifact.

The dirt cascades off in black ribbons and even before the yellow sports drink is done dripping off we see the words *Guthrie Gas and Power* written on a very damaged pipe.

First there's confusion on his face, then surprise. "I think we almost blew up the neighborhood," he says, smiling.

# TWELVE: THE NATURE OF THIN ICE, PART ONE

HER HAND WAS CLAMPED AGAINST the side of her head because, she said, in the movies they always said to keep pressure on it. The bleeding had mostly stopped on its own but her hand, caked with splashes of red, kept the rest of the blood at bay in case it decided to come pouring out.

"I got blood on my dad's hat. I was supposed to take care of it," Lump said.

"It's okay. We can clean it," I said as we worked our way down the dark path toward the main campgrounds.

"Why do you guys smell like my neighbor?" she asked.

My eyes flicked open wide. "Do we? That's weird," I said.

"Like mouthwash and skunky plants."

"So why 'Lump,' Lump?" Faisal asked quickly. He nodded at me as discreetly as possible, as if to indicate that he had thrown her off the figurative and literal scent.

"What?"

"Why do you go by 'Lump'?" he repeated.

"I wasn't very good at walking until I was four. I used to fall into things a lot," she said, looking at her feet like they'd been traitors until only very recently. "People at school started calling me it, and now it's just my name."

"Do you like that name?" I asked.

"Not really. I'm planning on getting a new one. But Mom said that if I didn't like what the other kids were calling me and if telling them I didn't like it only made them call me it more, then we would *repurpose* it," she said.

We were between worlds: one hundred yards into the dark between fire and civilization. Somewhere off in the woods, something made a cracking noise. Lump skidded to a stop and stared into the dark.

I said, "It's okay, it's pr—"

"Shh!" she said, cutting me off and running to the edge of the trees. She pulled some branches out of the way and listened more closely, still looking into the black of the woods.

"Did you hear anything?" I asked Faisal under my breath.

"Yes. But I'm still kind of high. This is terrifying."

"Shit," Lump said, walking back to us.

"Hey," Faisal said, trying to commit to his role as a responsible Camp Buddy. "Language."

Her face was still pale but her eyes were less worried than before. "I thought it might be bears. My mom said that I don't need to worry about bears, but we're out in the woods and bears live in the woods."

"If you're worried about bears, why is your first instinct to go *to* the bear noises?" I asked as we walked in the darkness.

"My *mom* is worried about bears and told me that *I* didn't need to worry about bears, but only because she worries too much about things like bears. Did you know that I had an Uncle Thomas who used to fly planes?"

It was safe to say that we did not know about her plane-flying Uncle Thomas.

"I never met him, not even when I was a baby, but sometimes my parents talk about him when they worry about me liking bears. Also he wasn't really my uncle. He was my grandma's brother and I've seen pictures of him standing next to big planes and when I ask Grandma when the picture was taken she says Korea, which isn't a time. It's a country. But, like, also two countries."

Faisal looked at me with eyes that said, "I am high and this child is freaking me out."

"But so my not-uncle Thomas used to drink alcohol and so when Mom was my age Uncle Thomas got sad and tried to drive his farm-plane—the kind that drops water and stuff—into space, but farm-planes don't have nearly enough to gas to get to space, so he crashed but no one ever found him or saw him again. Grandma says he was trying to get to the moon and sometimes Dad says he was already there and then Mom hits him in the shoulder but they laugh. She doesn't actually *hit* him. My mother doesn't abuse my father," she said, looking up from me to Faisal.

In the middle distance behind us, Test was trying to get the kids to sing along to a campfire song that I couldn't quite make out. All I could hear between Lump and the wind and the woods was the not-remotely-tuned guitar playing the same two alternating notes. Lump's hand was pressed against her head like a DJ listening to one headphone.


She scrunched her face up and breathed short blasts of air through her nose as I dabbed her head with a cotton ball soaked in rubbing alcohol. Faisal was making a ton of noise banging around in the cabinets looking for bandages while Lump sat cross-legged on the counter. The hard-plastic medical kit above the sink had only contained cotton balls and a yellowed plastic bottle of rubbing alcohol with a label that was cracking because it had, apparently, been purchased during the Reagan administration.

"I think they got this stuff in the Reagan administration," I said to her.

Her mouth formed like she was going to say something, then stopped. She squinted. "Ray gun administration?" With her big hat removed, her hair stuck up in every direction like an explosion made out of bed-head.

"No, like Ronal—never mind. Your version's cooler. But don't worry, isopropyl alcohol lasts forever.[10] Sorry this stings."

"It's okay. I don't even feel it." Her left eye kept twitching and her jaw clenched every time the cotton ball dabbed the side of her head. "Is it still bleeding?"

"Just a tiny bit, but it's okay."

"Do you think I need stitches?" she asked. "And where's my hat?"

"I don't think you'll need stitches. Plus. You know. If we had to, we could use super glue."

She lit up before I had a chance to try to hold her in suspense.

"Because they used to use glue to keep people's guts in!" she said. "I saw a documentary on the Internet about how, in a war, soldiers would get their guts blown out and then the field doctors

---

10 Not literally forever, obviously. The shelf life of isopropyl alcohol—rubbing alcohol—is more about the bottle's integrity. As well-intentioned as rubbing alcohol may be, burning away that which seeks to hurt you, the liquid will inevitably eat the bottle away until there's nothing left and everything comes spilling out.

would use glue to put them back together! Are we going to use super glue? My hat!" she said, looking over my shoulder.

Faisal was rounding the corner with an armful of bandages and a box of Band-Aids in his mouth. Lump's hat was pulled snug onto his head and, as he spit the box of Band-Aids onto the counter, he said, "We're going to have to amputate."

"Also, you smell like farm poop," she said to me, ignoring Faisal.

"I think you should be more concerned about your impending limb removal. Impending limb removals are a lot more important than what I do or do not smell like."

"You do smell like cow shit," Faisal said, unwinding an arm's length of white bandage before doing a double-take at Lump, who was trying not to smile. "Poop. You do smell like cow *poop* is what I meant."

I sniffed at my coat. Cow shit was definitely one of the smells layered into its fibers.

"It's from working the petting zoo earlier. I had to pitchfork shi—manure all morning."

"Right, Mike was saying you guys were working out there, playing with tiny pigs. Give me a hand, Lumps," he said, placing her hand over the square of cotton pressed against her ear. He ignored her as she corrected her name, and spooled the bandage around her head.

"Yeah, one of the deer busted loose.[11] Went tearing out past a broken-down fence."

"A deer is loose?" she said, trying to twist toward me.

---

11 Even under the bandages, I saw the words grab her attention. Like everything else suddenly went mute in her otherwise rapid-firing, circus-parade, caffeine-brain.

He straightened her head and pressed her shoulders down. "Shh. Mummies can't speak," he said, and wrapped the bandage down under her ear and over her mouth.

"Ith id a babvy deer?" Lump asked over the cotton, her eyes locked on mine.

"Yeah, but I'm sure they'll fin—"

She clawed the bandage from her mouth. "What about its mom? The baby is out *there*? In the *woods*?"

"Deer love the woods," Faisal said, nodding from me to Lump. "Remember Bambi? Bambi was all about the woods."

"Not a baby deer without a mom!" she said, loudly, throwing her hands out and almost knocking the ancient bottle of rubbing alcohol to the floor.

"Bambi didn't have a mom!" Faisal said, entirely invested in the argument.

"Bambi did too have a mom! And also especially because the baby deer is domes—doomes—destic—" She bunched up her eyebrows as her mind tried frantically to articulate the word.

"Domesticated?" I asked.

"Domesticated!" she said.

"I thought you were on my side," Faisal said to me.

"For your argument with the eight-year-old?" I said, egging him on even though I'd known him for less than a day.

"I'm eight and a half."

"For your argument with the eight-and-a-half-year-old?"

"I'm not the one who let the adorable little deer escape into the vast and unforgiving wilderness."

"I was holding teacup pigs."

"Did any of the pigs run away?" Lump asked, like she was making a checklist in her head.

"Great," Faisal said. "You were like Hitler's next-door neighbor. 'No, honey, it's fine—*all* the little neighbor boys goose-step around their backyards, barking at the Goldsteins.'" She looked up at him like she didn't understand what he was talking about. "I'm saying it's his fault because he could have prevented a disaster. Like how if Little Hitler's neighbors had just . . . you know . . ." he made his hand into shooty fingers. "Never mind."

"No, the pigs are fine," I said. "Is that your criminal origin story for Hitler? That he barked at the Jewish neighbors and his neighbors should have assassinated him? Does Little Hitler have the mustache too?"

"Of course not—children can't grow mustaches. But he drew one on, yes." He kept wrapping Lump's head in white bandage as we talked back and forth. Any traces of panic or fear from the bean-bomb had long since fallen away. Instead, I could see that there was a plan forming in her head. It was a look I recognized.

"But what about freezing to death?" Lump asked.

"All the better. No World War II."

"No, the deer!"

"Deer are good at not freezing to death," Faisal said. He put her hat back on her head and her shoulders relaxed a little.

"I think I need to help the deer," Lump said definitively. The way she said it made it seem like she wasn't talking to us anymore. Like she was back in her own head.

Like she was seeing a way out of her name.

"I think you missed a spot," I said, pointing at her head, which was almost completely covered in bandages.

"Got it," he said, covering a small patch of hair in the back before covering her mouth and chin in bandage.

Nobody said anything for a few seconds.

"You know she's going to ask again," he said.

"I think she can hear you through the bandages," I said.

"Matty. About your life story. She thinks you're real interesting. Wouldn't stop talking about you earlier."

I looked out the window to see if Test was nearby, hoping he would come in and force the subject to change, but the only thing I could see in the black glass was my reflection.

The glass was probably just warped, but where my reflection should have been all the unremarkable inches of my face, everything looked distorted. My eyes looked sunken, my face looked off-kilter and wrong.

"Yeah, I still can't believe anybody watched the Olympiad," I said to the window.

"Except she didn't ask about the Olympiad, she asked your life story," Faisal said. He picked up the pinkish-white cotton balls off of the counter and tossed them in the trash one at a time. I stared at him. "Look: you don't want to talk about . . . whatever it is, that's fine. But she's going to ask again. I'd have an answer ready, is all."

I was very aware of my hands and my tongue feeling funny, and the weed-paranoia had the suspicious feeling of being legitimate paranoia. "What don't I want to talk about?"

"Dyoovveapenthil?" Lump asked us. "Ahndpaypuh?"

I pulled the bandage down.

"I need a pencil and paper."

I put the bandage back over her mouth.

"I'll see what I can find. Here, take this," I said, and pulled the green Sakura marker out of my pocket. Even after Charlie, the habit of carrying that goddamned marker around was hard to break.

"I don't know what you don't want to talk about. But I've been coming to this camp long enough to know that it's partnered with community outreach programs." Faisal said. "Either way, I saw the way your face changed when she asked. And I think you look familiar too, but trust me: I didn't watch any fancy science-Olympics. I'm not trying to bust your bal—" He looked at Lump, stifled a pseudo-cough into his fist, and said: "—your chops or anything. Really, I'm not. I'm just saying."

Test came whipping through the door like a man who's used to sneaking up to doors and blasting into rooms. "Is she okay—why is her whole head covered in bandages?"

The small mummy with the aviator hat had to turn with her shoulders to face him.

"Thrvvadrrobaloov!" she said from behind her Claude Rains bandages. I reached over and pulled down three or four layers. "There's a deer on the loose!" she said again.

Test's face softened. "Are you all right, little lady?"

"I'm fine, but there's a deer on the loose! It escaped! Hours ago!" She said it like she was in a room full of assholes preventing her from doing her job.

"I know it, and so do the Buddies and the groundskeepers." He walked over, his eyes on us. "We'll find the little guy in no time." He bent over and pulled the bandages down, tucking them under her chin. "How's the head?"

She took an exasperated breath. "I said it's fine. I need paper. I need to make flyers about the deer. What if a hunter sees her and shoots her?"

Test's eyebrows raised and he thought about it. "How about this: you go see the nurse—get an official all-clear—and we'll get you all the paper you want. I think we even have some wanted posters somewhere—"

"No wanted posters! We don't want to give the wrong idea, especially to hunters." She was already pulling her coat on.

"Deal: no wanted posters." He looked at Faisal and said, "Shelly's in the rec hall. You remember Shelly, right, Mr. Al-Aziz?"

"Nurse Shelly." The words sounded like they'd been learned the hard way.

"Right."

"The one who I talked to after the arrow thing."

"Right again."

We all turned to leave.

"Not you," Test said to my back.

Right there: the two words that summed me up. Two goddamn words that never failed to remind me that I wasn't just a teenager dealing with normal teenager problems.

"All right."

And I knew, basically, what he was going to say before he said it:

"We have to talk about that cracking noise you keep hearing. The one under your feet."

Under other circumstances, it would have sounded like he was asking if I was all right. Asking if I needed to talk, asking if I was still holding all of my pieces together. But it was never going to be that. Not then, not with Test.

I looked at Faisal, who looked at the ground. He put an arm around Lump's shoulders and ushered her toward the door. "Come on, Lumps. Amputation time."

The door opened, the door closed, and it was just Test and

me. I was ten-months-tired, and ten-months-tired is too tired to tell yourself to unclench your jaw before your teeth shatter from the pressure.

"Follow me."

"This one of those thin-ice talks?" I asked as we headed down the corridor. There were pictures on the wall of campers and Buddies and counselors, and as we walked the length of the hall the pictures time-warped, going older and older, the crisp, time-stamped digitals changing to fading film with fading, deteriorating color.

He didn't answer.

Test unlocked the door to his office and said, "Sit," gesturing to the chair in front of his desk. I did. He walked over to an old humming fridge on the other side of the small room, pulled the door open, and took out a paper plate covered in blue Saran wrap before sitting down across from me in a large swivel chair. The kind of chair you imagine a judge using.

The only light in the room, up until that point, was the yellow slice thrown in from the hallway and, briefly, the glow from the fridge. When he clicked his desk lamp on, the room appeared, and it was everything you'd expect a camp administrator to have: poster-sized prints of nature scenes and state animals and plants, photos of different Buddies throughout the years participating in all of the staple activities, framed leaves, sports gear, survival equipment, and ponchos.

Directly under the lamp, though, was a tiny clear plastic box with a little brown shape in the middle.

When Test saw me looking at it, he said, "Mexican jumping bean. My nephew loves them."

He pulled the blue plastic wrap neatly off of the sandwich

on his desk and set it aside. The sandwich in the middle of the plate was packed with meat and vegetables.

I nodded.

"Why are we sitting here?" he asked me as he removed the top slice of bread from his sandwich. He picked a strip of crust off and ate it. Under the lamp, the little brown bean jumped with a *tick!* sound. A second later, the bean moved again with the same horrible noise.

I didn't say, "Because you told me to follow you here," but I didn't answer fast enough either, because you could see the blood going to his face even though he was trying to play it cool.

"Allow me to rephrase: do you know what my job is here?" He tore off another piece of his bread.

*Tick!* I flinched.

"Your job is to keep the kids safe and happy. Especially around court-ordered Buddies like me," I said, making myself look at him instead of the dying larva stuck in place.

What I didn't expect was for him to laugh. It wasn't exactly a good-natured laugh. "Please. You're more than smart enough to know that you wouldn't be allowed to even set *foot* on the grounds if anyone thought those kids weren't completely safe around you."

*Tick! Tick tick!*

His eyes looked huge under his glasses and the magnification was apparently so strong that it sniper-scoped his vision past the smudge of soot on the corner of the right lens.

"Okay," I said, like an intelligent and articulate individual.

My phone buzzed against my leg, a small burst of vibrations overlapping each other since Test's office was apparently one of the few places at camp where I got service. I slid out my phone and took a sidelong glance at it; there was a text from an un-known number, a notification about a system update, and a text from my dad. I put it back in my pocket.

"To answer your question, yes, this is one of those thin-ice talks. I get the impression you think being here is a punishment. Allow me to clear that up: it's not. You're here to do something positive, not make up for something negative. But if you keep insisting on playing the tough guy, I can't help you. You'll crack through the ice all on your own. It's the 'and then . . .' you need to worry about here, Mr. Hill."

And then.

And then.

And then.

I pictured the fabled golden halls of Guthrie Community College. The one building in Guthrie, aside from the hospital, that was more than three stories tall, conveniently located right across the street from the actual no-shit graveyard. I would drive by that stupid bowling alley on the way to class every day.

The tiny bean sitting in the plastic cube rattled back and forth, and I could feel Test staring at me—looking at me like I was just another little prick who couldn't accept help.

He pulled another length of crust off, balled it up, and ate it.

I figured, fuck it, I'd tell him about Charlie. The real story. The story that I tried and tried and tried to tell when everything first happened, but nobody would listen to. He thinks this is a chance for me to do something good?

*Let me tell you what happens when I try to do good things. Or maybe you saw the story on the news?*

"Look, I'm n—"

"No, you look, *mister*." He pointed at me as he called me mister. "No more crap. No more sneaking around and smoking cigarettes or giving me attitude." He cleared his throat. "I saw you," he said.

My eyes stayed on him and his smudged glasses, and my face turned to blank porcelain. I erased every line of emotion from the history of my face; I scrubbed every fault line clean away and let the muscles relax. I took a breath. Let him tell me he saw me on the news, long before the courts told him I was safe and would be attending his camp. Let him be another victim of mine who bravely tells me that they forgave me but never forgot me.

I waited for the jumping bean to start jumping again.

He continued: "The way you went to Allison when she got hurt." He pulled his glasses off and his eyes shrank to human size, and I cracked. He breathed on his smudged lens and wiped it on his shirt.

"What?"

"Lump. The girl all the kids call Lump. When the can exploded. That kind of noise—with all the sparks and the fire, everybody running around—nobody knew what it was. Not at first, anyway. Sounded like an artillery shell, and your first move was to help."

"She was hurt."

He nodded. "Despite your attitude, you deserve to be here as much as anyone else. Besides, you don't know Allison. She came here last year—youngest kiddo we ever had. Some of the other kids gave her a hard time for it and she kind of just closed up. And this year she's actually trying to make friends. I think it probably has to do with what's going on at home with her dad."

He took a breath, almost seemed like he wasn't going to say anything else, then added, "She needs friends, especially since she's still younger than a lot of the kids this year; and now that's you. Since you don't have a cabin to head, you get Allison. Welcome to Lump Detail."

"Her dad?"

He looked at me, tired, and said, "We have one week here, Moses. One." He fit the glasses back on his head and squinted for a moment, readjusting his vision. He pulled something out of a greasy-looking laundry bag next to his desk and tossed it at me. "Tomorrow's field day. You're on flag football."

I uncrumpled the wadded-up—but surprisingly clean— referee shirt and Test gestured for the door. He went back to deconstructing his sandwich and I never got my answer about Lump's dad.

By the time I left Test's office, the flames were out. The fire pit was an inky, sooty pool, because the children were all thoroughly convinced that they were the only ones that could prevent forest fires. I pulled my phone from my pocket. The text from my dad said:

> Hey Buddy,
> I just wanted to touch base and let you know how proud of you I am. It's nothing Moses the Magnificent can't deal with, I'm sure, but I'm still proud as hell of you for handling this like a man. Anyway, talk to you soon.

Dad had impeccable texting etiquette on account of working in the tech industry since the '90s. Even when I was a kid and we didn't have cell phones, he would send fully punctuated messages to the beeper we kept on a key ring next to the front door.

I typed out "I love you" in binary[12] and knew that, when he got it and when he got a chance to send a message back, I'd get a message that said 01001001 00100000 01101100 01101111 01110110 01100101 00100000 01111001 01101111 01110101.[13]

The next message from the unknown number said:

Moses. This is Michael. We need your help. Cabin B.

I didn't know how they had gotten my number but I didn't care. I not-quite-ran toward their cabin, uncomfortably aware that I'd only known these people for a day and was already almost-running through the woods because they needed help.

The cabin was actually two cabins—two A-frame cottages connected in the back by a large bathroom—and when I got there Matty was standing in the front cabin's walkway talking to Michael through the screen door.

"Moses!" she said, smiling and waving, when she heard me jogging up.

I tried to slow to a walk when I realized no one was panicking, so I waved and tried to regulate my breathing. Michael mashed his face up against the screen.

"Moses? Thank God you're here."

I extended my exceptionally casual wave to Michael.

---

12 01001001 00100000 01101100 01101111 01110110 01100101 00100000 01111001 01101111 01110101
13 "I love you too"

"He won't let me in," Matty said, switching from goofy melodrama to clinical, factual conversation seamlessly.

"It's for your own good!" Something behind him crashed down and he spun to face the noise, pointing a bright green water pistol that was steaming from the barrel. "It's not safe here, Matty!" He turned back. "If I don't make it out of here alive, I want you to move on—"

"Move on?" she cut in, moving right back into the schlock.

"Move on! Live your life. And when you get the choice to sit out or dance . . . I hope you dance."

Matty threw herself against the screen, her hands pressed against the frame. "How can I dance without my other half?"

He placed his palm flush against the screen.

"Can you open the door for just one last kiss? A final kiss?" she asked him.

"Hush," Michael said, placing his finger against the screen.

Matty turned and looked at me, switching back to somewhere between clinical and casual. "A war broke out between the cabins. Lots of casualties. Why do you have a referee shirt?"

"Football tomorrow. Test gave it to me. It looks pretty quiet over there," I said. The cabin in the back had seemed absolutely empty and silent when I'd gone tearing by it.

"Of course it does!" Michael said through the screen. "Faisal rules with an iron fist; he rules with fear."

"Michael is more of a Tom Hanks kind of leader. You should have heard the bumbling-but-inspirational speech he gave to them earlier," she said, trying to keep the smile from her face the best she could, like she begrudgingly loved him despite his being a jackass.

I looked past them into the bright cabin. Five or six children were positioned on and around beds, all peering past the fluorescent bathroom into the pitch-black square of nothingness that was Faisal's cabin.

"Are you sure there's anybody over there?" I asked.

"Oh, he's over there all right. Waiting. He already taught them guerrilla tactics like killing the lights and farting. I think one of his kids shit his pants at us."

"Why aren't you in there?" I asked Matty.

"I've already lost too many people I care about," Michael said, looking into Matty's eyes and stroking his hand down the screen. One of his child soldiers said, "I hear something!" and all the tiny bodies went rigid with wartime adrenaline. "Also it's No Girls Allowed," Michael added.

Matty made a fart noise with her mouth and said, "He won't unlock it. Also it's almost lights-out so I need to get going anyway."

From the dark of Faisal's cabin, a small orange shape came clattering across the floor. It skittered into the bare feet of one of the kids, who held it up lovingly while someone else said, "It's a Reese's Pieces!"

"You put that down, Goblin Joe—put it right down," Michael said, pointing his steaming water pistol at the child.

"I have so many questions," I said to Matty.

She nodded toward Michael and said, "Water gun's steaming because it's got hot water in it, but he told them all it was pee. And we call Goblin Joe 'Goblin Joe' because . . ." She nodded toward the kid who was slowly raising the bathroom-floor-candy to his mouth while maintaining eye contact with the Buddy pointing an alleged pee-gun at him.

All of the features on my face collapsed into a display of disgust.

"Goblin Joe. Kid'll eat anything. They're lucky though. I think Faisal would have really peed in the gun," Matty said.

Another piece of candy bounced out of the darkness toward Goblin Joe.

"Damn it, he's like E.T.," Michael said. "Faisal! You know he'll eat anything you throw—quit trying to poison him!"

A few seconds later a handful of socks sailed out of the dark and landed at Goblin Joe's feet.

"Do not put those in your mouth!"

To his credit, Goblin Joe did not put the socks in his mouth.

Another piece of candy appeared, this time closer to the darkness; Goblin Joe followed the candy. A moment later and another piece bounced out, even closer to the wall of darkness separating the cabins. Michael was about to threaten him with the pee-gun again when Matty interjected, "Michael! I have boobs and I have to leave."

Michael immediately forgot about his platoon.

Goblin Joe bent for the fourth piece of candy, his jaw still working on the previous one, when a Nerf arrow sliced out of the dark and hit him in the eye. Michael's hand was out of the door when he turned to see the child hit the tile floor, clutching his face.

Matty grabbed the door open, clutched Michael's wrist, and swung him to the floor while turning off his cabin's lights. They never stood a chance: an army of ten-year-old girls came pouring into the cabin full of disoriented boys, pulling makeshift blindfolds off, firing Nerf guns, and swinging wet socks like medieval morning stars. Cabin A—along with Matty's reinforcements—

was a swarm, a plague, and as Michael turned to look at Matty she pulled a Nerf gun from her coat and stuck the barrel under his chin.

"You?" he asked.

"Me," she said, and pulled the trigger.

# THIRTEEN: MACHINE BOY

"NO, NO, WATCH, HE LOVES this, watch," my dad says.

Half of the family is in the dining room, spilling over into the kitchen, talking and laughing and cleaning up after Easter dinner. The other half is crowded into the living room, relaxing, drinking, and mostly tuning out the classic rock playing on the radio.

"Moses! Stick 'em up!" he says, right as Angus Young rips into the opening chords of "Back in Black."

I'm sitting on the floor on the other side of the room, playing with Charlie, and I've got a red towel tied around my shoulders. I whirl on cue, standing and putting my fists against my hips as my dad fires off a Nerf dart that bounces off my chest with a soft *plap* noise.

I smile, because if there's one thing they've drilled home with me, it's that I'm their superhero.

The Magnificent Moses.

Moses the Miracle.

Machine Boy.

Since Dad moved back in, I fill the gaps in the conversations.

Whenever things get too drawn out or quiet, the conversation inevitably shifts in my direction.

I look down at Charlie to see if he saw, if he watched the Nerf dart fall harmlessly away, but he's mouthing AC/DC lyrics and staring down at the toys on the floor and I can't tell if he's laughing or crying about me taking another bullet to the heart.

# FOURTEEN: THE NATURE OF THIN ICE: PART TWO

"THEY REALLY DIDN'T GIVE you a cabin to lord over?" Michael said as he dealt the next hand. The cabins had agreed on a cease-fire on the grounds that Faisal had threatened to suffocate one of them if they didn't at least pretend to try to sleep. On account of official lights-out, we'd set up the card table under the harsh fluorescents of the connecting bathroom. The lights made the stark contrast of the black and white bars on my ref shirt even more defined.

"Nope. They needed Buddies, but Cabin Lordship was full up," I said,[14] picking up my cards. I risked a look at Faisal, who didn't have the same "You're a bullshitter" look on his face from earlier because he was staring into his cards.

"Wait. How much are tens worth?" he asked Michael.

"Tens are worth ten."

"And nines?" Faisal asked.

"Nines are also worth ten," Michael said, helpfully.

---

14 . . . lying. Even if Test was telling the truth about camp not being a punishment but community service, they still hadn't given me a cabin.

"Are eights tens?" he said, visibly trying to sort the rules out in his head.

"No, eights are eight. I told you."

"This game is nonsense."

"Unless," Michael continued, "it's an eight of clubs. Then it's a ten."

"Awful, unwinnable, horseshit nonsense."

"It's better than Porns—"

"You shut your terrible mouth!" Faisal said.

"It's not my fault you don't understand Tens."

"No one understands Tens! Hey: remember that time your girlfriend betrayed your trust and murdered you in front of a bunch of kids?"

"I have an Uno card," I said, holding the card up between two fingers.

Michael whistled. "Bad news, man. Bad news," he said. "You have to go elbow-drop one of Faisal's kids."

"No he doesn't," a voice said from the darkness behind Faisal. A chorus of small voices shushed the kid and outright told him to shut up.

"Shut up or we'll come search under your mattresses," Michael said without looking back.

"What do you *possibly* think you're going to find under a kid's mattress?" Faisal said. "They have all of the porn already. All of it. Inside of their telephones." He turned his attention to me. "So what did Test do to you?" he asked me as he laid a card down.

My stomach turned into a brief sour knot and I wanted to ask him why he couldn't leave it alone, but I realized that his not talking about it would have been just as conspicuous.

"You can't play reds yet," Michael said.

Faisal stared at him and didn't pick the card up.

It was pure eye contact and zero sound.

No breathing.

They burst into a lightning round of Rock, Paper, Scissors that Faisal immediately won; he fist pumped and Michael said "shit" and one of the kids in the dark told him that he wasn't allowed to say "shit."

Faisal marked ten points on his scorecard, muttering, "Tell *me* I don't understand Tens; I'm the motherfucking king of Tens." He looked at me and said, "Future reference: there's usually a bluff clause in his games—he tries to build his cheating ass a loophole into *any* games we have because he is a bad fucking person. Anyway. Test."

"Right: he just wanted to have a few words with me about the nature of thin ice." If he pressed the issue, there was enough truth I could give them without giving it all away. I lined up my options: lie and tell them that I was on Test's shit list because he thought I smelled like weed; tell them he was just trying to break me in; tell them anything except the fact that Test knew my whole story and was telling me that I belonged here too.

How would that conversation even go? *Hey, guys, Mr. Test was telling me to drop my attitude because I deserve to be here too. Oh, right, because I inadvertently helped burn down a bowling alley right before watching my cousin get shot.*

Still, even Test had thought we were only talking about the thin ice underfoot and not the ice that had somehow found its way into all of the beams that held me up.

"Ooh, I know *that* talk. Did he call you 'mister'?"

"He did," I said.

"He seems especially vigilant about his hard-on for you," Michael said. "I mean, I get him hating Faisal—Faisal shot him with a bow and arrow."

"Test loves me," Faisal said. "I tickle his *fancy*. I'm the Test Tickler." He heard what he said, smiled before going very serious, then pumped both of his fists up and exclaimed, "I *am* the Testicler!" and the darkness around us busted up.

"Not really sure why he's got it in for me. Guess I just have one of those faces. By the way, did you get Lump to Sheila?"

I knew the nurse's name was Shelly. They didn't know me and they didn't know that I was supposed to be a miracle or a criminal and it was stupid and little but it felt good to act like I didn't know what the nurse's name was. It felt good acting like I knew how to just be someone playing cards past bedtime who had nothing special or unique about him, not even a good memory.

"Is that the girl whose ear fell off when the can of beans exploded?" Michael asked. "I never knew her name was *Lump*. Also who's Sheila? Do you mean Shelly? The nurse?"

"Right, Shelly," I said, nodding. "She used to fall down a lot. Lump, I mean," I said.

"She's fine. And her ear didn't fall off," Faisal said. "She wouldn't stop talking about that deer. Shelly didn't have any paper for her to make flyers, so I think she's doing it tomorrow in Arts and Crafts. Kept saying that after she found it, her new name was going to be Katniss."

The darkness behind Faisal spat forth a child made of shapes, and his hair was a latchkey-kid hatchet job, the same kid Faisal had been cracking up on the bus. He walked past our table without saying a word, clenching his briefs, ignoring us and the catcalls behind him. He shuffled up to the low urinal as close as possible and pulled his underwear down around his ankles. The faces in the dark laughed like shitty little hyenas and the kid at the urinal kept his head down until the dribble in front of him tapered off.

"Trevor, my man, how you doing?" Faisal asked the kid when he'd finished and had started scrubbing his hands with pink liquid soap.

"Fine," he said with his back to us.

"Moses, this is Trevor. Now, me? I hear Trevor's a card shark; one the fifth-grader babes would *not* stop talking about it," Faisal told us in a very loud and confidential voice. "Up for a game of cards, Trev?"

"No, thanks," he said as he walked back into the cackling darkness.

We were quiet for a moment until Michael started dealing another hand.

"That's Trevor," Faisal said to me. "Trevor has to pee a lot. According to WebMD it's an anxiety thing."

"You WebMD'd Trevor?" Michael asked.

Faisal pointed at him and cocked his head to the side, his eyes big and accusing. Michael fanned his hands out and raised his eyebrows until something clicked and he said, "Goddammit."

"He doesn't believe me that he has a problem with turning everything into verbs," Faisal informed me.

"Michael or Trevor?" I asked and let them take it away; I leaned back and let the natural waves of their conversation ebb and flow.

"Mike. Trevor just has to pee a lot."

"It's not a problem. Saying it's a problem implies something negative. It's not my fault I'm a word-birthing grammar wizard," Michael said matter-of-factly.

"You're not a grammar wizard, you're just too lazy to put together a complete sentence with real words and you have a God complex."

"I didn't come up with WebMD as a transitive verb!" he said, leaning into the card table.

"To say nothing of your God complex," Faisal added.

"Well."

"And no, since you asked. Trevor told me on the bus. Hang on." Faisal tossed his cards facedown on the table and walked over to the urinal. In one swift motion he had his pants pulled down all the way around his ankles and proceeded to take the longest, loudest piss I'd ever heard, and all the darkness laughed. It was a laughter so complete that even Trevor had to have been part of it.

Michael leaned over to me so that all the ears in the abundant darkness couldn't hear what he said. "We like Trevor. Some of the little shithead kids here don't." He said it to me because, somehow, I was still there and I was still involved.

I picked up my cards and pretended to be figuring out my next move when I said, "Which ones?"

"You'll know them when you see them. Mostly Bryce and his little douchebag friends. You probably heard them, swearing and being little monsters in the back of the bus."

Faisal sat back down. "Getting the skinny on Bryce and his little douchebag friends?"

"Yep," I said. "I remember them from the bus."

"We still haven't figured out how to get rid of him," Michael said. "We should make shirts. It'll just be a picture of Bryce's face with the text *WHAT A PIECE OF SHIT* written in all caps over the top."

"I still like Matty's idea."

"The piñata full of bees?"

"No, covering him in honey and bear pheromones and leaving him in the middle of the woods."

Forty-five minutes later—after the cabins had gone completely quiet—they were still telling stories about the things Bryce had done last year. The stories had started off nearly silent so none of the students would hear them, but after a while they drifted up into a comfortable semi-whisper. Stories like how last fall, even though he was in the younger set of kids at the time, he had stolen three different cell phones and a 3DS from the older kids' cabins.

And about how, when the Buddies had set up a Scrabble tournament and Trevor eliminated him in the first round, Bryce's two-part revenge mission had consisted of (A) finding the trunk where they kept all the games and ripping them all in half before (B) beating up on Trevor until Trevor wet his pants.

"What've we got on him?" I said. Something in my stomach was cold; somewhere far in its fluid depths, there was a slithering, icy rope winding around my bones. Not because of the many juvenile injustices done to Trevor, but because I was starting to feel like it was any of my business.

This was how it always started with Charlie.

Always and without fail.

There would be something that one of us saw as some kind of injustice, some wrong we could right, and the stupid, caffeine-fueled plan would start to take shape.

"Got on him how?" Michael said.

"Like his weaknesses?" Faisal said.

"Sure," I said, even though the last time I'd started making elaborate plans, I'd watched my cousin and my best friend get shot. Despite that fact and despite the sour knot in my guts, I started going through the catalog of classic rock songs to which the heroics would have to be set. One of the ass-kickers, one of the heavies, like "War Pigs" by Black Sabbath. "Paint It Black" by The Stones.

"The good news is that I think he has the same weaknesses as most fifth-graders," Michael said.

"Like, for example, the awkward, fat-but-gangly, almost-puberty physique. Not really sure what to do with their hands or how to use their different-sized feet," Faisal chimed in.

"Really his only advantage is his low center of gravity," Michael said. "Which doesn't mean much if you hit him with a car. Although I do remember him being afraid of the dark."

The only sound from the cabins was the occasional creaking of old mattresses and bed frames that sounded like they almost couldn't hold the weight of those sleeping in them. The kind of creaking that makes you wonder if the ground will hold.

But even if the ground did break underfoot, I realized that I wasn't trying to make my mouth smile to look normal; I wasn't nodding along to a conversation I didn't care about to keep them from asking questions or thinking I was weird or out of place.

I was just being me.

# FIFTEEN: NO SERVICE

WE HAVE A SMALL SERVICE for Charlie. We don't call it a service—just the family geting together to try to start the healing process. But we all know it's a service.

Afterward, all of the aunts and uncles and parents are in our living room, while the younger kids play video games in the basement. I find Jordan in the rec room, looking small next to the pile of coats.

I find him because I hear him crying. Like he's still crying, and hasn't stopped since Christmas dinner. He's leaning over into his arms, crying big, ugly, hard tears, and as soon as he looks up and sees that it's me who found him, he buries his face back into his sleeves.

"He was my brother," he says, just like the time before, except this time there's no fight in him and his mouth sounds full. He's drowning and falling apart at the same time, like he can't help dissolving.

Jordan, who once snorted so many Pixy Stix that he started puking up blue.

Jordan, who kept a pet frog in a shoebox when he was thirteen and we were twelve.

Jordan, who doesn't know I can smell the booze on him.

When he sways, and retches, I think:

*Why haven't I fallen apart like this?*

*What kind of broken excuse for a person* doesn't *disintegrate?*

*This is what they whisper about me; they know I'm not like them.*

*They know I'm a bullshitter.*

Some superhero.

# SIXTEEN: INTO THE FIELDS

I STRETCHED AND CHECKED my phone and there were still ten minutes before my alarm was set to go off. I turned it to silent so it wouldn't wake up the groundskeeper, Nathan, who was asleep in the bunk next to me.

In the five or so minutes where we'd both been awake in the same cabin at the same time, we'd silently agreed not to talk about the uncomfortable age gap or the subpar living standards of his shack.

I pulled the heavy curtain open to check outside. Dead flies were piled up against the dirty glass. They were stacked four high in the corners, like the survivors of the apocalyptic insecticide incident refused to believe the dead bodies were evidence that no one gets out alive. Most of the bugs were long dead—dead to the point where their already fragile wings had since turned to particles floating on angled slats of sunlight. The rest of the bodies were just dust holding shape.

The heap shifted. Something moved in the bottom of the pile and a dead bug rolled silently from the top.

From the stacks and stacks of little dead bodies, a fly crawled out. It twitched back and forth, moving so fast in such a small space that it looked like it was glitching—like everything it did was edited out and I could only see the consequence of its movements.

The bug turned in a fast semicircle, wiped at its alien face a few times, then took flight. It clattered off the glass a few times, never understanding that windows get nailed shut. But it tried and it tried, and when I thought it was going to give up and resign itself to the mountain of bodies, it flew off into the dark of the cabin.

Outside of the window, past the empty, backlit trees, the graying, shotgun-blast clouds were rimmed with gold. The pieces of sky that you could see though the black trees had a color like the clouds were melting into the blue and diluting it. It was a patchwork of pale blue fighting to be seen through branches that looked like Rorschach ink blown out of a straw.

I fumbled through the dark with my arms stretched out in front of me. Aside from tossing my bags in there the first morning, I'd only seen the inside of the maintenance bunkhouse at night. Besides the antler racks and the old-fashioned bear trap on the wall, the only thing I knew about the interior was that it was cold and that Nathan slept with extra blankets that only served to overheat him and make him stink with night sweat.

Hugging my towel and body wash against my chest with my left hand, I dragged my free hand along the wall until I found the only door other than the front entrance.

It was dark in the quarters but stepping on the cold tile floor of the windowless bathroom felt like stepping on midnight, like the tiles were colder and sharper and more immediate than the cold of Nathan's weird little apartment. Wading into the infinite void of the bathroom made the dark of the quarters look gray, and if I could've seen anything, I probably would've seen my breath.

I tried the light switch at the door but it didn't do anything other than make a dry snapping noise each time I flicked it up or down. The potential heat of the shower outweighed staggering around in the dark and trying to keep both feet off the ground as much as possible.

After the shower sputtered and hissed to life, I realized it had two settings: boiling hot or off. I felt around for another knob but there was only one handle in the center of the tiny, coffin-shaped shower stall.

At first I just leaned forward with my hands against the wall, letting the water hit the top of my head while I stared into the nothingness in front of me. I stood there until the air around me began to change—until the air got thick and warm and when I turned around, the water poured down around my collarbone, covering the puckered spot of scar tissue above my heart.

When I couldn't stand it anymore because it felt like the water was going to wash me away, I crouched down and wrapped my arms around my knees. The searing water hit the back of my neck and my shoulders. I moved my head up and let the water wash down my face and around my eyes, pooling in the small cup where my arms hugged my knees like a baby in a strange womb.

It was too dark to see the water but it was impossible not to feel it because, despite the lack of light and despite the expanse of freezing tile, there was undeniable heat in the blackness and I was slowly waking up.

# SEVENTEEN: BEATLES VS. STONES

I HUNCHED MY SHOULDERS TOGETHER and held the Styrofoam cup of motor-oil coffee at chest level while Matty and Michael talked next to me. I pulled on the bottom of my striped ref shirt, momentarily stretching the wrinkles out until I let the fabric go. On the field, Faisal was standing between the two teams, talking and gesturing from one group to the other.

Since Matty had convinced a solid half of her cabin to come play football, the teams were divided roughly between the two-and-a-half cabins, with Faisal as captain of one half and Bryce as captain of the other. No one had protested that Bryce was leading a team, since he had volunteered, and since Faisal was looking for an excuse to demolish him.

Bryce, the legend himself, had been picking on Trevor all the way from the cabins to the field. Having walked with the group, I got to see the little fart in action, starting with small annoying shit like flat-heeling Trevor and throwing pinecones at kids I hadn't met.

As we got everybody separated on the field and ready to play, Goblin Joe ran into him, got tangled up, and fell. Bryce decided to help him up by lifting Joe's shirt off and tucking it into his own flag football belt.

Joe didn't even try to take his shirt back. He just got up, crossed his arms to hide his chest, and looked like he was about to cry.

"*Bryce,*" Matty said. "*Now.*"

Bryce smiled photogenically. "We were just messing around!" he said, tossing the shirt back to Joe.

Faisal finished what he was saying, nodded, and the two teams separated. I looked at my stopwatch, let the final six seconds of their time-out tick away, and blew the whistle. Faisal's team headed for the twenty-yard line and got into formation, but Bryce kept talking to his team. I blew the whistle again, harder, forcing the air out of my lungs and calling him a fucker at the same time.

I added "Total willingness to punt a child into a volcano" to the list of things I'd have to atone for at some point.

He looked over at me, smiled just enough to let me know he heard me, then turned back to his team and kept talking.

I spat the whistle out of my mouth and started toward him but only managed a half-stride before his team broke for the line. He positioned himself in front of Faisal, leaning forward and bracing himself on three fingers.

Faisal looked back and forth, nodded, and yelled, "Football!" before faking to his left and running right.

The teams fanned out and Bryce went gunning for Faisal.

Behind everyone, Trevor walked to the end zone. Nobody saw him; he wasn't a threat to anyone. Right as Bryce went crashing through the no-touch defenders and jumped toward Faisal, Faisal flipped the ball behind his back.

It spiraled sloppily and unevenly but it fell, perfect and awkward, into Trevor's flinching embrace.

Everyone on the field went quiet and Trevor looked around amid the wild silence until Faisal shoved Bryce off of himself and yelled, "Trevor!" triumphantly right into Bryce's dumb face.

I remembered my job and blew the whistle.

Faisal jogged from the center of the football field to where we stood. "This is amazing," he said, pulling his sweatshirt off. "I get it now. I *get* it."

"Which thing do you get?" Matty asked.

"Football. I never liked football." He balled up his sweatshirt and tossed it next to us. "Or I never thought I did."

"This doesn't count as football," Michael said. "You're twice the size of the biggest kid out there."

"I know. It's perfect. I'm Too Big to Fail. I am *destroying* them." He turned and faced the two teams that were loosely huddled together, kicking at leaves and doing the odd handstand, and yelled with a surprising amount of authority from behind his smile: "No mingling!" He turned back to us. "I'm going to make the losing team write letters to their parents apologizing for the shame they're bringing down upon their families." He grinned.

"Faisal!" one of the kids yelled, waving. He pronounced "Faisal" like "fizzle." It was impossible to make out all the words the kid said except for "cold."

"Gotta go. Kids are getting cold; can't have the little animals going all *Lord of the Flies* on Trevor."

"Moses! Tonight: The Entertainment?" Michael said.

"Yes," I said. Then: "No. I don't know. I don't understand the question." The wind was hitting me in the eyes so I looked more suspicious than I meant to.

"You don't know The Entertainment?" Matty said. The disbelief in her voice was utter.

"Is that a wrestler? Like professional wrestler?"

"They're only *the* seminal David-Foster-Wallace-related band in the Midwest and they're only playing *one town over*. For a *porch* show. Our yearly delinquency trip has never been more important."

"I guess I wouldn't miss it for the world, then," my mouth said before my brain could formulate a bullshit excuse for not going. Because this was after Tens and this was after talks about thin ice and this was after being put on Lump Detail and goddammit, this was after Charlie. And *they* were asking *me* if I wanted to be with *them*. I wanted to see more of Matty and Michael. More of Michael and Faisal. More of Matty and Faisal. If that meant learning about David Foster Wallace fan rock, then I was going to learn about some David Foster Wallace fan rock.

Their dynamic felt familiar and I kept thinking about Matty calling Michael a Tom Hanks kind of leader. It was just an off-handed joke, but she'd said it and it was the same kind of thing Charlie would have said about himself, even if Charlie would have chosen a different celebrity. Someone harder, someone more rock and roll. Where he'd have called me the Beatles, he'd have called himself the Rolling Stones.

And she'd called Michael her other half.

And she'd shot him—albeit with a Nerf gun.

Their dynamic, all three of them, was like looking at all of the constituent parts of my relationship with Charlie with just enough new pieces to make it different and new.

But like a version of us that worked.

While the two teams walked back to the starting line, Bryce kept staring Trevor down, which Trevor kept trying to ignore. Even after everyone lined up and waited for the play to begin, Bryce kept staring at him.

Fifty yards away, past the archery range, the door to the crafts hall burst open. Lump launched out, hurdling the stairs and hitting the ground mid-stride, aiming for us before the door had time to slap shut. She was a fantastic blur, pumping her free arm while the other held a stack of bright papers snug against her chest. With the sun at her back, her shadow was a thousand miles long—long like it could reach up and touch the light that made it. One of the Buddies emerged from the crafts hall and called after her to slow down.

If nothing else, people saw her now. She would have been fine after the bonfire and exploding can, but somebody had seen her when she'd needed to be seen, and now she ran like she knew she wasn't invisible.

It's not all the time that you get to do right by someone and actually see the result.

Right when it looked like she was going to dash in front of the tiny archers, she hooked around them. As she closed in on us, I waved to the Buddy she'd escaped from, who gave an exasperated wave back.

"Hi, Lump!" Matty said as the running child came to a dramatic and skidding stop in front of us.

"Hi. I need to keep borrowing this," she said, mostly ignoring Matty and holding up the marker I'd lent her. "For the posters. I promise I'll keep it safe."

"Can I see one?" I asked.

She held out a bright yellow flyer from the multicolored stack. It had a pixelated stock picture of a baby deer glued under the word "LOST."

"I couldn't fill out the description part because I haven't seen the deer yet so I need your help. With the diss-ting-wishing features and all," she said, enunciating the word carefully to keep it from tumbling apart.

"I think you got it down pretty well," I said. "This picture looks just like him," I said, not quite lying. The picture looked like the deer because it was a picture of a baby deer. What made this lost deer different, though, was that somebody was trying to find it.

"Exactly like? Or just mostly like?"

"Baby deer all look pretty similar. Their genetics are pre—"

"We don't want the wrong deer. We don't want to steal a baby deer from the wild."

"That's a good point. But I think these'll work."

"Here," Lump said to Michael and Matty, holding a couple of flyers out to them.

"Guys!" Faisal yelled to us, waving his free hand while the other one cradled the football in the nook of his arm. A small army of children was huffing in his wake, some still running after him with streaming flags at their waists, but most dejected or bent over and out of breath. "Guys! I'm about to win foot—" One of the smaller kids had decided to play from the sideline, silently jetting around in front of him and diving at him head-on as he stared over at us. He let out a *hrrk!* noise when the small bony bundle of destruction hit him in the solar plexus, sending the football bouncing away.

If it were regulation football, the players would have returned to a planned formation where they would strategize their next play. But this was the jungle. International waters. Prison rules. The ones still running to catch up caught up, hurling themselves through the air, bellowing warrior-cries as they did. The ones who'd stopped, too tired to chase on, snapped back to battle mode and went screaming toward the downed Faisal.

"Guys!" we heard, muffled. "Help! This isn't football anymore—"

The kids piled onto him.

"Should we help him?" Matty asked, leaning over to see better, popping a handful of trail mix into her mouth.

"Nah, he's got it under control," Michael said with his hands shoved deep in his pockets. We heard a yelp as one of the children stood tall, yelling and holding up a triumphant handful of hair. "Oh. Yeah, no, we should help him."

I blew the whistle again and started to go with Michael and Matty to help Faisal, but Lump grabbed my sleeve. "Can you help me pass these out? They said I need an adult. We have to go to the barn where it happened."

She looked at me and shook the stack of papers a little, like, "Okay, come on," and somewhere Test was off wearing creepy shorts and somewhere Charlie simply wasn't, and it was just me.

"Look," I said. "Right now, I've gotta do this football thing."

I was the one who'd told her about the deer—if anybody else had brought her to get her ear bandaged up that first night, she would have never found about the missing animal. At the same time, there was still that stupid, assholish prerecorded message running through my head telling me to mind my own business and keep my head down and get through the week and maybe I could put everything behind me.

"Can he help me put up flyers?" she yelled over to Matty, who turned and shrugged and said, "Sure!" before immediately turning back to the kids mauling Faisal.

I breathed out through my nose.

I caught Matty's attention and tossed her the whistle and stopwatch.

Michael pulled two kids off of the pile while Matty hunched in front of the kid who'd tried to scalp Faisal. The kid held out the handful of hair to her but she shook her head and kept talking to him.

There was an honest impulse to use the *Lord of the Flies* death match in front of me to my own advantage and leave Lump to find someone else to help her. But then a burst of cold, pre-winter wind weaved its way through the field and it made me think of the seasons changing, which made me think of the line from the Blue Oyster Cult song about how seasons don't fear the reaper, and I knew that this was it: this was Lump Detail. Fuck the rest.

"How many posters did you make?"

"Almost a hundred."

"And you want to put them all up?"

"How else are we supposed to find the deer?" She handed me a small slip of paper like I really wasn't grasping how simple this was.

"Okay. Let's do it."

"Good. This is my phone number in case we need to split up and you run out of flyers and need more. What's yours?"

# EIGHTEEN: THE NUMEROUS HEINOUS CRIMES OF CECIL BENSON THE EIGHTH

WE'RE IN SEVENTH GRADE and we're in the Chicago History Museum for a field trip about industrialization, which is a topic neither one of us can even remotely pretend to give the faintest shit about. Our class is big enough and the museum is hectic enough that we take the first opportunity that presents itself to slip away and explore on our own.

That first opportunity, it turns out, is down a mock turn-of-the-twentieth-century street, complete with a cobblestone road, gas lamps, and old-fashioned pickup trucks loaded up with wooden barrels.

We're just looking for any kind of way to split off from our school group, but when we realize we're in a gangster exhibit called "Booze and Bullets" that comes with a content warning, Charlie goes, "Fuck *yes,* we're going learn about whiskey and machine guns."

We walk down the road, passing glassed-in displays of crime-scene photos and artifacts.

I'm checking out one about Dillinger, his stark, blown-up mug shot staring out at the steady trickle of passersby. There's a picture of his death mask, as well as a handkerchief that was dipped in his blood after he was shot down behind the Biograph Theater. "We should go check out the theater where they shot Dillinger, dude," I say, reading an old news clipping. Charlie doesn't answer, even though I'm aware of him in my peripheral vision. "Hey, you hear me?"

But Charlie's looking at a murderer's exhibit. I walk up behind him and see a huge picture of a man named Cecil Benson the Eighth being led out of his house by two expressionless cops. Benson's in a white T-shirt with suspenders hanging in loops at his side, and there are spots of blood on his face and clothes. He's a mess, but I know Charlie's looking at the feet in the background, sticking out of the doorway, the body mostly in the house. The articles list Benson's crimes, murder included.

The picture we're looking at was taken the night he killed his cousin.

He starts when he sees me, then says, "Let's get the fuck out of here," without much tone or emotion. So we do, and we don't talk about Cecil Benson the Eighth or any of his heinous crimes, but nobody outside of Charlie's other half would have heard the waver in his voice when we left, or noticed how much eye contact he didn't make the rest of the day.

# NINETEEN: ANTHONY THE ASSHOLE

AFTER STOPPING AT THE MAIN OFFICE for tape and staplers, we set off.

"Because animals need our help!" Lump said. She had very enthusiastically already passed out ten or so flyers to the group at the archery range. "Especially baby animals. Did you know that when I was in second grade we had a cat named Helicopter that Mom and Dad thought ran away? This was before Grandma moved in because Dad got sick. Dad has ghost hair because he has mesothelioma."[15]

Behind us the archery group were making stupid goddamn faces and pointing to the posters in their hands.

"But so anyway, the cat, Helicopter, that Mom and Dad thought ran away, didn't actually run away. He only ran away to the front yard and tried to hide under the hood of the truck because it was warm there and it was winter outside so it was cold everywhere else. Here," she said, handing me some more

---

15 Caused primarily by exposure to asbestos, mesothelioma is a rare form of cancer that develops in the lining that covers many internal organs, and she pronounced the word flawlessly. She didn't explain what ghost hair was.

flyers. "We should ask the people on the rock-climbing wall to put some flyers up top, or maybe have them make them into paper airplanes and throw them down to everybody."

"We can put some up in the mess hall," I said. "Lots of people, lots of eyes. Maximum exposure," I said, trying to shift gears as fast as her.

"Good idea. We also still need to go to the barn. Anyway, so Mom told me to go warm up the truck so that she could drive me to school and we didn't know that Helicopter had crawled up around the engine."

"I can't see this ending too great for Helicopter."

Her tone never really changed from fast-paced conversational. There weren't many ways this could turn out well for Helicopter the cat, and when I looked at her to see if she was tensing up for the inevitably grisly outcome, I saw someone who might as well be recapping a mildly interesting movie. Something as fucked up as watching your family deal with mesothelioma probably has that effect on you. I should know: the punch lines for half the jokes at any of my family gatherings, at least growing up, involved little kids getting shot.

"And I turned the car on but it sounded funny so I pressed the gas pedal all the way down even though Mom said never play with any of the pedals or buttons but I did and then Helicopter sort of blew up on the windshield."

"*Je*-sus." As a responsible Buddy, I tried not to smile at her delivery of the story but it sounded like every joke I grew up on. Jokes like, "Take out the trash or I'll finish what your cousin started," and "I knew he should have bought a bigger gun."

Jokes that we all thought were legitimately funny too.

"I don't warm up the truck anymore." The way she said it,

she knew it was fucked up and terrible but you could tell she thought it was a funny story too. At least a faraway kind of funny. That "a lot of the other parts of my life are destabilizing bullshit so I'm going to laugh at cats that explode" kind of funny.

"I don't blame you," I said.

"Not unless I bang on the truck first with a hockey stick, but Mom says that gives her pre-mat-sure wrinkles which doesn't make any sense because old age gives you wrinkles and she's forty-three."

And I couldn't not laugh; I laughed my real laugh.

We headed for the mess hall and handed flyers out to the stragglers we passed. I taped a *LOST* flyer under the word "Nakwatuk." Test was inside, standing in front of a wheeled-in whiteboard, lecturing a group of older campers that I didn't know. Kids from one of the other buses.

"Maybe we should come back later," I said to Lump.

"Why?"

"Because Tes—" I cleared my throat. "*Mister* Test is in there talking to the older kids." It seemed like the right thing to say to make her to think I was a responsible and capable adult.

"That's perfect!" she said and flung the door open, like she wanted to show me how to be a responsible and capable child.

Test stopped mid-sentence, his hands still up, and the group of nine or ten kids all turned and looked at us at the same time.

"I need everyone's attention! I have an announcement!"

Test gave me a look that said, "Seriously?" before softening and looking at Lump. "Allison, you can make your announcement when I'm finished. I have the floor right now."

Lump's face went deep red. "Don't call me that."

"I'm sorry?" he said, placing his loose fists on his hips and trying to look as parentally intimidating as possible.

"I said, please don't call me that." Some of the fire went out of her voice when she tried to match Test's authority. Still, the words came out made of iron, even if they came out quiet.

Test nodded and asked the group in a sweeping, semi-rhetorical voice, "Where were we?"

"You okay?" I whispered to Lump.

"I don't like it when other people call me Allison."

Before I could say anything else, and before Lump could tell me who calls her Allison, Test went on. "Right: you're walking in the woods. Right. So. You come to a split in the trail and standing between the two paths is an old man. He greets you and says that you have two choices." Which was obvious because it was a two-pronged fork, and wrong because there are always other choices. "Choice one." He drew one large red arrow veering left and one veering right, and pointed to the left arrow with his marker.

"He definitely needed the giant dry-erase board for this," I said to Lump. Some of the red faded from her cheeks.

"You go left and you will be given one *billion* dollars. With a *B*." The students looked back and forth between each other. A small grin slunk across his face and you could tell he was thinking, *Got these boys eating out the palm of my hand.* After a very dramatic two-second pause, he said, flippantly, "Or you go right and you get . . ." He fished a dingy penny out of his back pocket and held it up between his thumb and forefinger. After everyone saw the coin, he tossed it to the nearest fourth-or-fifth-grader. "But: if you choose the penny, your money will double every day for a month. A penny the first day, two pennies the second, four pennies the third day, eight on the fourth, and so on." He shrugged like, "That's it; pretty lame, I know." He looked his audience over. "The tension at the crossroads is palatable as the old man looks you in the eye and waits for your answer. What do you do?"

I leaned down to Lump. "Tension's not palatable; it's palpable." I considered telling her that, despite his best efforts and sly intentions, a billion dollars was without a doubt the correct choice here, but settled on the abridged, "Also, choose billion." Her color returned to normal.

"Who says go left?" he asked. All of the hands went up.

"C'mon. Let's go put up some flyers. We'll come back when they're done."

We made our way around the hall, dropping flyers where people would see them. On the sneeze guard over the empty salad bar; taped to the microphone stand on the stage; on the fire exits.

"What about through here?" she said, standing in front of a large wooden door marked "Staff Only." She twisted the knob but the door didn't move.

"If it's staff only," I said, taping a flyer to the window, "it's probably . . ." In my peripheral vision I saw a Lump-blur run shoulder-first into the door, rattling it on its hinges with a sound loud enough to echo through the hall. "Holy shit, Lump."

I saw Test looking at me from his makeshift stage through the porthole window on the connecting door. I tried to convey that things were still okay in here by flashing a smile and giving him two thumbs-up.

She was backing up and getting ready to batter the door down. "Lump, *stop*," I said. The red started creeping back into her cheeks. It wasn't much, but it was there. I took a breath, clicked my tongue against the roof of my mouth, checked to see that Test had returned to talking to the kids, thought, *Fuck it,* and said, "Hang on."

I handed her the flyers and tried the door. It was locked, but just barely. I took my wallet out and found a rewards card to a place called Bonnie's Café; I pushed the card between the door frame and the latch bolt and forced the door open.

"*Yes!*" she said, pumping both of her fists, still holding the papers. We couldn't see anything past the door but that didn't stop her from heading straight for it. I grabbed the back of her coat, said "Hang on," again, and felt around for a light switch.

The switch was high up on the wall, hidden in the cool, dry darkness. I flipped it on and we were looking at ten steep stairs leading to a maintenance tunnel.

"Can we?" she said, her eyes wide.

I jogged down the steps, looked down the tunnel, and came back up.

"Nobody's going to see them if we put them down there," I said.

"They might!" She looked at me until she scrunched her face up. "Fine. Can I look though?"

When I didn't answer right away she shoved the flyers into my hands and sprinted down the steps. "It's creepy down here!" she said without looking back at me.

And it was. The tunnel ran for maybe forty or fifty yards and was supposed to be lit by bare yellow bulbs every ten feet, except all of them but two had burned out: one bulb at the bottom of the stairs and one at the end of the tunnel. Under the last bulb there was a mess of tables, folding chairs, and decommissioned camp equipment.

I could hear Test and the campers wrapping up. "Lump. Go time!"

She ran up the stairs two at a time and we headed back toward Test, Lump moving somewhere between a power walk and a jog.

The whiteboard had a section of tallies under the left arrow and then what was supposed to be a mind-blowing equation under the right, except you could tell he'd realized his mistake during the presentation and had tried for a more creative math angle. He saw us approaching and asked the students to hang on a minute.

"Hi. Okay. Thanks. I have an announcement." She studied their faces and waited for a response.

"What's your announcement, Lump?" Test said. She didn't tense up when he called her Lump.

"There is a deer missing. She's just a baby and she escaped yesterday. I looked it up on the Internet . . . before, at home, because we're not allowed to be on the Internet here . . . and the nightly average temp-er-rature has been in the record lows."

"It's just a deer," one of the kids said. He was, inevitably, the Bryce of whatever cabin he belonged to.

The color filled her cheeks again. "She's just a baby. She needs help."

"Or," the asshole kid continued, "maybe it'll get hit by a truck and there'll be one less deer to worry about."

"Anthony—" Test said, stepping toward the little shit.

"There's a reward," I heard myself say before Test could move any closer, which was a thousand times better than what I had thought I was going to say. Test gave me the same "Are you kidding me" look from before.

Lump looked up at me and her eyes flashed. "Of a hundred . . ." she started to say until she saw me glaring at her. "I mean. Of fifty dollars." She looked at me and I couldn't keep glaring. "Yeah. Fifty dollars. We know what she looks like. What she exactly looks like. So don't bring us just any deer."

The righteous confidence in her voice was a booming, thunderous "fuck you" to the little bastard kid.

Since Charlie wasn't around to high-five her, I took on the responsibility.

# TWENTY: SIX-MILE THOUGHTS

WE'RE JUNIORS AND IT'S MID-OCTOBER and we're in the north suburbs because we heard about a party where a kid we went to school with was planning on raising the dead in his backyard.

Eddie Carlo's dog died three days ago and, after a series of Dark Web rabbit holes, he's convinced he can say the right combination of words in the right combination of languages to bring Bluebeard back to this world, and return to his mortal dog coil.

If there's one thing Charlie and I know about, it's defying the void.

Eddie Carlo is and always has been the nicest kid you could hope to meet, so Charlie doesn't have a hard time convincing me that Eddie should have friends around when his dog doesn't come back from the grave, and plus, Eddie Carlo has a pool and his parents are out of town.

And everything is good, aside from Eddie's dog's untimely fate. The air is warm for October and the sun sets early so it's warm and dark and the strands of Edison lights in Eddie's backyard make everything look like the World's Fair, even when we gather around Eddie and the circle of stones he's placed around Bluebeard's grave in his backyard.

But mid-ritual, while Eddie's stuttering through a Latin incantation and trying not to cry, I realize that I've lost Charlie. And the more I look around, the more I realize that I've lost most everybody else.

It's just me and Eddie Carlo and two people making out on a bench in the garden, because everybody else who showed up is jumping in the pool and drinking shitty beer.

But not Charlie.

Charlie is gone.

Charlie has taken the car and bailed because Al Stinson told him he could score some weed.

So I stay, and the dog stays dead, and Charlie never comes back or answers his phone, and it doesn't take the whole of the six miles walking home to realize that a sizeable part of you hates—at least in part—someone you're supposed to love.

It takes a whole lot less than six.

# TWENTY-ONE: SOMEWHERE IN BETWEEN

"ARE YOU SAD?" LUMP asked me as we stapled and taped more flyers up around the barn.

"What?"

"You seem sad. Or mad."

"No, Lump, I'm not sad or mad." I didn't know how to tell her I was somewhere in between the two and that, more than that, I was something else as well. That I was furious and heartbroken but there was something extra that I wasn't familiar with. It was something that *felt* like happy, even if happy wasn't quite the right word. Something like distracted, or like a pace being changed. Different air finally getting breathed in.

"Is it about the deer?"

"Lump, I said I'm not sad."

"It's just that you keep putting the flyers up a certain way like you're doing one thing but thinking about something else. Like when grandma talks about Uncle Thomas and then ends up dusting everything and cleaning the sink even though the sink never gets that dirty because we order pizza a lot."

I smiled without opening my mouth. It was cold but the sun

was bright enough to make you unzip your coat and take your gloves off.

"I'm just thinking about the deer," I said. "Want to make sure these flyers are in all the right places. Tall places so the adults can see them, short places so the kids can see them." I demonstrated this with my hands.

"Are you worried because you were there when the deer got away?"

I aggressively stapled another flyer to the barn doors. The fence where the deer had escaped was blocked up with a few bales of hay.

"A little. But I'm also thinking about how, after he got away, the other deer is back at the barn, safe, and it's nice out and it's sunny and it's like nothing is wrong."

"How do you know the deer was a boy?"

"What?"

"You said 'he'—how do you know he was a him and not a her? Were you sexting the deer?"

I stopped and faced her full-on. "What?"

She squinted one eye shut and spoke like she was reciting something she'd read: " 'I-dent-ifying the gender of a deer or other baby animal is called sexting.' I read that on the Internet last night even though we're not allowed to and even though the Internet drains my battery and I have to use data to get the Internet from satellites. My phone connects to satellites," she said confidentially.

"Sext . . . *sexing*. There's no T. With a T it's something else."

She knew what she was trying to say, she'd just said it wrong. Like the time I'd mixed up the words "primal" and "carnal" on an essay question about *To Kill a Mockingbird*.

"It looked big for a baby deer so I assumed it was a boy."

"Girls can be big. Bigger than boys."

"Very true. What are we calling the deer? Does the deer have a name?"

"Not one that she knows yet. Right now her name is Amelia Earhart."

"Because she's missing?"

"No. Because she doesn't believe in fences. She can go wherever she wants, whenever she wants."

"You should name the deer Jimmy Hoffa. I think Jimmy Hoffa the Deer has a nice ring to it."

"Mom says it's important to have strong role models that aren't on the Internet or TV or drugs," she said, ignoring my joke about Jimmy Hoffa the Deer. "And Amelia Earhart . . ." She placed the flyers down reverently and unzipped her coat. The front of her shirt had a picture of Amelia Earhart standing atop her Lockheed Model 10 Electra, waving to an unseen audience, her red scarf caught in the wind and blazing behind her. "Amelia Earhart is a hero. But anyway, you shouldn't be sad because you can't stop deer from escaping." She zipped her coat, picked the flyers up, and wiped away the flecks of dirt and earth from the bottom page.

"Then why are we putting flyers up? If they're just going to run away again, right?"

"No."

"No what? Why not?"

"Because this time she'll know she has friends."

I checked, and all of a sudden, the mysterious other feeling, the one that wasn't quite happiness but somewhere closer to distraction, simply wasn't there anymore. Now it was the same anger and sadness that had been hanging around for so long.

"You think he didn't know he had friends? What about the other deer that tried to escape with him?"

"Her. Maybe they just weren't fast enough."

"The other deer was plenty fast. Just as fast as the one that got away," I said, indignant. I told myself to relax. "What if he knew exactly what he was doing and was just being an asshole? Like what if the deer was a pattern asshole and was always doing stuff like this to the other deer?" I asked the eight-year-old. Then, "Sorry I swore."

"Huh?"

"I'm saying, what if that was the deer's plan all along, because that deer was always doing stupid stuff and making the other deer pay for it? Like making a break for it and not telling the other deer. Because the other deer tried to escape too. You could just *tell* the other one wanted to run away."

One of her eyebrows raised up a little and her mouth became a thin line, like she didn't know why the supposed "grown-up" was talking to her like she was a therapist.

Instead of just saying, "Dude, shut up," she very generously said, "I guess she was being selfish. But. I think probably she was just scared—probably like all the other baby deer—and just did what she thought was best."

This mysterious other not-quite-but-almost happiness feeling was a million miles away. We weren't walking in the warm sun or talking about funny things to name missing deer anymore. This wasn't cards at night or smoking on top of decommissioned ROTC equipment. This was the Ghost of Charlie Baltimore, flickering just outside of my line of sight.

I stapled another poster up with what I hoped was less aggression.

"What is *that?*" she said, looking over my head toward the tree line. A splash of orange and white was flitting back and forth in the wind, just past the trees. "Is that a *windsock?*" It was. "Usually at night airports shine bright lights on their windsocks," she continued. "Probably so planes won't run into them but also so they can tell which way the wind is blowing even though it's nighttime out. I like that the wind wears socks."

Which it doesn't, because the wind is not a sock-wearing thing. But that didn't stop her from staring at the piece of orange-and-white fabric riding the invisible air currents, trying just to sail off with the breeze, where it could always point the direction of the wind for the rest of us.

# TWENTY-TWO: MOM AND MY OTHER HALF

A WEEK AFTER THE FIRE—A week after I was arrested and fingerprinted and released into my parents' custody—Mom is driving me to my first court appearance and she's crying.

She says things like "I love you so much, baby," whenever we pull up to a red light. Things like, "It's okay to cry," on all of the occasions she notices I'm not crying. And now she's doing it again. "I just . . . I keep thinking about how you lost your other half. And how you saw it happen right in front of you." She wipes the side of her thumb under her eyes, one at a time, then looks over and gives me the hardest excuse for a smile I've ever seen: her lips make a crooked line, and her eyes are pooling over, and she's trying so hard to actually smile because that's what a parent does—tries with everything they have to keep their kid from knowing how much pain they're really in.

"It's okay, Mom," I say, knowing that she'll just take it as me trying to comfort her.

This is the truth: as terrible as it all is, I am okay.

I can be okay.

I can be okay without Charlie. Or, at least, I want to be able to be okay without him.

And that feels so fucked up.

The light changes to green, but she doesn't move. She just looks at me, the devastating smile going tighter and flatter as the car behind us gives a short and polite reminder honk. "You don't need to be okay, baby," she says.

"Light, Mom," I say, motioning toward the traffic signal.

"Sweetie," she says, and this time the car behind us lays on its horn. She reaches back between the seats and gives the car behind us *not* the middle finger, but the index finger—one that says, "Just a moment." Her eyes are locked on mine when she says it again: "You don't need to be okay. It's okay to be everything else too."

"Mom, the light changed."

The car behind us backs up, angles its wheels, then dramatically zooms around us, the driver giving us not the index, but the middle. The light turns yellow.

"I love you so much," she says. Her face is composed, but there are silent tears coming down her cheeks.

"I know, Mom. And I love you too."

My eyes are dry. The light clicks to a deep red, washing over us.

# TWENTY-THREE:
# HARRIET TUBMAN

JUST AS WE RAN out of posters, the dented metal speakers on top of a utility pole started playing a tinny, old-fashioned horn melody that meant lunch. The bright squares of paper on the tripod archery targets were impossible to ignore.

"Those little shitheads," I said, pulling a flyer down. Each one of the bull's-eye targets had a brightly colored *LOST* flyer stuck to its center with an arrow. She pulled one down and looked at me through the hole in the paper.

"Shot right in the head," she said.

"They're just being stupid, Lump. Don't worry about it," I said, more to my feet than to her.

"You just called them shitheads though."

"I did. And I shouldn't have. I'm the grown-up here."

"It's okay. They're just kids. Plus, this way more people will see the flyers. They'll know what we're looking for." Her voice was void of angry, huffed air, which was the opposite of how I would have handled it, whether at her age or now. At her age, I would have deflated, and now, as an almost-adult, I would have been boiling. Lump, though, was anything but deflated.

We headed for lunch.

"Twelff," Michael said carefully as he maneuvered the twelfth grape into his mouth.

"Thirththeen," Faisal said, fitting a thirteenth into his.

"So what was the Korn kid like?" Matty said to me.

I put my can of soda down and looked at her. ". . . corn kid?"

Lump had disappeared once we'd gotten to lunch, but not before grilling me about identifying marks on the deer; she'd run off to make more flyers. The Buddies didn't have to sit near the campers, but it was encouraged. And since they were bigger than the campers, the Buddies could move their herds accordingly. Matty was in charge of the table of girls who kept giving Faisal and Michael's table dirty looks whenever Goblin Joe would eat a piece of gum off the bottom of the bench.

"At the Olympiad. He placed third or fourth, I think, but I remember him. Mostly because I didn't expect a Chemistry Olympian to be wearing a Korn shirt, but also because I remember his mom in the audience holding up a banner with his name on it and being real cute."

I still hadn't wrapped my head around the fact that anyone had watched the Olympiad, school mandated or not. The idea that anyone other than our immediate families and local science teachers had anything to do with our viewership was unbelievable.

"Oh! Right. Number Eighty-Two."

"ThKorkidthnabewaseightydoo?" Faisal asked, then said: "Forththeen," and pressed another green grape into his mouth.

"I don't know his actual name. I still can't believe you watched the Olympiad. I'm pretty sure my own parents only watched half of it."

"Full disclosure: I probably paid more attention to it than the rest of my class because I was laid up in bed for three days with mono." She looked over at Michael, who pointed at himself with both thumbs, smiling as much as he could with a mouth loaded with fruit.

"Shgeefrewupaytduyms."

"He says I threw up eight times," she said. Michael nodded the same smug way Charlie would've. And she kept going strong the way I like to think I would have.

Michael looked around at us. "Idwuhuhiysgore."

"He says it was the high score. Anyway. It was when we were on vacation up in Wisconsin and our cabin didn't have cable or the Internet so I ended up watching the entire Olympiad. So: Korny Eighty-Two," she said, refusing to let Michael sidetrack her.

"Kid was a sweetheart. We didn't talk much, but he was nice to everyone—called people sir and ma'am. Kind of guy me and my cousin would have been friends with, " I said truthfully, feeling my stomach flip over at Charlie's mention.

I'd said thirty-one words to these people. In a row. About my past. I'd spoken them with varying cadence and total honesty. I'd spoken to them like we were all teenagers sitting at a table together at a youth camp.

Faisal slapped his hand to his pocket and pulled out a buzzing phone. He held up a "Hang on a minute and shut up" finger to Michael and spit all of the grapes out onto the table while Matty made a barf face and muttered, "Boys are so gross."

"Hey, Mom," he said, smiling a little. "Yeah, everything's good. Yeah. Yep. I think it was in the garage, last time I saw it." He nodded along to a voice we couldn't hear and ushered a couple of shiny mouth-grapes around in front of him. Then he smiled full-on and said, "He did? Yeah, no, I told him we'd be in Michigan by now. All right. Yep. No, that would be great. I will. I will. Love you too. Yep, bye."

He held the phone out, hit a button, and buried it in his pocket. "Mom says hi."

"Hi, Mama Al-Aziz!" Matty said into her sandwich.

"Ibabazeez," Michael said. He started chomping sloppily down on the grapes.

"This is my boyfriend," Matty said to us like an aside.

"We loave eesh other," he said, his cheeks mushing up under his eyes.

"You take me. You take me right now."

"Mom says hi to you too, Moses," Faisal said.

"She did? Oh. Hi." It had been a while since I was in the fold with pleasantries. Lately, it had been "Tell Moses to stay strong," or "Tell him we're keeping him in our prayers." When people didn't think I could hear them, it was more "Did you hear what he did?" and "Motherfucker's crazy. His cousin got shot over how crazy he is."

Nobody just said hi.

"Also, what are you smiling about?" Matty said, pointing at him. "This is camp, we don't smile here."

The guy who peed in front of everyone, the guy who could scream porno titles at the heavens and fire wayward arrows through our superiors, dropped his eyes and shrugged a little. But the smile only got bigger. "He brought flowers over."

Matty beamed.

"Those flowbers're gonna be suber dead by the time we ged home," Michael said, still working on the grapes.

"Nah, my mom's putting them in water."

"Do you guys know how goddamn cute you are?" Matty asked, smacking Michael in the chest and making him almost choke. Her smile made her cheeks and eyes scrunch up.

Detail after detail of their personal lives, and they didn't seem to hide them from me for even a second.

"I never said they weren't super cute," Michael struggled to say, just before coughing up a half-eaten chunk of grape.

"Okay, well," Faisal said with finality. "This cutesy shit is getting old. And I have to pee. Also, you swallowed your grapes before you beat my record. Is it dark in here, or is that just my immense shadow that you'll always live in?" He and Matty fist-bumped.

They gave each other shit and they were weird to each other, but they did it without explosions or a blast radius.

Faisal stood up and took a bite of his sandwich. "Don't let Goblin Joe touch my food."

As he walked by his cabin's table, Goblin Joe looked up from spitting into his own hands and went for a weird two-handed high five and Faisal twisted out of the way. Goblin Joe scuttled after him and jumped on him, so Faisal put him in a headlock. He let him go and, even though the room was loud enough to destroy their conversation before it reached our table, you could see he was explaining to Joe how to put someone into a full nelson.

"Oh. Hey. You," Matty said, poking Michael in the forehead. "My dad wants to know about Thanksgiving."

"It's not even Halloween yet. *That's* the next holiday."

"Yeah, exactly. He needs to know how intensely he should be hunting this weekend."

Which was where I expected the exasperated deep breath from one or both of them. The sigh before the argument.

"I don't think your dad operates on an intensity level of less than one hundred percent."

"That's not tr—"

"Remember what he does to home invaders?"

"We never *had* a home invader."

"*Exactly.* They all know about your dad."

I watched the conversation bounce back and forth from behind my sandwich. Matty rolled her eyes and looked at me. This had to be where she'd ask me to give them a minute because she needed to talk to Michael in private.

"Last year, around Christmas, there were a bunch of home invasions in my neighborhood," she said, "and Mike and I thought it was a good idea to play Santa and set the gifts up for Christmas morning." She looked at him, asking him silently if, so far, this wasn't all true; he gestured with a "by all means, please go on" motion. "And we were up at like three or four in the morning wrapping gifts and putting up stockings, making everything all Christmassy—"

"And he didn't know about any of this?" I asked.

"That's debatable," Michael said, throwing little jabs at the story that she knew were coming. They told the story together like it'd been done a hundred times before.

"No, it's not debatable: he had no idea. We came back late

after Mike's family's dinner, way after Dad went to bed, so it was just the two of us. Mom'd died a couple years before so Christmas mornings weren't as traditional as they'd been growing up, so I was trying to make things, you know . . ." she waved her hand slowly, filling in the gaps. Michael didn't add jabs or licks to the story when she said it either. He stayed quiet, completely solemn for the two and a half seconds it took her to talk about her mom.

"Anyway, Mike and I, we pooled some of our money to buy him one of those punching bags that's shaped like a guy with no arms."

"Uh-oh."

"*Yeah, uh-oh,*" Michael said, right back in the mix. She shot him a look that was half smile, half "I'll kill you."

"Well, Dad heard us farting around downstairs so we killed the lights and hid when we heard him moving around. And he comes tearing down the stairs and he sees the outline of a weird motionless guy standing in his living room leering out the window and all I remember is us hiding behind the couch and hearing my dad go, 'Hey! *Hey! Hey* mother*fucker!*' And then the sound of him attacking White Tyson. We named the dummy White Tyson."

"That's terrible—he wasn't even . . . armed . . ." I said, and slowly raised my hand for a high five. Matty high-fived me back but when our hands clapped together it was a thunderclap.[16]

When I pulled my hand back it automatically snapped back to rub the spot where Charlie's brother had choked me until I

---

16  Like catalyst gunshots.

blacked out. That place on my neck had had a bruise shaped like a spider—a dark middle with lines extending out to points.

"No. No high fives," Michael said. "He didn't *attack* White Tyson—he *butchered* White Tyson. We turned the lights on and there was a fucking *ax* sticking out of the small of White Tyson's back."

"An ax? Like an ax-ax? Like a lumberjack ax?" I said, forcing my hand to do something completely and utterly normal like fidgeting around on the table and tapping my fork against my plate.

"In the *small of his back!*" Michael said. "Not only does he *sleep with an ax* but he tried to chop the dude's spine out. That's some serial killer shit."

"So, Thanksgiving . . . ?" Matty said to Michael.

His phone went off in his pocket and he dug it out. "I just don't understand why he always asks me how much I weigh every time he gets back from hunting. It's terrifying," he said as he clicked his phone on to check the text. His forehead wrinkled. "It's Faisal. Trevor's eating lunch in the bathroom."

"They're still picking on him?" Matty asked.

"Yeah. They painted his nails last night. We got them to shake hands eventually but you know neither one of them meant it."

"Bryce?" Matty asked. It was barely a question. Even after hearing all of their stories about Bryce, it was different seeing his aftermath in real time.

"Yeah."

"Come on. Got a plan," she said, standing up. "Think, life-size Mouse Trap, but instead of dropping a cage on a mouse we're going to drop a bag full of scorpions on a ten-year-old."

Michael slapped a hand against the table in an "About time, here we go" motion, then stood up to follow Matty. Before either of them could go anywhere, though, Faisal came out of the double doors that led to the bathrooms. Trevor was right behind him.

Michael and Matty sat back down, joined by Faisal and Trevor. Trevor's fingertips were pinkish red with raw spots here and there, like he'd been scrubbing at his fingers for hours. He was exactly the kind of person Charlie would have heard about and insisted we do something for. Knowing Charlie, it would have involved a corkboard with pinned-up pictures, psychological warfare, and classic rock.

Like "Locomotive Breath" by Jethro Tull.

Like "Dirty Deeds" by AC/DC.

Like any badass, burn-a-motherfucker-down song that Charlie would have suggested we throw on before deciding on how to bring the world crashing so righteously down. Each song I thought of brought my heart rate up, matching the mad drums of the classic rock ballads, turning my hands into fists.

Even though I knew that the feeling was overblown and completely about getting premeditated revenge on a child, it was a familiar and maybe even exciting poison.

A small fist punched me between the shoulder blades. I looked up at Michael to see if his face said, "Swing low" and in which direction, but it didn't.

Instead, it was Lump. She was out of breath and had a fresh stack of papers with her. She held one out, shutting us down before we could converge on Bryce. Like a levee that wouldn't break.

"It's updated! I have the description you gave me and everything. They said they don't have security cameras so I couldn't find a real picture of her. *And* Mr. Test said that I could announce it during lunch. Do you have any announcements you want to make?"

I read the flyer over. The description of the deer was the description of every baby deer. She'd printed off a photo of a deer using a standard printer, so the ink was still wet and there were lines running through the picture. She'd written, "This Is Just An Example" above the printer photo. It took me out at the knees.

"I think you've got it all, Lump."

"Are you sure?"

"Yeah, I'm sure," I said, my righteous anger at Bryce fading to the background.

"Okay. Good. Pass that one around," she said, pointing at the flyer in my hand. "I'm going to the other tables, then I'm going to give a speech."

"You wouldn't know it, but she makes a fantastic Cabin Defender," Matty said. "She keeps everybody in line. Really, you guys should invest in Lumps. Last night she told me about the time her dog threw up," she said, nodding in an "Enough said" kind of way.

"Must be nice," Michael said. "We have to worry about Goblin Joe chewing through electrical wires. But we've been teaching them a new game called 'hold your breath until you get sleepy' which is also not a bad investment."

Lump was a tiny and chatty rocket-powered force, only stopping at the tables long enough to explain that there would be more information shortly. Eventually she wound her way to the stage, where she fumbled around for a full minute adjusting the microphone stand. No one was watching her except us, and every time one of us got her attention to see if she needed help, she shook her head back and forth and said, even though we couldn't hear her over the crowd, "I can do it."

"She's doing better this year," Matty said as we watched Lump try to get the microphone into place.

"Test told me she had a hard time making friends last year," I said.

"Yeah, I guess you could say that. It was more like she didn't really even try. But this year she's talking to people. Coming out of her shell a little. I'm proud of her."

"Hello, everyone," she eventually said into the mic. There were a few cursory glances. "As many of you know, there is a baby deer missing. You may have seen my flyers. After sexing the deer—" A few tables started laughing. Bryce's table the loudest. Lump steeled herself. "I said sexing, not sexting." She explained that sexting with a T is different than sexing without a T, but the tables laughed even louder this time. "She is missing and we need to find her," Lump said, more loudly. The murmur of the crowd returned to normal levels. "She went missing the day we got here. We still have time. She escaped from behind the barn. There are more flyers there, but they aren't updated. The updated ones are in front of you."

Next to the entrance, Jeffrey the Travel Guide Buddy raised a battered old brass bell up and started ringing it. He had a look on his face that said, "I know, right? *An old-timey bell!* I am such a card." Mostly, everybody ignored his smug, shit-eating grin and headed toward the door, knowing the bell meant the end of lunch. The tables began to clear.

"There's a reward!" she said. A couple of kids craned their heads back as they walked out, but they still walked out. She stepped down from the small stage, almost proud until she saw the tables littered with her flyers. Most had just been left behind, but a lot of them were folded into airplanes or hats, and some of them looked like the kids had tried to see how many times they could tear the paper in half. She looked like a flock of blackbirds that had scattered out of formation. I hated it. The Trevors and the Lumps of the world didn't need asshole kids tearing them down any more than life already did.

"That was good, Lump!" Matty said. We were the only Buddies left in the cafeteria. Trevor was sitting at our table finishing off his bagel sandwich.

She didn't answer.

She started piling up the flyers that hadn't been destroyed, and after a minute, Trevor and Matty joined her.

"Do you know who Harriet Tubman is?" I heard Matty ask her. "And, follow-up question, do you know what a hero's journey is?" Lump shook her head and kept picking up scraps of paper; Matty smiled. "All right, girlfriend, let me tell you what a woman can do when she puts her mind to it."

"Is she an inventor?"

"Kind of. She invented being the biggest badass of all time."

Lump smiled a little under her giant hat. "That's not an invention. And plus also it's not true because Amelia Earhart already invented that. Not that it's an invention."

Trevor had found a trash bag and was raking the piles of multicolored paper scraps off the tables with the crook of his arm. Lump walked over with an armful of paper.

"Amelia Earhart didn't invent it—she refined it. Made it modern. Harriet Tubman was a black woman in slave times who escaped slavery, on foot, and then came back for other slaves. Not once or twice but *nineteen* times. And she saved three *hundred* slaves doing that." The more she talked about Harriet Tubman, the faster the words came out: the exact and polar opposite of someone reciting facts that they couldn't care less about.

"The Underground Railroad?" Lump asked suspiciously, like a grown-up was trying to trick her into learning something.

"That's right. But that was just her doing her own thing. Eventually she became a spy for the good guys and was the first woman to lead an armed expedition where seven hundred *more* slaves got rescued. Lump: are you wrapping your magnificent little head around how awesome Harriet Tubman was?"

Lump kept avoiding eye contact and still hadn't dumped the damaged flyers into the bag that Trevor was hovering below her hands. The pile of paper precariously balanced over the open bag inflicted a look of stress across Trevor's wide face.

"She was a *spy*?" Lump yelled, throwing her arms up, the erupting Paper Vesuvius going everywhere but the trash bag. "Like with secret codes?"

For the next ten minutes she grilled Matty about Harriet Tubman while the rest of us cleaned up paper plates and left-over food. Matty told her that it sounded like she was on her own hero's journey. That the deer was both her call to action and her magical protective figure. And that yes, Harriet Tubman and the Underground Railroad used tons of secret codes.

"Moses!" Lump said from across the room.

"Yeah, Lump?"

"I know the deer's name! Me and Trevor figured out the deer's name!"

"Come talk to me, Lump!" I yelled from across the room while scraping pale macaroni into an already-fetid trash bin. She was making friends, and if I was on Lump Detail then, goddammit, I was doing something right.

She sprinted over like maybe her birds were flying in formation again. "Moses! The deer's name!"

"Is it Harriet Tubman?"

"Of course it's Harriet Tubman! So don't feel bad."

"What?" I stopped scraping the camp food, but a huge glob of it lurched off the plate with a splattery sound.

"Harriet Tubman came back to rescue the slaves before she became an Underground Railroad conductor who *never lost anyone*. You just didn't know what she was planning."[17]

I couldn't answer as fast as I wanted to because everything inside of me suddenly felt tight. But then I said, "I like that name. That's a good name for the deer, Lump."

"And did you know that people also called Harriet Tubman 'Moses'? Like you and the deer mixed together!" She shifted gears at the speed of Lump: "We have too much garbage," she said, shaking the half-full bag of trash. I breathed out, one more full breath of air away from the subject of the deer's name and who'd left who behind.

"The bag's half empty. We can still fit more."

"No, I mean in the world. There is too much garbage. Look at Trevor over there," she said and pointed. "I don't mean that Trevor is garbage. I like Trevor. I mean, look at what he's doing."

Matty was supporting him by his armpits as he stood in the trash can full of paper, stomping up and down.

"Why don't we send all the garbage to the sun?" Lump asked.

"Because we have a dumpster."

"But the sun would burn it all up forever."

"Really want to know?" I asked. She nodded, and I had no

---

17 It's impossible to know.

doubt that if I used words she didn't understand, she'd look them up on her own or insist I repeat myself. "Because it's not just paper we're getting rid of. That kind of stuff is biodegradable and will eventually go away on its own. Money aside—which, daily, would be more than the US's annual GDP of any year ever— the big problem is the nuclear waste. That's the stuff that has a half-life of forever."

"So?"

"So we're just not good enough at rockets. We can't even reliably get a rocket full of people to space. Even if we were ninety-nine point nine nine nine percent sure the rocket would get there without a problem, it's still way too risky."

"But it would be all of our trash. Gone. Away forever. Trevor wouldn't have to stand in the trash can." She said it so plainly and truthfully that you had to think that maybe it was right. Like risking total annihilation just to keep Trevor from stamping down trash was absolutely the best move.

"If it didn't work, though, we'd be looking at the single biggest disaster the world has ever seen. Like ever, this side of the dinosaurs getting wiped out. There would be no way of telling how far the nuclear waste would go, and for how long it would ruin everything. Basically it would be real bad."

"I think the risk is worth it."

"You're probably not the only one, Lump," I said, listening for the thunderous drums deep below my surface, beating out music I hadn't heard since Charlie. But it didn't look like she heard me; her attention was on something else, deep inside and out of sight.

# TWENTY-FOUR:
# BUDDY BEHAVIOR

THAT EVENING, WE CARVED pumpkins in the rec hall without Lump. She'd told Test that her stomach hurt and that she needed to rest up in the infirmary.

Just as I got to the big double doors, I heard a pair of voices, one male and one female, come up from behind me. I turned and nodded at the pair of Buddies walking over. Both appeared to be dressed for an Arctic tundra and a sleepover—big coats, boots, and pajama pants.

"Coach sent us. You're Moses," the guy said plainly. When he wasn't talking his mouth hung open a little, so you could see his braces.

"*Who* sent you?" I said.

"Mr. Test?" the girl said.

"Oh. Okay. Great."

"He said to make sure you guys stayed in line," the mouth-breathing Buddy said, looking at his friend like he was the hottest shit in the world. His tone was everything I'd spent almost a year dealing with. Condescending, pitying, self-righteous bullshit. "It's all right, this is a tough job. Takes a lot of responsibility—"

"Fuck off, dickhole," I said, suddenly feeling beads of sweat forming on my back.

His mouth clicked shut. The girl lowered her coffee and stared at me.

I rubbed my eyes with one hand. "Sorry," I said reflexively.

I realized I was grouping the Buddies and the campers into Us and Them. Mouth Buddy was a Them, just like Bryce, just like the ones that had shot Lump's pictures or torn them up. Just like the ones Charlie and I were always railing against.

They edged past me, not saying anything, but clearly making mental notes about avoiding the weird new guy.


"In your defense," Faisal said, "that guy *is* a dickwad. Like a big, squishy fistful of dicks."

Faisal and I were in charge of carving; Matty and Michael were on design and crowd control.

The kids were all sitting at child-size tables covered in clear plastic, the same as the tiny table Faisal and I had to sit at because all the adult tables had been set up in the mess hall. My knees rose up six inches over the lip of the table, but not over the backlog of grapefruit-sized pumpkins arranged in a pyramid on my right. Faisal's pumpkamid was on his left.

"Dick*hole*," I said.

"You say hole, I say wad. Guy's the king of dick nouns. Speaking of which, I think this one is supposed to be balls," he said, showcasing a small pumpkin. "I think this kid wants me to carve balls into his pumpkin." There were two very distinct ball-like circles on the pumpkin.

"I'm pretty sure this one wants me to carve him stomping

on a school. Or an orphanage. I can't really tell." The picture on the pumpkin showed a stick figure stomping on a small building that was erupting into flames while even smaller stick figures flooded out. I stabbed the top of the pumpkin for the thousandth time, poking slits into the tough orange skin.

"What's up with jack-o'-lanterns, man?"

"It's probably cabin fever," I said, still stabbing the top of the pumpkin.

Every time I readjusted my feet they'd bang against the table and threaten to send the pumpkins rolling off the table. It was impossible to get comfortable without toppling them.

"No, not these ones in particular. I mean in general. Like, why did someone think, 'Hey, I should carve a face into this gourd and then put some fire in it'? You're the brains: what's up with pumpkin carving?"

"I don't know."[18]

Just past a table full of girls, Matty and Michael were doing the best they could to manage Bryce and his amazing, charming, diplomatic friends.

"I'm surprised they're holding it together around Bryce," I said, pointing with my chin toward Matty and Michael.

"When it comes down to it, they're clutch. They're good, non-murdering folk."

"They remind me of some people," I said out loud, instead

---

18 Which was another lie. We domesticated hard-shell gourds ten thousand years ago because they were good for almost exactly that reason: carving and containment. But we do it for other reasons than just art and storage. We do it to keep the monsters at bay and because some people believe that jack-o'-lanterns represent all the souls in purgatory and sometimes we just do it to light the way.

of just thinking it like I meant to. I saw him nod in my peripheral vision. "Like a different, healthier version."

"They're good together. Oh hey, by the way, I got a text from Matty earlier. Said she mentioned her mom to you." He said it not quite looking at me, his lips not quite smiling.

"Uh, yeah, offhandedly. Said she died." I didn't know why he was looking at me like that.

He nodded, his smile defining itself just a little more. "She doesn't talk about her mom. Pretty much ever, at all, to anybody. If she mentioned her to you, then you're doing something right."

"I imagine that's a pretty tough subject," I said, thinking about Charlie's parents. About Jordan. Thinking about how Charlie and I are the skeletons in their closets. How we probably don't come up in their conversations, and if we do, it's major.

"Especially for someone like her. Listen, what I'm about to tell you, you'd find out anyway. And I already asked her if I could talk to you about it. But her mom died pretty suddenly; Matty was eleven." Unlike the story about the house in the woods he'd told around the campfire that first night, this time he treaded lightly, searching for solid footing in each sentence and syllable like he wasn't used to telling this story and didn't know where to start. "She was having—Matty, I mean—was having a birthday party at this place called Duncan's World of Water. And we were there all day, running around, going down the slides, making up names for the flips off the boards—just, you know, kid stuff. And we're getting ready to go and they're clearing the pool out, and Matty gets this look in her eye after seeing that everyone's mostly out of the pool and says 'hang on,' and goes running back toward the diving board. But her feet gave and the only two people that saw her go down were me and her mom, but *everybody* heard her head hit the tiles before she fell in."

"Holy shit."

"Holy shit is right. So her mom goes tearing though us and jumps in the pool and pulls her out of this little red cloud she's floating in. And they give her CPR even though she was only in the water for a few seconds, and an ambulance comes, Matty has a mid-sized concussion, and that's . . ." He trailed off and watched his friends. "That's where it should've ended. Except Matty's mom cut her arm, just, I mean, the smallest bit, like just a scrape, on something in the pool—probably a piece of metal under the diving board or one of the water filters, something. Up near her armpit. And it got infected and got in her blood. She died about a week later. One of those one-in-a-million things, you know?" He breathed out through his nose and I put my hand down when I realized I was rubbing the front of my throat.

"I don't really know what to say," I said, honestly. And I didn't. Here was somebody who'd been through one of the most awful tragedies, the worst possible types of defining moments, and yet you'd never know it from talking to her. It was the kind of situation where you could convince yourself that it was your fault and let that guilt eat you from the inside out, but Matty was solid. At least as far as somebody on the outside could tell. "I know it was a long time ago, but that seems like the kind of thing that would change a pretty fundamental part of you."

Faisal leaned toward me, just a little, his eyes on the floor between us and his hands rotating the small, uncarved pumpkin in his hands. "It was a long time ago, but she dealt with it. And, I guess, *still is* dealing with it. But she's doing good. Better. Anyway. Thought you should know."

Nothing about her seemed to be pretending though.

Trevor waded through the small tables, past Matty and Michael, his pumpkin held close to his chest. Trevor's nails were clean and clear after Matty had sat down with him and a bottle of nail polish remover.

"What's a blow job?" Trevor asked, looking at both of us and setting the pumpkin down.

"Um," I said. Having never dealt with children, I decided to let the seasoned expert handle this one.

"Bryce was talking about them but he didn't seem to really know either," Trevor added.

"It's a . . . joke," Faisal said. "Just a joke."

"Like a gag?"

Faisal opened his mouth to say something but just nodded for a second before saying, "That's definitely one way of looking at it, yes."

"I heard a pretty good blow job earlier," Trevor said.

Faisal's face changed into the look of a man who had just eaten something poisonous. "Trev," he said and held out his hands with his index fingers pointed up. "I know I just said one thing, but listen to this new thing: don't ever say that again."

"But y—"

"I know. Just," he said, and shook his head. "Got a pumpkin?"

Trevor looked at the small pumpkin that looked bigger than

it really was in his small, slender-pudgy hands. There were no testicles on it, there were no giants crushing cities; there was one half-inch-thick continuous line running in a spiral and tapering off at the top.

"Can you carve this?"

"You don't want to make a face? Or something?" I asked.

"Not really. I like the spiral."

Faisal twisted the pumpkin in his hands, examining the line before saying, "I think we can handle this. We won't be able to cut the line all the way through at certain points." He looked at me.

"For load-bearing purposes," Trevor said. "Can you do the bottom too? So it can rotate?"

Faisal nodded. "Yeah, Trev, we can do that."

For the next twenty or thirty minutes we worked on the pumpkin, carving deep enough into it at certain points so light could get out and only carving the skin away at other points to keep the structure sound. When the spiral was done, we rounded the bottom.

I twisted in my seat to check the clock on the wall, and when I turned around Bryce was standing at the table. I squinted at him and his stupid pumpkin.

"Here's my pumpkin for you to carve," he said like a shithead. He had written "FAGGIT" in huge letters and the smirk on his face wasn't because he'd spelled the word wrong like an asshole.

"Are you smiling because you're an asshole?" I said, just to make sure that wasn't why.

Faisal rubbed his face in his hands and, before the ten-year-old could respond to me calling him an asshole, said, "We're not carving that."

"Why not? That one has balls on it," he said and slapped the testicle-pumpkin off the table. Goblin Joe's head popped up from two tables away, scanning the situation before disappearing again.

"It looks like an infinity sign to me," Trevor said.

"Shut up, *Trevor,*" Bryce said. "Why does Trevor get to draw a faggy line on his but I can't use a word?"

It takes a unique combination of angst, caffeine, and months of being told I'm a criminal or a sinner or both, but I am fully capable of deciding I want to smack the shit out of a child who is barely four feet tall.

He slapped another pumpkin off the table. When it hit the ground the stem broke off.[19] Trevor pulled his pumpkin close to his chest.

"Why are you so angry?" Faisal asked Bryce.

"I'm not angry," he shouted. He cocked his arm back like he was going to throw the pumpkin. Trevor shut his eyes and shielded his pumpkin; Faisal raised his finger and started to say something; I dropped my hands and exposed my chest and neck, hoping it would hit me and I'd have an excuse to go berserk on the little son of a bitch; and Goblin Joe sprang up and put him in a full nelson.

Bryce's pumpkin went spinning out behind him and shattered on the floor, spilling its orange guts everywhere.

"Let go of me!" he said. We couldn't see his face but the words sounded wet, like he was crying or about to be crying. Goblin Joe looked up at Faisal, scared.

---

19 Sincerely just smack the ever-loving shit out of a child in front of fucking everybody.

"Let—let him go, Joe. Let him go."

Goblin Joe's hands shot toward the ceiling like he was getting arrested, and Bryce swung back up, staring at us, his face burning red. His eyes were shining when he swiped Joe out of the way and walked out of the room, throwing the connecting door open and heading for the empty half of the rec hall. Before the door had a chance to swing shut, I saw Matty and Michael look over at the angry child and follow him into the other room.

"Way to be on crowd control, Joe," I said and put my hand out for a high five that he immediately and awkwardly fist-bumped.

"I'll go get him," Faisal said. "Make sure he's all right."

"No, hey, I'll do it," I said, standing up fast. I thought about all of the shit Bryce and his friends had said to Lump and Trevor, all of the shit they'd keep saying for years and years, and I realized I had an opportunity to do something about it.

I heard Charlie's familiar voice in my head, egging me on.

"You just called him an asshole."

"No, I know—I should apologize anyway. I'll go bring him back."

"Faisal?" Trevor said. "Do you still have playing cards?"

I wanted to hug Trevor. Not just because he was all of the little kids that would spend the rest of their lives fighting off the Bryces of the world, and not just because kids like him need to celebrate the fucking novelty of coming out with their pumpkins intact, but for the purely selfish reason that he'd distracted Faisal. Because I needed Faisal to be preoccupied with doing good by him and Joe and the rest of them, while I went and dealt with Bryce.

I turned as I walked away and said, "Need some more coffee?"

Faisal was opening the deck of cards he'd pulled out when he said, "I'm good, thanks."

And I was in the clear.

# TWENTY-FIVE: WWCD

MATTY AND MICHAEL WERE TALKING to Bryce when I walked in. He was standing between them, staring straight ahead into the middle distance with eyes that were angry white holes in the red expanse of his face.

Matty was crouched in front of him, and as I walked up Michael saw me and tried to smile. Matty looked up and tried the same.

"I'll handle it, guys," I said. "Gotta get Bryce here a new pumpkin, that's all." Bryce still hadn't said anything. "You guys want to go see how Faisal's doing? See if he needs any backup?"

Michael didn't think about it. He just nodded and said, "Yeah, all right. Thanks."

"Let me know if you need any help in here," Matty said, locking her eyes on mine.

"I will," I said, smiling until the door closed behind them. I waited to make sure they didn't come back through. "All right, gotta get you a new pumpkin, huh?"

Bryce didn't say anything back. His jaw was clenched at an

angle and his eyes were still focused on whatever he was seeing a million miles between us.

"Look. I'm sorry I called you an asshole. I shouldn't have done that. Just been a long day. Let's just get you a pumpkin and we'll carve it up, yeah?" If I'd said it any friendlier, he might have figured that something was up.

"I don't want to."

This time, when I smiled, it was real. Because he was dropping his horseshit act and talking to me.

"Come on. It's okay. We'll carve whatever you want into it." He looked at me.

"Whatever I want?"

"Mostly whatever you want."

"Fine."

"Fine?"

"*Fine,* let's carve the stupid pumpkins."

"My man. All right, go get one."

"What?"

"Just through there," I said, pointing at the staff-only room Lump and I had found.

"What about the ones in there?" he said, pointing back to the room filled with kids.

"What ones in there? Those are all taken. Yours got busted so you need to get another from the staff pile. Means I won't get to carve one, but that's the job, right?"

The dramatic color had gone out of his face, but he was still looking at me like I was lying to him.[20]

"It's staff only."

---

20  Which was fair.

"So?"

"So you're probably going to tell on me."

I breathed out heavily, only half-faking being frustrated. "Why would I tell on you? I just told you to do it. Pumpkins are down there next to the confiscation box at the end of the tunnel. Just be quick." I opened the door that nobody had bothered re-locking and hit the light switch.

The only two bulbs that worked buzzed on as I let the keywords work their way into his head, slowly but steadily convincing him that A) it was a good idea to do what I said because B) it was an independent act of free will that would put him somewhere he wasn't allowed to be and C) in the direct vicinity of a whole box of contraband while also D) depriving me of a pumpkin. He edged up to the doorway and looked down the stairs.

"It's dark in there," he said.

I answered him even though he was more than likely just thinking out loud. "So?"

There was enough sarcasm in that one word to shift his tone one hundred and eighty degrees.

"So *nothing*. I'll be right back."

And the little fucker steeled himself and stepped into the darkness, jolting and grabbing the railing when the first stair creaked under his weight. He paused for a tenth of a second at the first light's horizon, not looking back at me or dramatically shuddering, but pausing all the same.

He forded the darkness, one arm clutched close and the other reached out, his feet moving six inches at a time.

I waited until he broke into the light to step down. Under the second lightbulb, he was far enough away that he didn't hear the stair creak under my feet.

Beneath the lights, he was the Bryce we all knew: obnoxious, loud, and shitty. I reached up for the light nearest the stairs, the bulb that completed and ended the bridge of darkness in the long tunnel, and twisted.

He didn't notice; bent over with his face buried in the boxes, he didn't see the light nearest the stairs go out. But he would. He would turn around and he would realize that there was nothing for him in that tunnel except one small island-puddle of light in a cold, soundless, and otherwise pitch-black void.

He would hear me walk back up the stairs, one creaking step at a time.

He would hear the door close.

He wouldn't leave the dim light. Not when it was the only light he could see.

And eventually someone would notice he was missing and they'd eventually hear him screaming and crying and they'd open the door and find him, the pale-faced and whimpering little bastard who finally got what he deserved.

Charlie taught me a lot of things, not the least of which was the price and payoff of being a bastard. That there could be a reason to play the villain.

The bulb in my hand hadn't had a chance to get hot, to reach its full temperature, but it wasn't cold. Not yet. It had started to heat up even though it had only been on for thirty seconds.

Bryce stood up, scratched at his back, and said, "I don't see it." He went to turn around—to see all there wasn't to see—when he leaned back over to rummage through another box he had no business rummaging through.

The lightbulb was going cold in my hand.

I pictured staring up at Test through all of the thin ice I'd let myself fall through.

Bryce stood up.

And he started to turn around.

He turned and faced the apparently endless darkness.

I thought of that moment when little broken Charlie Baltimore brought me his Nintendo DS because he just wanted to mitigate the damage.

I thought about the dead things in Faisal's story that really maybe did contain life, and I thought about Lump still needing help, and how much I needed everything that had led to this moment to mean something. And I twisted the goddamn light back on.

"There's nothing down here," he said, not having a chance to register how close he'd come to being left in his own worst-case scenario.

With the bulbs working and me standing there, he walked through the tunnel toward the rickety stairs as shittily as ever.

"Everything okay?" Matty said from the top of the steps.

I flinched hard enough to almost rip the light out of the socket. She turned her head a little and said, "You okay? What're you guys doing down there?" For just a second in the dim yellow light, it was like looking into a crystal ball: she looked ten years older and ten times more badass. Like a noir detective, one hand resting out of sight on the butt of a six-shooter; calm, cool, and anything but oblivious.

Bryce walked past me and up the stairs, past Matty. "He told me to go down there to get another pumpkin."

"Oh. All right," she said, looking at me, her eyes scanning

for subtext. "Well, I think I saw some extras in the other room. With the other pumpkins. Where all the other pumpkins are."

"I don't want a stupid pumpkin anyway," Bryce said, breaking off toward his friends.

Matty and I sat down around the small table where Faisal was hanging out with Trevor and Michael. Goblin Joe was hovering around the table looking at all the pumpkin designs we hadn't gotten around to carving yet.

"Everything okay?" Faisal said.

"Yeah, everything's fine." I looked at Trevor and said, "Couldn't find him another pumpkin. I guess he doesn't get to have one."

And instead of smiling or telling me just how much Bryce should go fuck himself, Trevor said, "I think he's scared."

"Who?" I asked, even though I was sure I knew.

"Bryce," Trevor said. "He spends so much of his time being a blow job but I think it's because he doesn't know how to be sad and scared like everyone else." Like all the other machine boys in the world who don't hurt like they're supposed to.

"Why would he be sad or scared?" I asked, running through a mental list of reasons why someone like Bryce would feel anything like shame or guilt.

Trevor gave me a look that was, for Trevor, very sarcastic. "Because Lump is in the infirmary because of him. She told him that she's seen how mean he is to Joe and it makes her so sad it hurts. She's sad enough to be sick and he knows he helped make her feel that way."

"What?" I said, forcing myself to keep a straight face. I hadn't known her for very long, but Lump seemed like the kind of person who would emotionally gut-punch the Bryces of the world in defense of the Trevors and Goblin Joes.

"I'd be extra sad too," Trevor said, and Goblin Joe nodded his goblin-head in agreement. "Anyway, thanks for the pumpkin." Trevor looked us both in the eyes before nodding at Goblin Joe and heading over to Bryce's table. He handed Bryce his pumpkin.

# TWENTY-SIX:
# EMPTY SPACES

I PUSHED THE OLD METAL door to the infirmary open and saw everything I expected to see: a dingy old set of hospital beds with paper sheets, a faded medical kit on the wall, and posters featuring cartoon kids in cartoon woods dealing with cartoon injuries.

With no sign of Lump, I figured she was in a different room. Maybe sleeping on a couch in the back office.

Shelly was sitting at a desk cluttered with papers, her face lit up by her laptop. She was middle-aged with her hair in a messy bun, and she smiled a tired smile when she saw me walk in.

"Moses, right?" she asked. My hands started sweating the way they always did when people recognized me, but before I could get too far into my own head, she said, "Good to finally meet you. Unless you're sick or dying or need me to reattach something."

I smiled back. She was easy to talk to; she had a bedside manner, even out in the Michigan wilderness. "Nope, just looking for Lump. Er, Allison. Heard she was coming out here and I'm supposed to keep track of her. Faisal told me to come check over here."

"I still can't believe that child's mother calls her Lump," she said good-naturedly.

I shrugged and offered, "I hear it's a reclamation thing."

She took a sip from a steaming Styrofoam cup and made a "hmm" sound while nodding at me. Whatever was in the cup smelled like spicy flowers. "Well, in any case, haven't seen *Lump.* Hasn't been in."

"Oh. Huh," I said smoothly. "Okay. Thanks, then?"

"Tell Faisal I said hi," she said, getting back to her computer and not looking at me.

Nothing felt out of place. It was just a miscommunication, or Lump had decided that she felt fine, or she'd gone off to her cabin.

She was fine. Of course she was fine.

# TWENTY-SEVEN: DEAD LIFE

WE AGREED TO MEET at the rope wall after dismissal from the rec hall. It took candy to bribe children into guardian roles, but it took cash to bribe groundskeepers. It looked like this:

NATHAN: Where are you going? It's lights-out.

MOSES: Out.

NATHAN: Might be easier for me to forget you sneaking out if I had some extra beer money. Be a shame if Mr. Test found out.

MOSES: No.

NATHAN: What?

MOSES: Tell whomever you want.

NATHAN (SURPRISED AND A LITTLE HUFFY): You'll get kicked out, you little prick.

MOSES (PULLS OUT PHONE; BEGINS TO LIE): I just recorded you trying to blackmail me; I'm going out.

He would rat me out or he wouldn't, but something insisted I make the effort.

I found the group and made sure to make noise when I came through the trees. Michael and Faisal raised their heads up and waved. Matty's back was to me.

They nodded at each other and Matty turned to me, waving and smiling.

I stopped.

"Who—wait. When did you get massively pregnant?" I asked Matty. The only time it is okay to ask a girl if she's pregnant is when she goes from Not At All Pregnant to My Water Will Burst If I Sneeze in the span of six hours.

Her smile dropped and brought her face crumbling after it as her eyes welled up. Michael put his arm around her and made shushing noises into her hair before looking at me and scolding, "What's wrong with you?" Then, to her, "I love you despite your condition."

The icy October air went hot and thick. The only noise except for the wind whistling through the pines was Matty choking air down and burying her face into Michael's arm. It's nearly—if not literally—impossible to calculate the exact number of words in the English language; there are, however, according to the Global Language Monitor, more than one million and twenty five thousand of them. Of those one million and twenty-five thousand–plus words, the only the two I could think of were a stuttered version of "Oh, fuck."

"Look at his eyes," Faisal said out of the corner of his mouth.

Matty looked up from Michael's coat and wiped her tears away with the backs of her thumbs. "I don't know why we didn't think of this before," she said, beaming and cracking up.

The air around me thinned but nothing made any more god-damn sense. Faisal walked over and flipped up the bottom of

Matty's shirt, revealing a pale and very pregnant stomach that wasn't the same color as the rest of her. On the flanks of her belly were large elastic bands that held her womb in place. His fingers seemed to disappear into the topmost point of her enormous stomach before they pulled a flap open with a ripping Velcro noise. He reached in and pulled out a red can of Woodsmith's beer.

"Want a Woody?" he asked.

"Okay, *what*?" The amount of effort and foresight it would take to get a replica stomach and convert it into a cooler big enough for multiple drinks and snacks was something I'd have expected contestants from the Olympiad to come up with.

They were the kind of weird I knew.

It was same kind of outlandish shit me and Charlie would have come up with.

"The pregnancy pouch!" she said, throwing her hands up. "We've been working on it for months and we finally get to use it for something other than getting good seats at Applebee's," she said, high-fiving her boyfriend.

"Did . . . how . . . you converted a fake pregnant stomach into a *cooler*? Where did you even *get* a fake pregnant stomach?"

"My mom works at a health center," Faisal said. "And they had these for those presentations they give at high schools, but they upgraded. So I rescued one."

"It's great for sneaking food into movie theaters. Like lots of food. Like if you want to bring a whole roasted chicken and drinks."

"This is amazing," I said, more to myself than anyone else while checking out their invention. The inside was lined with silver insulation that kept the beers cold. I cracked one open. It's hard to argue with extremely cheap beer from the inside of a uterus.

"Plus, if we get caught, bam: pregnant and crying," she said, pointing to her face, which was legitimately puffy. "Thank you, Freshman Drama Club."

"You guys are like an evil brain trust," I said as we headed into the woods, putting more and more distance between ourselves and our responsibilities. Allegedly evil brain trusts were in my wheelhouse.

"How's Lump?" Pregnant Matty asked as we worked our way through the trees.

"Oh, she actually wasn't there. I think we just missed each other."

Her brow knitted up for a second before she said, "Huh. All right."

And before we could talk any more about it, Michael said, "We've got about a mile hike before the farm we have to trespass through, then we're pretty much in town. Shouldn't take too long to get there."

We trekked into the night, winding down the utility roads that eventually spilled onto the backcountry highway. We followed the signs for the town of Bannister, back the way we drove in but before the freeway. It was dark and it was snowing.

"Hey, is there still a Snickers in there?" Faisal asked Matty.

She opened the pouch and poked around for a few seconds before holding up a bag of fun-size candies. "There are five little ones. It's like a full-size one, but made up of fun little constituent parts that you have to painstakingly open one at a time. Here," she said and held the bag out.

He pinched his face together. "I thought there was a full-size." He shook his head after thinking for a second and said, "No, wait, I remember there being one. We bought it at the first stop on the way here."

"Ate it," Michael said from behind us.

"What?"

I smiled as I brought the can of utero beer to my mouth. Listening to them bounce back and forth—listening to them riff and play on each other—was like watching a stylus find the groove on an old record. One I hadn't heard in a while.

"I ate it. Hence the bag full of little Snickers. To make up for it."

"You think five little Snickers is the same as one big one? A *king* size?"

"Yes," he said definitively.

"You have never been more wrong." Faisal opened the bag and full-speed threw one of the candies at Michael, who managed to catch it while simultaneously ducking.

"That's probably not true," he said, opening the candy and eating it. "It's math! It's just fractions. Five-fifths is more than equal to one-ones. That's algebra; I just algebra'd you."

"You think you can verb your way out of this?" He threw another candy that Michael tried to catch.

*"I can algebra."*

"No. Look: if I have half a cat and you have half a cat and we mush them together . . ." He brought his hands together, interlacing his fingers. "We don't have a full cat; we have two floppy, dead halves of a cat." His hands fell apart.

The beer and the miles between me and the town made me laugh out loud.

"I would say we have a full cat. Unless it's two ass-halves; then we just have an ass-cat." Michael said, sneaking a look at me and then making his face go deadpan when he saw I was laughing.

"I would say that just because the components are in place doesn't mean the machine works, you candy-thieving mother-fucker."

"Wait. Is it a robot cat?"

"What? No."

"I just thought components—two halves, even if they were ass-halves, of a robot cat might work."

"No. This is a very dead, freshly sawed-in-half cat."

I made a note in my head to tell Lump about the robo cat with two butts. As a kid with an unfortunate familiarity with feline trauma, I figured she'd appreciate the ass-cat.

Matty sipped on her beer, smiling, taking knee-high steps through the snowbank and leaving craters behind her. Partly because of lake effect, partly because of how far north we were, and partly because of freakish cold snaps, there was more snow in October than I'd ever seen.

But it didn't seem to affect them. In the miles and miles of freezing expanse all around us, they were warmth. *We* were warmth.

Every quarter mile there were utility poles with dingy yellow lights fixed to them: old streetlamps that the county hadn't up-graded to arc sodium. One of them winked out as we walked under it.

"There! See?" Matty said, pointing at the light with her fully extended free arm. The filament inside the glass was a glowing orange sliver. She pointed at Faisal with her hand holding the beer, shaking both arms for emphasis.

"Matty thinks she causes lights to turn out when she walks under them," Faisal said to me. "She's got powers."

"I never said I have powers." She said it in a way that made it sound like maybe she did, in fact, possibly at one point say that she had powers. Her face was red, but only from the cold, and she couldn't stop smiling.

I remembered lying in bed when I was a little kid and thinking about my secret superpower. I'd lie there and imagine standing in line at a bank right when a man in a ski mask would burst in. Everybody would freeze or panic, but I'd puff out my chest and tell him he picked the wrong day to be a bank robber. And all of the bullets he fired at me would rain down off my chest, dented and crooked.

"Do it again," Faisal said, nodding toward the next light down the road.

She turned to me. "I can't do it on command. It just happens."

All superhero origin stories are the same: it's never by choice, it just happens. Sometimes you get bit by a radioactive spider and sometimes you're a wealthy billionaire vigilante, but sometimes your cousin just happens to miss your heart.

"I looked it up once," Michael said. "It's called 'streetlight interference phenomenon.' People think it's a thing."

"See? Streetlight—what?"

"Interference phenomenon."

"Interference phenomenon. I don't make the rules. I just break them. The rules of physics and science—I destroy them."

"Moses?" Faisal asked. "You're the science-y one. Is Matty a wizard?"

"Could be. Maybe some people just operate on a different frequency or burn more cosmic energy than others. It's not lights turning on, right? It's them turning off. Maybe you're just a magnet for energy. Like an X-Men villain. But for light bulbs." I said the entire unfiltered thing without thinking, without reminding myself that this is how you talk to *friends,* not acquaintances.

"Like Dumbledore!" she said.

"Which X-Men villain do you think Dumbledore is?" Michael asked her. "This is very important for our relationship."

I smiled into my beer.

"No, he's got the light-switch spell thing! From the movie! It's like the Clapper but for wizard sticks."

"Wands," Faisal said.

"Which reminds me: Moses, I have a question,"[21] she said.

"Shoot," the Human Bullseye said.

"Well. This is a conversation that we have a lot, which means it's important to know where you stand, so be honest."

"I know where she's going with this one," Michael said.

"If you could hav—"

"—kill one person and get away with it, who—" Michael said but stopped when we all looked at him. "I thought it was the murder freebie question. It's not the murder freebie question?"

Even though I could still see Charlie's head kicking back, a red-black hole appearing as Plastic Buddha ruptured . . .

---

21 If she asked for my life story again, Faisal wasn't going to stop her. Eventually questions have to be answered, especially when you're breaking rules and drinking cheap beer.

Even though I wasn't sure my ears were done ringing and I could still feel the wet red hitting me as Charlie crumpled over . . .

Somehow I heard the words and I expected more of a gut punch from them but there was something about the sound of all of us laughing that made the hit fall short.

"It's never the murder freebie question, man," Faisal said.

"Don't you act like we haven't talked about murder freebies. I would say murder fre—"

"Michael!" Matty said. "No one is talking about murder. That's not my question. My question is what kind of superpower would you have?"

"An oldie but a goodie," Faisal conceded. "You know Matty's is turning light bulbs off and Mike's is a weird blank check for murder—"

"Those aren't the powers we chose!" Matty said.

"Yeah! That's not the power Matty chose!" Michael said.

She glared at him but couldn't hide the smile behind her eyes. Whatever cold snap was coming off of Lake Michigan wasn't letting up but neither were we.

I could feel Charlie in the wind, but I was here. I was with people who wanted me here. I was standing up in the sideways wind.

"Also," Matty said, holding up her hand while she started counting off on her fingers, "no flying, no invisibility, no Wolverine claws, and no time travel."

"Wait, why can't we choose Wolverine claws?" I asked.

"Too easy," Faisal said, picking up a stick and whipping it into a field. "Same for the rest of them. No simple answers."

"Mine, for example, is not actually lightbulb manipulation. It's spiders," she said with a slight nod.

"Spiders," Michael said. "Which is why she wears the pants in this relationship."

"How do spiders work as a superpower?" I asked.

Faisal grinned and Matty pointed at him. She said, "He's smiling because he's responsible for this and he knows it."

An advantage to having a low alcohol tolerance is that it didn't take much beer for me to start thinking that we were all best friends and that the night should go on forever.

That this is what normal felt like.

"I'm like the guy that shot Batman's parents." He didn't look like this was regrettable.

"He showed me *Arachnophobia* when I was a little kid and now I'm terrified of spiders."

"It's a classic movie," Faisal said.

"Yeah, except for the lifelong terror it induces."

"One might argue, that's *why* it's a classic."

"But so there's this scene, right, where a photographer guy is in the Amazon on some spider-finding expedition or something and he goes to sleep in his tent that is *on the ground. Where spiders live.* And obviously a spider crawls into his tent and then crawls into his sleeping bag and bites him on the foot and then they find him in the morning and he's all rotten and dead and claw-hand-y." She grimaced the whole time she described the dead photographer.

"Because Oreo-sized monsters are apparently enough to terrorize a town in movies," Faisal said, rolling his eyes.

"But, *anyway,* I still sleep with my blankets wrapped under my feet. It's not even a conscious thing anymore; I don't wrap myself up specifically to keep spiders from biting my ankles and killing me in my sleep, but it's the underlying cause. It was a means to an end, and fuck that; I want the control back. I want to manage my monsters. That would be my superpower."

Before I had a chance to answer—to tell them that if I could have any power in the world, it would be to not have a super-power, to be more than the unkillable aftermath, more than a walking reminder, and more than a machine that couldn't be turned off—we saw it.

Faisal slowed down and craned his neck to look at the shape a little less than half a lamp's length away. "Uh-oh," he said, walking up ahead of us to the broken, spiky shape on the side of the road. "It's our porcupine."

We caught up to him and Matty squatted down, resting her hands on her massive stomach. "I get that you aren't supposed to swerve if a deer goes running out. That makes sense—"

"Especially with a busload of kids," Michael added.

"Right. That makes sense. But this little guy was walking *down the road*—which was the dumbest thing he ever did—the driver could have gone around him." She said it quiet.

There was a pink landing strip down the length of the por-cupine's back where the bus had shaved its quills off and a thick dusting of snow on the rest of its spikes that made it almost in-distinguishable from the white bank next to it. Michael tromped into the tree line and pulled out a thin branch.

"What are you doing?" Matty asked.

"Rolling him into the woods." He finished his beer, belched, and handed the can to Faisal. He positioned the stick under the animal like a lever. "Porcupines are nature's tire shredders. Like how banana peels are nature's oil sl—"

The animal kicked its broken, pathetic leg at the stick pushing into its side. Matty jolted and fell onto her butt.

"Fuckfuckfuck," Michael said, grabbing onto Matty's coat and sliding her over to Faisal, who had his own hands pulled up and away from the animal.

It didn't hiss or try to crawl away or do much of anything else.

The wind picked up and weaved between us and the not-dead animal, whisking away all the words that none of us said. We stared at it.

*"Fuck,"* Michael said once more, more consonant and glottal stop than fleshed-out word. "What do we do?" he finally asked.

No one said anything.

"I can't believe it's still alive," Faisal said. "It got hit by a *bus* full of baby fat and luggage. Jesus Christ."

"Can we fix him?" Matty asked. It had started to snow again and she was still sitting on the ground.

"If he hasn't moved, it's his back. His back is broken," I said.

"So: can we fix him?" she asked again.

"No," I said. Not without gleaming doctors and EKG tones that refused to monotone.

She stood up and pulled her hat off. "Then we have to put him out of his misery."

Michael groaned. "Why did you have to walk *down* the road! What were you *thinking*?" he asked the porcupine, like he expected it to answer.

"He's been out here for almost two days," Faisal said. "I thought for sure he was dead."

"Mike, I need you to find a big rock, okay? Can you do that for me? Or a big, big log," she said.

He kept looking at us, one at a time. "Do we have to?"

"Yeah, we do," she said.

He nodded and went looking for something heavy or something sharp. Faisal went stomping after him. They disappeared into the gloom beyond the moonlight.

Matty went over to the broken animal and whispered something to it. She petted its nose and stroked its quills, going with the grain and breezing her fingers through the sharp points. The animal's eyes were glassy and far away but it managed to sniff at her hand.

"My dad had to do this years and years ago," she said with her back to me. "Same kind of thing. He hit a possum and pretty much tore it in half."

I crouched next to her and let the animal sniff me. It stopped paying her any attention and tried to lick my hand.

"He likes you."

The darkness felt too complete, like it had swallowed Michael and Faisal and was just waiting for us to wander in after them. I couldn't feel the snowflakes falling around us.

"Anyway. He got out of his car and realized he had to finish the thing off, even though he didn't want to and never asked for it, you know? But he didn't have his tools with him or his gun because he was just going to pick up lunch. Basically, all he had was a shovel in his trunk."

I cleared my throat. "Does Michael know this story?"

"Oh, he knows it. Dad likes to tell this one. Turns out, possums are really hard to kill. And every few minutes when a car would go by he'd have to stop and pretend he was just shoveling some roadkill out of the way because he didn't want the people driving by and seeing some lunatic going nuts on a possum with a shovel." She let out a humorless little laugh. "It's funnier when he tells it. Or it was, anyway, before I met this little guy."

"Sounds like your dad has a lot of stories." It sounded like her dad would fit right in at any of my family reunions.

"He does." She kept stroking the porcupine's nose. "He tells them all the time. It's how he deals with things, I think."

Michael and Faisal clawed their way out of the woods. Michael was out of breath, like he'd gone jogging around looking for the right tool. Faisal had an armful of small-to medium-sized sticks, and said, "We couldn't find any big sticks or rocks. It's all pines in there."

"Okay. That's okay," Matty said. She unzipped her coat and pulled the pregnancy pouch open before fishing around and pulling her keys out. On the ring, surrounded by bronze- and silver-colored keys, between the drugstore scan card and the tiny flashlight, there was a small Swiss Army knife.

The blade was only two or so inches long.

"Moses, hold his head back." When I hesitated, she looked me in the eyes and said, "If you can't do it, it's okay."

The drums in my chest were pounding.

I let his nose follow my fingers up until his throat was fully exposed because I was exhausted from seeing Charlie in everything. She kept the porcupine's chin up with the pinky on her left hand and went up on her elbows, pushing her weight into her hands and flicking the small blade. The porcupine clawed distantly at her sleeve. After a final push, she leaned back and brushed her hand through the animal's quills until it went slack and stopped pawing at nothing.

She took a deep breath and wiped the hair out of her face with the heel of her hand. "You can move him off the road now."

# TWENTY-EIGHT: CHOICES

AFTER WE'D PASSED A TINY bottle of hand sanitizer around, Matty had insisted that we all have another beer since we were drinking her baby weight away. No one argued; no one said anything for lamps and lamps. The moonlight filled the pines around us and it was bright enough to see our breath.

"Do you want to talk about it?" Faisal eventually asked.

"I'm all right," Michael said, sounding more legitimately upset than I'd expected him to.

Faisal looked at him but Michael was staring into his beer. Faisal cleared his throat. "Right. *Matty,* do *you* want to talk about it?"

"I'm okay," she said. There was a sad, distant smile on her lips that didn't quite reach her eyes. "It happens. And we did the best we could. Sometimes you can't save them. I just hate it."

I fumbled with my coat, trying to work the zipper down without taking my gloves off. I expected to open my coat and see flames pour out of me between the black and white lines of my referee shirt. It was adrenaline. It was beer. It was the glowing coals and the melting gods. I pulled my hat off.

My gloves were sticky. I couldn't see anything against the black fabric but it had to be blood. I turned my hand around and tried to find red, but it was invisible on the black gloves in the primal dark. Some engine inside of me started working harder, pumping my heart at more beats per minute and making my stomach vibrate and churn. There was no good way of getting the terrible gloves off. If I pulled one off with the other it meant getting the sticky blood on my skin where it would stain my wrists and work its way up my arms and eventually cover every inch of me and everyone would know that I was covered in blood that would never wash off. The other option was pulling the gloves off with my teeth. Pulling the gloves off with my teeth and getting the blood in my mouth until it drowned me or until it transfused all of my blood. The engine deep inside me that made my heart beat faster started making my breaths come out on hobbled legs and clipped wings.

"Gotta pee. Hang on," I said. I clamored into the woods, deep enough that they couldn't see me, and dropped. I had to get the fucking gloves off. I looked for a branch or a stick or some leaves, anything I could use to pry the bloody gloves off, but they'd been right: it was just pine needles. My breath was matching my heart and my mouth was dry and the gloves were wet and I finally stepped on my gloves and pulled my hands out. They were red from being dragged under my boots but I couldn't see any blood. Until the fingerprints. There were traces of blood around the pads of my fingers.

"Matty, can you throw the hand sanitizer in here?" I said, and then threw up.

———

When I came out they were hunkered down on the other side of the road by an old and battered wooden fence tangled in barbed wire. They were sitting with their backs to it, drinking beer and eating snacks out of Matty's stomach. Past the fence and past the thin line of trees, there was a field that was all frozen mud and splotches of tall, dead grass moving lazily in the night breeze. At the far end of the field, lit by the crisp moonlight bouncing off the fresh snow, there was a busted-up barn with its roof blown mostly off.[22]

The way the moonlight came through the trees, the three of them were in a clean ray of light, separate and divided from the other shadows.

"Better?" Matty asked me.

"Much. Thanks," I said, holding up the bottle of sanitizer and tossing it to her. Behind the pines, I'd counted until I felt my chest stop shaking.

"Okay," Michael said to me. "This is the tricky part."

Fifty yards away from the broken-down barn there was a single-story home with a bank of windows emanating soft yellow light. One of the darker windows was lit by the colored, flashing light of a television.

"Farmer Browning," Faisal said, the way you say the name of your oldest adversary.

"Browning because he's got a shotgun," Matty said.

---

22 Even in that light you could tell it was the kind of barn that had been built fifty, sixty, a hundred years back. The kind that someone had built one plank at a time, with a purpose in mind. The barn was defiant though—even after all these years and countless roof-tearing storms and brutal winters, it was still standing. Unshakable. Resolute. Old barns are like that; they're practically invisible and just part of the Norman Rockwell backdrop of any road trip, but they are there. Despite outward appearances, they are there.

"Are you kidding me?"

"He shot at me last year," Michael said.

"He shot at you? With his *shotgun?*"

"Right. Last year."

"And we're back at the same farm?" I said, not trying to hide my disbelief.

"He's old. We weren't sure he'd still be alive."

"And," Faisal added, "to be fair, Mike touched his horse."

"I didn't *touch* his horse."

*"Why would you touch his horse?"* I said.

"You didn't even buy it dinner it first. You didn't even bring it a salt block," Faisal said.

Michael directed his attention at me. "Obviously that was before we knew about the shotgun."

*"And,"* Matty said, "since he's a thousand years old, he can't really shoot all that well. Especially at night."

"None of you are making this sound any better."

"You've got that look in your eye," Faisal said to me.

"Which look?"

"The 'Why don't we just go *around* the guy with the shotgun's house' look. We've all had the look."

"It's a reasonable look," Matty said.

"The road we need is right through his property. Right on the other side. You can't see it because of the trees, but his house is on a little land bridge that cuts through the marsh back there. It would be an extra mile or two to take the road around the property since it's swamp that way," Michael said, pointing, "and it's all *lake, that* way," he said, pointing the other way. He looked at me to see if the answer had worked. "He's still got the look in his eye."

Matty smiled. "Because it's important. He called us animals the first time we snuck across his property, a couple years back."

"Animals?"

"Animals. And I don't know how to describe it, but you could tell he meant it. It was a bad fucking word for him, you could tell."

"And this was before Mike touched the horse's bathing suit area," Faisal chimed in.

"I don't molest horses," he said, like someone trying to talk their way out of a speeding ticket.

"But so now it's important. We do it to know that we can and to prove that there's nothing wrong with being an animal. Especially if being an animal means smoking weed and loving your friends and not arbitrarily calling someone 'Coach.'"

"It's reclamation," Faisal said. "If we're animals, we're going to show him why he should be jealous."

"Plus, look," Michael said. "He's watching TV—I don't think he's going to bother getting out of bed to murder a bunch of kids."

"He would be in his legal right though," Faisal said.

"More of a legal gray area, probably," Matty said.

"Fuck though," Michael said, pulling his hat off and scratching the back of his head. "I don't feel like dealing with that asshole tonight. Not after we mercy-killed a porcupine."

Faisal made a "pfft" noise and mumbled, "*We.*"

"Moral support," Michael said, pointing at himself. "And also Weapon Getter."

"*Failed* Weapon Getter," Faisal said, also pointing at him.

"What do you think, Moses?" Matty said. She didn't have

the same energy and color about her that she'd had when we left, but her eyes were still bright.

"I don't mind walking around," I said. Most of me just wanted to keep the walk going—to keep hanging out and laughing—and that part really didn't mind walking the extra distance. The Charlie part of me, though, was shaking his head and calling me a coward. The Charlie part of me saw a missed opportunity for adventure.

As we skirted the farmer's property, the lights came on one at a time. Almost immediately we saw someone appear in the big rectangle of the farmer's living room, staring out at us, followed by faraway barks.

He was watching us and his dog knew that we were out there. Even though we couldn't see features, the figure and his dog stayed in that window and watched us until we were out of sight.

# TWENTY-NINE: DOGFIGHTER

WE'RE WALKING INTO TOWN, which is only a mile or so away, and it's the kind of long summer afternoon that goes on forever because we're twelve and only ever worry about everything and nothing at the same time. My Superman shirt is still baggy on me, but at least it doesn't cover my knees anymore.

"Yeah, but the tunnel would lead to the fort," Charlie says.

"The fort should be in the tree though," I say. I don't have to tell him which tree I'm talking about. Three houses up, there's a big dog asleep on the front lawn.

"A tree fort with a tunnel system."

Neither one of us looks at the palm-down-palm-up high five but it gets the dog's attention, making it raise its head up and twitch its ears.

"We could put lights in the tunnel. Like, string lights through it. And a sound system," I say.

"And snakes. Gotta buy some snakes."

"Snakes?"

"To keep intruders out."

"I'll see if we can buy snakes online." The dog doesn't take its eyes off of us and as we get in front of its house, it scrabbles to its feet and starts growling. "I wonder if a dog could live in the tunnel," I ask him.

"We should find out," he says, and I hear the volume rising in his voice midway though the sentence and I'm aware of the increasing upswing of laughter on the words and I even feel his arms brace against my shoulders, but I still don't realize that he's about to push me toward the dog that is easily three-quarters as big as me.

I hear three things as I catch myself, hands braced out and eyes to the ground:

Charlie laughing.

Charlie's footsteps as he runs off.

And growling.

I pull back with my hands out, and I say, in the calmest voice possible, "It's okay. It's oka—" but the dog jumps at me anyway, simultaneously pulling me down and pushing me back.

I don't expect to hear the next sound: me laughing. Even as the dog's claws dig pale red trenches into my arm while I try to keep its head pushed back, even as it shoves me further back onto the lawn and starts shredding my pant leg, I can't stop laughing.

Even as a faraway part of my brain registers that my best friend just made this happen.

The claw marks are starting to spill over, sending red teardrops down either side of my arm, and the dog has managed to pull my pants all the way off, whipping its head back and forth, when Charlie comes screaming back, yelling "We are the champions, motherfucker!" adding twenty extra syllables to "motherfucker" as he tackles the dog into a low hedge.

And I can't hate him because I am invincible and my Superman shirt isn't even torn. I can't imagine any other way we're supposed to be around each other.

An hour later we're playing video games like nothing happened and he leans over and says, without context, "Plus, now we know dogs can't hurt you either."

# THIRTY: HERE
# BE TIGERS

EVENTUALLY THE ROAD SPILLED us into Bannister and we headed for the first business that we saw: a Dairy Mart.

The Dairy Mart was every Dairy Mart in the world. It had a bright storefront and a big illuminated soft-serve cone on the roof that spun lazily clockwise and signs about liquor prices in the huge windows. On the door was a neon *OPEN* sign that lit up one letter at a time before flashing a few times and repeating the cycle.

This particular Dairy Mart was on top of a hill, higher than the rest of the city and everything else. When we got past the dumpsters and to the curb, we could see it all:

Miles of wet street and blinking traffic signals and apartment buildings with lights at different heights clicking on and off like the universe's audio equalizer and a stream of headlights so thick and wavering that you couldn't tell if you were looking at a dazzling literal river of light or a figurative bloodline of glowing plasma or just a stream of cars packed so completely with complex lives that, for just a second, they became one refulgent mass of temporary oneness.

When the cars drove past trees or turned away from us, little pockets of blackness would appear in the light like Morse code reminders: there's darkness too. It's never just light. There will be dark as well.

Along the street, storefronts were adorned with skeletons and witches; city flags with pictures of harvest gourds hung from streetlights, while snow-capped billboards advertised haunted hayrides.

"Do we need supplies?" Michael asked as we crossed the mostly empty parking lot. "Matty? Pregnancy supplies?"

"I would be a more believable pregnant person if I was eating a jar of pickles," she said, nodding.

"Maybe. But these are hipsters we're dealing with here," Faisal said. "Half of them will think you're quirky and ironic and the other half will legitimately, wholeheartedly hate you."

"For eating pickles?" Michael asked.

"I mean, them hating someone eating pickles is probably just a symptom of a deeper sort of self-hatred, but yes, because of pickles. Not to mention drinking cheap beer while hugely pregnant."

"My baby, my choice," she said, the empty beer cans and candy wrappers rattling around in her womb. The door made a *bing-bong* noise when we stepped through and the girl behind the counter didn't look up until she noticed Michael stop and flip through the magazines by the door. The tip of her nose was colored black and she had whiskers drawn on over orange circles on her cheeks. We dispersed into the store.

"They have a magazine called *Weed and Butts*," Michael said, holding up the magazine for us to see. It was, in fact, a magazine called *Weed and Butts*.

The girl with the tiger makeup behind the counter gave him

a look that said, "I'm sick of teenagers and you're probably going to steal something and it's been a long shift so I won't have a problem running you down with my car if you try any shit."

The first time I looked up from the racks and saw Tiger Woman behind the counter watching me in the convex, disk-shaped mirror, nothing was weird. The third time I looked up and made eye contact with her, I knew she was watching me and waiting for me to stuff something in my coat. The look was a distant relative of the look people give you when they think you're a damned-to-hell arsonist.

Behind Tiger Woman, a small flat-screen TV was playing the news with the volume turned all the way down.

I looked up as Faisal leaned down and picked up a pecan pie—the sweaty, stale kind that comes in a box with a clear, flimsy plastic top. He shuffled the box around a couple of times, making the pie bounce around like a hockey puck, before holding it up and saying, "You guys ever look at a pecan pie and think it looks like some kind of horrible STD?"

Even though she was deliberately not looking at us, Tiger Woman made a disgusted face where she half-closed, half-fluttered her eyes and turned her chin toward her shoulder like she was fighting back hangover resurgence. Faisal noticed and did a small double take.

"Why are you trying to ruin pie?" Matty asked.

"No, I mean—I don't mean it like that," he said, pacifying the air around us by shaking the awful, now-I-can't-not-see-STDs pie at us. "I mean, it looks like something you'd see in a medical file. Like a photo of someone who was in the Amazon and then got bit by some exotic insect and then the insect laid eggs in them."

Michael peeled back the top of a little blue French-vanilla creamer and drank it before saying, "Or like gonorrhea. That's what I imagine gonorrhea looks like."

"Pecan pie is not gonorrhea!" Matty said, scolding both of them with her eyes. Tiger Woman, who assumed we were all stealing things, looked relieved. "It does kind of look like an impacted butthole though."

Michael drank a green Irish-Cream creamer and high-fived Matty from two aisles away with a little nod and proud eye contact. She nodded back.

"Moses," Faisal said. "Weigh in here. STD-riddled butthole?"

My first thought was, *What would Charlie say?* but I realized I didn't need to know. Fuck what Charlie would say. "I'm on Team Butthole all the way."

Fuck Tiger Lady's suspicious looks.

Fuck the thin ice Test insisted I was choosing to tread on.

Charlie was stuck in my head and demanding I see him and our fire in everything I did, but I could live my own life too.

After a few minutes of poking around, we converged on the counter where the clerk had her painted face reburied in her phone like she'd never been watching us. I set the small bag of chips on the counter.

"Anything else?" she asked.

Taped to the front of the cash register, next to a sticker for a local DJ called DJ Apache Whirlwind, there was a piece of green paper with a drawing of an anthropomorphic cigarette saying, "You must have been born on or before today's date . . ." followed by another piece of paper taped below it with what was supposed to have the current year. Instead of the year, though, the piece of paper had fallen and was hanging facedown.

"Nope. Just the chips. I think you need more tape," I said, flipping up the felled piece of paper. I expected to see a date, but it was blank, and she gave me a tight-lipped smile that said, "Thanks, I definitely need your help with my job."

And I noticed the TV. For one terrible second I saw Charlie's and my courtroom with the looped footage of the burning building followed by the mourners mourning followed by them coming together as one solid community in WARMTH shirts. But then it was something else—footage from a new and different courtroom shit storm unfolding in someone else's life.

I realized Tiger Woman had said something.

"Sorry, what?"

She breathed out through her nose. "For the chips. Ninety-nine cents."

I handed her a five but kept looking at the piece of paper that insisted I had been born at some point between right now and any time in the past, and at the silent television behind her.

It's a weird feeling, finding yourself missing the shittiest part of your life. Like some stupid part of you misses the incredible low because it was closer to the time before you did something irrevocable. The antithesis of pining for the glory days—pining for rock bottom.

Even if that pining is rooted in something toxic, like being addicted to your shitty old life.

As she gave me my change, my phone started going off in my pocket.

I managed to take my change and get my phone.

It was Lump.

"I don't think you're supposed to have your phone out," I said as I answered. I caught Matty's attention, mouthed "Lump," then stepped outside.

"Hi, Moses!" she whispered as loudly as she apparently could.

"How's it going? I thought you were staying with the nurse tonight."

"Oh. No. I felt better and then I went back to the cabin."

Through the door, I saw Matty hand Faisal the candy bar she wanted and a small wad of money before stepping outside with me. Her face was serious and nervous since Lump was in her cabin, but she knew that if something had gone horribly wrong, Lump would have gone for an adult, not called me.

"I know, I just wanted to call and see if you could help put up more flyers tonight."

I had to admire the kid's total disregard for camp policy.

I smiled what I hoped was a relief-inducing smile at Matty and said, "We can't put more flyers up tonight, Lump. It was lights-out forever ago."

The tension evaporated from Matty's face and shoulders.

"I know. I was just wondering." She was still whispering, but something sounded different. There was no enthusiasm, no adventure in her voice. It sounded different than a kid who had just been told that they could have those adventures in a few hours, when the sun was up.

"You okay?" I asked.

I didn't want Matty worrying, but I had to ask. I saw the nervous creep back into her posture.

"Yeah," she said, obviously lying.

"You know we can put them up in the morning, right? I didn't mean to sound . . . you know."

"I know."

"Then what's going on?"

She hesitated, just breathing for a moment. And when she breathed in through her nose, it was a thick sniffle. She swallowed before saying, "Can I talk to you?"

"Yeah, hey, of course you can talk to me." I said it both for her and Matty as I leaned my back against the metal cage that had propane tanks for sale. I tried to tune out the world for just a minute. All I had to do was talk to this kid who needed a friend.

"Will you promise not to tell anyone?"

"Yeah, Lump, I promise." I had an idea of what she was going to say, and it wasn't about lost deer or mean little kids. It was about ghost hair.

Matty and I didn't break eye contact while Lump started talking. She was reading my face.

"My dad is sick. And I'm scared about that."

Even though I'd figured that she was going to say it, I still didn't know how to respond. So I just tried. "Mesothelioma, yeah, you mentioned that."

I saw Matty smile, just a little. Just enough to show that she was relieved that this sad, lonely kid wasn't calling because she was in trouble, but because she just needed to talk to someone.

"Mom says not to worry because they've got good doctors." She stopped abruptly. Like she didn't know what to say or how to say it.

"It's okay to be scared, Lump. Everybody gets scared."

"That's what Mom says."

And I thought, *Our moms would get along.* Her voice was thick.

"I don't know too much about your mom or dad, but I bet

they'd be really proud of you for caring as much as you do about that deer. And as much as I know they don't want you to worry, I bet they'd be proud of you for worrying about them."

She didn't say anything back but I could hear her crying.

"Let's put more flyers up tomorrow, okay? I'll tell you about how I get scared too," I said, finally breaking eye contact with Matty.

"Okay. That'd be good."

"Goodnight, Lump."

And I hung up. I'd had enough beers to think I'd done everything right. I even did a brief scan of what was probably happening at camp: the kids were all asleep, a handful of the Buddies were still awake, their faces illuminated by their phones, and Test was being Test—probably diligently flossing and wearing his monogrammed camp pajama shorts.

Still, the sober part of my brain kept telling me that for a kid like her, this was a courtesy call; she was going to do what she was going to do, with or without me.

Before I could think about it any more, Michael and Faisal came through the musical door.

We left the fluorescent storefront for the yellow streetlights. As we worked our way down the hill into the town's glowing streets, Matty reached over and squeezed my arm. Just once, and just enough to tell me that she thought I'd done something good.

# THIRTY-ONE: THE ENTERTAINMENT

WE HEARD THE CROWD from a block away. The houses we passed were old and they were big and each one was unique from its neighbor. As we got closer, the streets, driveways, and gravel parking lots became more and more full of cars. They were mostly bangers and junkers—the kinds of cars that college kids buy so they don't have to worry about backing into fire hydrants. Matty slowed down in front of a dirty beige pickup that had a jumbled mess of tools, coolers, and lawn bags sticking out of the back. A decal along the passenger door said "Home Grown Maintenance."

"You okay?" Michael asked her. She was looking at the truck and suddenly she was hundreds of miles away.

"Huh?" she said, swallowing and snapping back to us in an instant.

He smiled. "Is the baby kicking?"

"Nope. Everything is okay," she said. "Here." She opened her belly with a ripping noise and held out beers for us. "Baby beers!"

"Oh, shit, that reminds me," Faisal said. He patted around

on his coat before reaching behind his back and pulling out an empty Diet Faygo Cream Soda bottle. "Here. It's bad enough people are going to be smoking around your little bastard."

She laughed; we cracked our beers and Matty dumped hers into the bottle.

"See, Moses," Faisal said, "That's the difference between a third-wheel friend and a *load-bearing* friend. Gotta pull your weight."

We rounded the corner, right into the arms of a crowd of college kids mingling on the lawn, porch, and driveway of an old house. They were all laughing and talking and drinking out of plastic cups; it was a sea of flannel and Halloween costumes featuring brightly colored leggings and skinny jeans and facial hair and partially shaved heads.

The thing about small towns—like Guthrie, like Greenfield—is that everybody knows everybody's story. I know that my mail carrier, Mira Evans, miscarried three times before having her first kid; I know that my seventh-grade math teacher buys weed from my seventh-grade bully.

But here, in the throng of college students, I was nobody.

I was baggageless. I wasn't Moses Hill and I sure as hell wasn't Charlie Baltimore's cousin. It was one of the things I was feeling at camp too. Below the suspicion of new friends and authority figures in shorts, that strange weightlessness in the pit of my stomach was genuine anonymity. And it turned out that there was a whole world of it. It wasn't just a matter of pretending to be someone else in the face of sad, brokenhearted adults in line at Chicago convenience stores.

We headed for the packed porch. When we hit the wall of college kids, Matty started rubbing her stomach with one hand

and massaging the small of her back with the other, groaning just loud enough for people to hear.

The sea of flannel parted.

Matty led us up the stairs to the deepest reaches of the porch. When we got to the back, two guys sitting on the banister immediately got up and gestured toward the rail. The guy closest to us blew smoke out of the side of his lips and waved it frantically away.

"Shit. Sorry. Here, please," he said. He was dressed like a panda. After craning around and assessing whether or not he could fit his panda-body anywhere, he moved to the other side of the porch next to a wizard with a staff made of beer cans and duct tape.

"We should have worn costumes, guys," Matty said.

"You're already in costume," Michael said to her. "Or just flip that shit around your back and you can be a sexy hunchback."

"Yeah, but *real* costumes. I don't want to be a sexy hunchback."

"Everything is sexy and dumb," Faisal said. "Remember when everything wasn't always sexy and dumb on Halloween? Which also, by the way, is going to be the name of my memoir: 'Everything Is Sexy and Dumb: The Faisal Al-Aziz story.' "

A hipster in a winter hat and an ugly sweater whistled through his fingers before waving his arms. "All right! Guys! Next up, all the way from Milwaukee, we have The Entertainment. And just a reminder, if you're here to see Meat Bath, they're playing in the basement!"

The porch full of people erupted with applause before going silent in anticipation. I followed the rapt eyes of the quiet crowd and found that the band was indistinguishable from the rest of the people. The lead singer sat on the far end of the porch with his acoustic guitar; the woman to his right held a tambourine; the guy to his left cupped a harmonica to his lips. The lead in the middle looked back and forth between them, smiling and nodding, mouthing "One, two, three," before strumming into the music. The girl shook her instrument every few seconds, rhythmic and melancholic, the notes twinkling out next to the bare chords of the lead. The crowd didn't murmur.

I'd spent so long listening to classic rock with Charlie that I'd forgotten what it felt like to sway instead of thrash. The music on the porch didn't need to be cranked up or accompanied by blistering guitar solos.

Instead, there was poetry woven through the muted notes.

I took a long pull from my beer and somewhere, deep in the house, vibrations trembled their way out under our feet.

# THIRTY-TWO: THE LOVE SONG OF MOSES HILL

THE ENTERTAINMENT TAPERED OFF and the porch roared into applause but I could still hear the band underfoot.

I drank the rest of my beer and stared between my feet, my vision beginning to sway. I knew I was standing right above the forest from Faisal's story—the one that held out hope for all of the dead and ugly things—and I needed to see what the drums really were. Especially if it was too loud and too out of place to ask Faisal to finish his story and especially if I'd lost track of how many beers I'd already had.

I leaned over to the group and said, "Hey, I gotta . . ." but could barely hear myself over the music and the beer-colored excitement. Matty scrunched her face up and cupped her hand behind her ear. I shook the can and pointed at it, motioning to them that I'd be right back.

The band thanked everyone for showing up and said that the next song was called "Double the Flagpole."

I expected to hit a wall of people and noise when I opened the front door, not a small smattering of people talking quietly. The house wasn't silent though. There was still the deep rumble of bass somewhere and just off the main room in a coat-room under the stairs there was a parrot flapping and quoting poetry.

The living room was filled with hideous couches, and a young couple was sitting in the corner gesturing back and forth in sign language. The bass was coming from the back of the house, through the dim little kitchen where a handful of college students were huddled around a yellow polyurethane tub.

What I thought at first was a half-bathroom nestled in the corner of the kitchen was the door to the basement. I knew because it rattled on its hinges.

"This guy!" one of the college students said, pointing at me and catching me off guard. He had a top hat on. "I love this guy. He was in my poli-sci class last year and we . . ." He itched his face with the back of his hand. "But yeah. Give him a cup."

Top Hat's friend dipped a ladle into the strange tub filled with neon-colored liquid and chunks of tropical fruit and filled a red Solo cup for me. I was anybody; I chose to be someone who nonchalantly drank out of large colorful tubs. From the living room there was a *squawk!* noise followed by, "Do I dare! Disturb the universe!"

*"Quit with Prufrock!"* one of Top Hat's friends yelled over our shoulders.

Top Hat hugged me and I said thanks, but all at once I was invisible to the undergrads, who resumed talking about French cinema. The rattling door beckoned me and there was no one to tell me to fuck off or come on down, just me and the rattling door. Just me and the drums and maybe the answer to whether or not things can be dead on the outside and alive down below. I dumped the drink down my throat.

But the door was locked. The hidden drums were inches away and I couldn't see them.

On top of the beers I'd already lost track off, the new drink was working fast. The edges around my thoughts were starting to get fuzzy, but it was becoming increasingly important to find Faisal and tell him we could see the drums if we could just get past this goddamn door.

I weaved past Top Hat and his friends and opened the front door, caught between the warm air of the house and the cold wind of the open night. Ten feet away Matty, Michael, and Faisal were swaying in a small triangle with Matty in the middle. The sky couldn't decide whether to rain or snow but it felt like I had a say in it. Like I could make it rain when it had been snowing for so long.

They saw me at the same time and smiled and gestured for me to come over. Of all the people on all the porches in all the world, none were as unshakable or as complete as Matty, Michael, and Faisal in that rare, perfect moment. And I was welcome with them; they'd welcomed me since the start, even though I was convinced that we were all just seconds away from falling through the thin ice at any given moment.

They were warmth in an otherwise cold expanse. Looking at them, I didn't want to be Nobody or Anybody, I just wanted to be me. The same me with all of the history and scars. No lying, no pretending, just me.

Just like them.

The Entertainment tuned their instruments for their next song and the lead singer said, "This one's called 'Gately versus Demerol.' Two, three, four . . ."

The bass underfoot trembled in unintentional harmony with the music before us and the sound swelled and the lights behind the band backlit them into spectacular anonymity. When they finished and had managed to sincerely thank everyone for showing up, I edged through the crowd of people toward the trio.

"Guys," I yelled, showing them my cup. "We have to go inside—there are things inside that you need to see. Faisal! It's your house! From the campfire with the basement! We just have to break into the basement."

A faraway part of me was aware of the fact that I'd lost my handle on context and social norms. For example, instead of saying, "Hey, I'm noticing similarities between this house and the one you were telling us about at the campfire. Moreover, I want to explore what the drums mean to me on a personal, metaphorical level, specifically how I've spent the last year feeling, at best, robotic, and at worst, dead. Let's go check it out!" I'd decided on out-of-context alcohol-infused word bombs.

He smiled. "I don't know what that means, but I intend to find out. Why are your teeth green?"

"There are literal gallons of this stuff inside. But we need to figure how to get into the basement!"

"We should get going," Matty said, squeezing Michael's hand. "I'm exceptionally pregnant and my feet hurt. Plus I don't want to worry about Test figuring out that we're gone."

"What if I get you a cup of the hobo potion that Moses drank?" Faisal asked her, totally unfazed by the mention of Test.

"I just . . ." She groaned a little. "Okay. But then promise we're leaving or I tell my dad you got me pregnant," she said to Michael.

Michael's eyes flicked open wide.

"Moses, Faisal: it is very important that we are not in there for long."

The music under the house had changed. It wasn't gone, but it was different and we followed it.

# THIRTY-THREE: MIMICRY

"HUMAN VOICES WAKE US and we drown!" the parrot ominously squawked from the other room, tucked away under the stairs.

Faisal froze and tensed his shoulders up. "What the fresh fucking hell was that?""

"There's a bird that's been quoting T.S. Eliot since I came in earlier," I said. I figured that if I talked slow and enunciated every word they wouldn't know I was drunk. If they were as drunk as I was, they weren't showing it, and it felt wrong to be disproportionately more fucked up than my friends.

I caught myself smiling a stupid, half-in-the-bag grin because they were my friends and because there was a big cartoony bird quoting modernist poetry.

"This is a nightmare," Faisal said, leaning past us to see the bird. "I hate those things."

"Parrots?" I said.

"Even when they quote poetry like little Shakespeares?" Michael said.

"Yes, even then."

"What if it was quoting *Total Recall*?" he asked.

"You *know* how I feel about parrots," he said.

"But I also know how you feel about *Total Recall*," Michael said with exceptionally convincing eyebrows.

"Faisal's afraid of birds," Matty said to me.

I put on a very serious listening face.

"I am *not* afraid of birds; I just don't trust animals who have any kind of handle on human language."

"But it's just mimicry," I said. "Except for the ones that learn how to count and have a vocabulary of almost two thousand words. Those birds are . . ." I trailed off when I realized how heavy my arms felt and how if I turned my head back and forth it felt like there was a delay in my vision.

"What is it what is it what is it!" the parrot said to the coats. "Etherized!"

Faisal grimaced and made a "yick" noise. "Just . . . where's the basement?"

Across the room, an Imperial stormtrooper was whispering something to a girl dressed like a sexy tree. They were sitting on one of the ratty couches talking and he kept trying to flirt with her by taking her hand and resting it way up on his inner thigh. She'd pull her hand away, he'd lean in and say something to her, and he'd try to drag her hand back. Right as it looked like she was going to get up and leave, he braced his hands out, said something we couldn't hear, and pulled an Altoids tin out of his pocket.

Drunk Moses couldn't focus as concisely as he would have liked, but the still-pounding bass underfoot faded to background noise as the asshole on the couch kept trying to flirt with Tree Girl.

The sexy tree girl looked at it, looked at him, and eventually nodded with a tight-lipped, "quit being a douchebag" smile.

"There is absolutely no reason why you and that bird aren't best friends," Matty was saying to Faisal, leaning into the small room to get a better look at the parrot.

"I can think of every single reason in the world as to why me and that bird aren't even casual acquaintances," Faisal said with disgusted, fascinated horror.

Sexy Tree Girl's face read like she was about to punch the stormtrooper to death. He held up his hands, holding onto the tin and pacifying the situation before pulling a blue pill out of the Altoids container. He balanced it on two outstretched fingers and, just as she reached out to take it, pulled his hand back. He pinched it between his gloved fingers, motioning like he was about to throw a dart and aiming at her mouth.

"What if it was quoting *Tremors*?" Michael said.

"The bird doesn't get less awful the better it quotes movies, it gets worse."

The stormtrooper tossed the small blue shape and it ricocheted off her ear, bouncing toward us. His laugh came out muffled from under his mask. She stood up, almost fell back, and then made her way past us.

"Fucking asshole," she said as she made her way through the door. As she stumbled past us, I realized she was drunker than me. The stormtrooper bounded over to the door, still laughing, and he didn't seem very drunk at all. Drunk Moses felt his back get sweaty and his blood pressure start to climb. Drunk Moses started thinking about which classic rock song was appropriate for tackling drug-dealing sex predators.

"Wait! Come back— Ah, fuck it," he said.

I picked the small blue tablet up off the ground. It was about the diameter of a pencil eraser and there was an anchor carved into its middle.

"Matty?" the stormtrooper said through Faisal and Michael to her back.

Matty clenched her eyes shut at the muffled voice behind her and puffed a short, sharp breath through her nose. Michael and Faisal leaned back out of the parrot-room and looked over her shoulder at the stormtrooper.

"Matty," Faisal whispered. "It's a stormtrooper."

"Maybe I'm not the Matty he's looking for."

"Matty Gable?" There was no mistaking the excited familiarity in his voice.

"No, I think he definitely knows you," Faisal whispered.

She let out a slow breath and her face went pleasant as she turned around. When the stormtrooper saw her massive belly he jolted to a stop and pointed at her stomach.

"Jesus *Christ*."

I decided it was a good idea to loudly ask, "Who is this goddamn stormtrooper? Stormtrooper! Who are you?" He still hadn't noticed the tablet in my hand.

The stormtrooper lifted his helmet halfway off and rested it on the crown of his head; he was smiling a huge, open, and completely dead smile. Faisal's face went slack and Matty tried to keep looking pleasant.

"The goddamn stormtrooper is Dalton Emmory," Faisal said to me. The familiarity in his voice lacked any excitement and I decided that the most casual thing to do was to make unwavering eye contact with the drug-peddling, galactic douchebag.

"Oh. Shit," Michael said, not exactly laughing, not exactly not. "Hi, Dalton. How you been, man?"

"You're pregnant? That's fucking *crazy*," Dalton the storm-trooper said.

"Dalton," Michael said. "Relax, it's—"

"Fuck off, Mike," he said as though Michael was a little kid interrupting the adult. "You're pregnant? Is it mine?" he said, pointing at Matty. Her complexion had gone off-white. He looked back and forth between the four of us. "I'm kidding. Matty, Mike, guys, I'm kidding. Just, wow though," Dalton said. There was nothing in his voice that said he was actually kidding. What his voice actually said was that he was the kind of person who added "I'm kidding!" to very serious statements.

"Come on, guys. We have to get back anyway," Michael said with a more level voice than I would have expected.

Matty took a small breath, smiled, and diplomatically said, "It was good seeing you, Dalton." She took Michael's hand and started for the door.

"No, you know what: no. Sorry," he said, his tone going cold and loud. "This is fucking stupid and we have to talk about it. What is your goddamn problem? I just want to talk. We don't talk anymore," Dalton said, fluctuating back to a calmer, more reasonable tone.

"*Hey*," Michael said, stepping between them. "That's enough, Dalton."

Dalton wetted his lips and almost looked like he was going to apologize. To just let it go. Instead, he took a sip of his drink and said, "I cared about you, Matty."

"Are you really doing this right now?" Faisal asked semi-rhetorically.

"How much did you care? Would you have shot someone for her?" I said, enunciating everything. I figured it was a perfect time for a stormtrooper accuracy joke.

"What? Who the fuck are you?"

"Dalton," Matty said. "We'll talk about this some oth—"

"No, we won't. Because we don't *talk* anymore." He took a heavy breath in through his nose and sloshed his drink around in his cup. "And you're fucking pregnant?"

The stormtrooper joke I had lined up died halfway up my pipes; the sulking idiot in front of us was another one of Matty's defining moments. I'd been stupid enough to think that her mother had been her only one.

And even though I was drunk, I could see him fitting into her past. How he was a hurdle that she'd never asked for, and how we all get more than one defining moment.

Dalton was my bullet when I was eight, or Charlie's last year.

He was all the things that a little girl named Allison walked into that made her name Lump.

He was Test's desire to be command authority with a stupid new title like Coach.

Next to me, Michael was unambiguously not laughing. He kept half shaking his head each time the stormtrooper said something.

"Matty, come on, let's go," Faisal said.

"Shut up, Faisal," Dalton said. "This is a conversation we need to have."

Matty patted Faisal on the arm and gave him a shushing, calming look. "Dalton, this isn't a conversation I want to have right now."

"We dated for a year." His pupils were tiny black points.

"I remember." Her voice was iron.

"Do you remember how hard it was getting you to come out of your sexless little shell?"

Even as he said it, she didn't flinch. Her face didn't change at all.

The parrot behind us said, "No great matter! Great matter!"

As much as I wanted to go screaming toward the idiot, I knew that there was nothing I could add to the situation that Matty hadn't already brought. As much as we *all* wanted to jump in, she had it under control—everything Dalton said to her bounced off.

And still, the more that bird quoted Eliot, the more I wanted to scream.

"That's enough," Michael said.

"You barely held a boy's hand before me—I loved you and now you're knocked up?" The gears, somewhere in his storm-trooper head, turned. "The whole time: the whole time you were shooting off whore flares, but I didn't care."

"Then he said *whore flares*," Faisal said to nobody, shaking his head.

When she didn't fall apart or start crying, Dalton said, "*Good* one, Faisal." His responses were getting desperate. Matty wasn't folding. "I loved you, Matty—it took you almost six months to start loving me back, but you did. And then you broke my heart. And now you're doing it again." He flinched when he said it, like he knew he was barreling steadfast over a line he couldn't un-cross. Instead of shutting up and walking away, he said, "No, it's bullshit: Little Miss My-Body-Is-a-Temple finds out how much she likes to fuck, then breaks up with me and gets pregnant."

*"Dalton,"* Faisal said, like enough was enough, like he knew the whole story and needed Dalton to shut up as much for Michael's sake as for Matty's.

My moment—Charlie's moment—had come and left a gigantic, lifeless crater. But not Matty. Matty had had her huge, shattering moment with her mother before ever dealing with Dalton, and she had come out gleaming and vividly alive.

She was the life that refused not one, but two extinction events.

Who the fuck was I, lost and robotic in the aftermath?

Michael didn't say anything else—he was too busy staring at the stormtrooper and not blinking. When Dalton looked like he was about to keep talking, Michael cleared the space between us and the stormtrooper in two strides. He was only a couple of inches away from Dalton's face when he said, "Enough."

Michael wasn't Charlie, but the more he talked to Dalton, the more he edged into Charlie territory.

"What's the matter, Mike? Think you have something special with her? Join the fuckin' club." He was smiling but his face was pale and sick-looking.

"You're full of shit," Michael said, still just a couple inches away from the stormtrooper.

"Mike, stop," Matty said. And this time there *was* something in her voice. It's the hardest thing in the world, watching the ones you love try to take on your blowback.

"You don't know anything about us," Michael said. "About her."

Dalton's eyes darted back and forth between Mike's like he was reading every intimate line of personal narrative on his face.

"Holy shit. Holy *shit*," he said, smiling. "She told you *you* were her first."

"Fuck you," Michael said.

"Do I look like I'm lying?"

All of the frequencies in the house hummed down to one buzzing note—it was the house's beating heart in the basement. It was Matty breathing through her nose. It was the murmur of music and conversations from the porch.

Michael turned toward us. "It's true, though. Right? Matty?"

Matty winced her eyes shut for half a second.

"Mike . . ." Faisal said, his hands half-raised and his head shaking back and forth in a "just shut up, man" motion.

"No, I just want to make sure. Matty?"

Dalton let out a short, humorless laugh and Michael spun on him. "You shut up." He turned back.

"I know the baby's yours," she said, rubbing her stomach. She tried to smile but there was something nervous in her eyes.

"No, I'm not kidding. Forget the pregnancy pouch. I don't care that you slept—" He took a breath. "That's your business. But you told me I was your first. You lied."

"Mike . . ." she said.

"I thought that was our thing. Honesty and transparency. Whatever. I thought that was our thing. Why would you lie?"

"But he's a stormtrooper," I said, which I felt was the most obvious and important fact in the room.

"I'm sorry. I just— I need some air."

He walked out.

"Michael, wait—" she said to his back as he left, slamming the door in his wake. She didn't go after him; she turned her attention to Dalton. It only lasted a millionth of a second, but there was wrath in her eyes.

Then it was gone.

"We're leaving," she said to us.

"What? *Fuck you,* you don't get to keep walking away from me, Matty."

As we walked after Michael, I unclenched my fist and realized I was still holding the tablet. I held it up and caught his attention because I was still drunk and if I didn't do something, I knew I was going to start crying because I couldn't stop seeing the worst parts of my life replaying in front of me all the time. Whether it was a house show or a campfire story, everything brought me back to Charlie and it was exhausting. Right when you think you can escape your moment, you realize that it will always be able to hurt you.

He scoffed and, after a second, said, "Thanks," holding his hand out. I pulled it back.

"Is this what you were trying to give Sexy Tree Girl, *storm-trooper?*"

Matty stopped at the door and looked over her shoulder. "What were you doing over there?" she asked before he had a chance to respond to me.

"What do you mean 'what was I doing'? You don't get to be jealous of me, Matty. We broke up. You broke up with *me,* remember? And you, that's mine; give it back."

"Tree Girl's drunk," I said, less careful with my enunciation.

"So am I," he said like a smug son of a bitch.

"Not as drunk as her," I said.

"I asked you a question," Matty said.

"Matty, that's enough. This is starting to piss me off, okay? I was just having a good time with my friend."

"I don't think she wanted to be friends with you. Which is why she kept not wanting to touch your penis," I said, pointing between his legs in case he didn't know what I meant.

"Moses, can you hand me that?" she asked, pointing at my hand holding the pill.

"Oh come on, Matty, don't. Would you just let it go? And you," he said, pointing at me, "would you just fucking shut up?"

I handed it to her.

"What is this?" she asked.

"It is ecstasy," I said. "Methylenedioxymethamphetamine. MDMA and a shitload of syllables." I blinked a couple of times and then opened my eyes as wide as I could because my vision kept getting all blurry. We'd had to make anti-drug PSAs freshman year; it made sense at the time to read up on every illegal substance I could. "In 2007 it was ranked the 16th most addictive and 13th—no, *12th* most harmful recrea—"

"Thanks, Rain Man. I sell to her all the time, I wasn't doing anything she didn't want. Don't make this something it isn't," Dalton said.

Even as drunk as I was, I could see the wrath coming back. It flooded in from whatever oceanic depths were behind Matty's eyes and she said, calmly and unwaveringly, "What would your mother think?"

Matty was still standing, and it made me laugh in relief.

The parrot squawked, "Squeeze the universe! Bitten off with a smile!"

But I didn't squeeze the universe, and all I'd done for the last ten months was bite everything off with a smile; even now, as my guts warmed, as I realized how awake I was for the first time in months and months, I chose to simply bite the matter off with a smile and refuse to really tell them who I was. But the more I watched Matty, ceaseless against her clawing past, the more I wanted to.

Faisal inconspicuously reached over and tapped me on the elbow. When I looked over at him he whispered, "Watch this," then nodded toward Matty.

Dalton raised his eyebrows. "What? Whatever, Matty, it's good to see you," he said, the corner of his lip twisting into a faint smile, and he didn't go anywhere. "Good luck with your little brood."

She looked at the blue tablet in her hand before dropping it into a not-quite-empty, boot-shaped cup on the table next to us.

He sighed, tapped his finger against the rim of his cup, and said, "Great, good. Those aren't cheap. You win, I guess. Are you happy now?"

"I said, 'What would your mother think?' "

Nobody had thought to ask me that kind of question after the bowling alley. They were always much more interested in what God thought than what my mother and father thought.

"*What?* Look, I'm sorry I said that stuff in front of Mike. Probably shouldn't ha—"

"What the fuck made you think it was okay to put your hands on her?"

He laughed and his eyes were watery. "I already told you, she's a friend and I sell to her all the time."

"You still didn't answer my question," she said.

"What? What question?"

"About what your mom would think."

"So now you want to talk, huh? Can we talk about what we're really talking about? The little bundle of joy you and Mike made? Because *it's my business too*. Do you know how fucking ruined I was after you? You were the bomb that went off in my life, Matty."

She dropped her hand to her side, her fingers hovering over her pocket. As soon as the obviously-garbage-picked grandfather clock against the wall chimed midnight, she drew out her phone. "I forgot about you."

If her breaking up with him was the bomb that had gone off in his life, this was the nuclear winter that followed. "No you didn't," he said. He was drowning in her.

"I did. And I forgot about the pressure—I forgot about all the degrading little comments and the jokes and the secrets, all of the little weapons you used because you wanted to get off."

She used her words like a prizefighter uses haymakers, swinging heavy blows that pushed him against the ropes.

"They were *jokes*. I was *hurt*. I'm sorry. I shouldn't have made jokes. I mean, you did break up with me at my grandma's funeral."

I snorted.

"Something funny?" he asked me.

"It wasn't at her funeral," Matty said. "It was after. When I wouldn't have sex with you and you called me a cocktease."

"I was mourning!"

"You were horny. That's not an excuse. And that was how you did it every time: shame and guilt."

"I loved you. I never mea—"

"Stop making excuses."

"Matty, come on. I said I'm sorry, okay? If it helps, I'm not mad at you anymore. I forgive you. I just want you to forgive me too."

She pressed a button on the phone and placed it to her head before saying, "I don't need forgiveness."

Faisal grabbed an anticipatory handful of my sleeve.

"You gonna try to call Mike back? Fine. Good idea," Dalton said. "Give him a call. Great. Look, he's right: transparency is the key to relationships."

A college student dressed either like a pirate or a poet came in with a staggeringly drunk and exquisitely bearded wizard. The wizard kept leaning on him and mumbling into his ear, gesturing grandly with his staff made entirely of taped-together beer cans. Several cups and pictures were knocked off of shelves.

Matty held up a "hang on, I'm on the phone" finger.

"Hi, Mrs. Emmory?" Faisal and I both realized what she was doing at the same instant and both snapped our entirely undivided attention toward the stormtrooper; we saw all of the air come out of him. All of the bluster, all of the fire—he'd never stood a chance. "Hi. Sorry to wake you. I just wanted to let you know that Dalton still sells ecstasy. He used to keep it in the urn on the mantle. And he probably still does." She nodded, locked her eyes on him and said, "Yeah: that urn."

The things in her haunted past never stood a goddamn chance, and I wished I could be like her. I wished I could lay atomic waste to all of the footnotes of my life.

The tiny blue tablet with an anchor on it in the boot-shaped cup had dissolved to almost nothing.

"I—I'm on probation. Matty, what are you—what are you *doing*?"

He started to move toward her. He moved like he was dreaming. Like he was watching all of his bad decisions catching up to him. Matty's eyes went fierce. She stared deep into his devastation and pulled the trigger one more time, just for good goddamn measure.

"Mrs. Emmory? Your son treats women's sexuality like it's something to be ashamed of. He treats sex like a weapon and I know you raised him better." She hung up without looking at the phone or breaking eye contact with Dalton.

"Pardon me," the pirate/poet said, stepping between them. He had a piece of folded paper in his hands. "Sorry. I was told to read this to the . . . stormtrooper?" He pointed at the punch-drunk Dalton.

Dalton blinked a few times. "What?"

The parrot in the other room fluttered around and said, "I am Lazarus!"

"It says . . ." He squinted and unfolded the paper, leaning his head back to read through his glasses. "Faisal: dick punch."

Directly behind Dalton, the drunk wizard pulled his beard down and said, "Bluff clause, motherfucker," and in one fluid, downward motion twisted the stormtrooper helmet down and pantsed the awful asshole.

Faisal was a blur. The noise his fist made when he punched Dalton Emmory in the penis was not the sound of ham getting slapped, but the sound of victory. Dalton Emmory twisted around and tripped over the space pants around his ankles as he curled into a ball on the floor.

The trio bounded toward the door.

I knelt in front of Dalton.

First song that came to mind: "Back in the Saddle Again" by Aerosmith.

"In their defense, you were being churlish. And you have a really stupid fucking name." I let the words slur where they needed to slur and stay in focus where they needed to be in focus. I just smiled.

"Moses! Come on!"

As I ran for the door, I yelled at the bird, "Fuck you, Prufrock!" with as many extra syllables as I could fit before I ran out of breath.

# THIRTY-FOUR: SNOW

WE EXPLODED INTO THE NIGHT, clearing the porch steps three at a time, and went running back the way we came. The crowd of students and monsters faded behind us.

We skidded to a stop in front of the beige truck with all the tools in it.

"Holy shit," Faisal said.

There was a pickaxe sticking out of its hood. Faisal pulled his phone out of his pocket and took a picture of the truck's new hood ornament.

"I realized whose truck it was when he started talking to us," Michael said. He pulled the wizard robe off and tossed it in the bed of the truck, followed by the beard. "We should get out of here."

Every part of Michael's plan felt like something Charlie would have put together. From the bluff clause to the disguise to sinking a garden tool into some asshole's engine block.

Seeing Charlie back was like seeing a mountain of black thunderheads on the horizon after a drought: it would be a solution until it was a problem.

"You came back. As a wizard," Matty said.

He shrugged. "I love you."

She smiled. "I know."

They were holding hands. Behind us, hidden by the town's skyline, behind the buildings mottled with bright windows, a pair of lights climbed up and into the night. The lights grew like someone had punctured the night's pressure and was letting the dark drain away; they grew until they were over us and the small plane droned past, pushing its sound and light toward the wilderness we were headed for.

"That was the most gangster shit I have ever seen," Faisal said. "Mike! It was the most gangster shit I have ever seen! You missed it because you were off organizing your own gangster shit, but Matty was the most gangster of all gangsters."

Matty nodded and said "Nice," and then high-fived herself.

When we reached the Dairy Mart, Faisal asked for the time and asked if we needed to get any cabin supplies.

"I spent the last of my money paying off that wizard," Mike said.

I turned my phone on to check the time and the home screen showed a small backlog of texts: the first text message I'd missed, two hours previous, read:

Hi moses its lump! Reminder that thing that went missing?? I have a plan. Cant talk about it here. Msg me back!!

"Thank God," Faisal said to Michael. "I thought it was some kind of twist ending where you'd been the wizard the whole time. Plus I don't think that clerk wants to see us anymore."

The next message, sent fifteen minutes after the first, read:

[page 1/2]Hi moses! My phone has automatic correct on it so
I didn't mean to say reminder when I meant remember. Okay.
That is all. You might be asleep which
[page 2/2]is okay because it is getting late but I made a up a
code so we can talk about the plan. Just like the underground railroad!!

"No, he was super okay with it. Probably because he was
really drunk. And probably broke."

The next message, forty-five minutes after the last, said:

Hi moses! My phone is about to die but I am going to look for
the thing. Don't tell Mr. Test and don't be mad!
112 518 447 9826 55 3119 421

"Moses, you got the time?" Faisal asked me.

The final message, sent thirty minutes after that, was a voicemail. I hit play and shoved the phone against my head.

The message was just crunching and static.

"Oh, shit," I said, staring at my phone.

They didn't hear me because Faisal had started reenacting
hitting Dalton Emmory in the penis by crouching down and
punching his open palm before shaking his head and saying,
"No no no. That wasn't it, that wasn't it." I heard him punch his
palm again and say, "There! That was the noise! That was the
noise when my fist touched his penis!"

"*Guys.*"

The swimming, floating feeling in the pit of my stomach
was nothing new. It was the same feeling I'd had when Harper
saw us steal his Jesus, the same as any of the innumerable times

Charlie and I found ourselves getting deeper into trouble than we'd meant to.

They looked at me, still laughing a little.

"Something's up."

They went serious and I clicked through the menus on my phone until it asked if I wanted to call the number that had texted me. I hit "call."

A mom-sounding adult's voice immediately answered. Sobriety wild-fired through my body, bouncing off the blurry, drunken sludge writhing around in my head.

"Hi, this is Allison's cell phone that her parents are generously allowing her to use while she is away at camp. Leave a message and I'm sure she will get back to you in a timely fashion whenever she is done with her important and stately business or decides to charge her phone."

Just beyond the familiar feeling of Oh Shit, though, just past the final semblance of order, floating around my periphery was a quiet, heavy darkness that insisted we no longer had any control. And that was a feeling I'd only felt twice, both times marked with a gunshot.

"Moses?" Matty asked.

"Lump is out looking for the deer."

The sky settled on snow.

# THIRTY-FIVE: MONSTER LIGHTS

WE INCHED UP TO the tree line of the shotgun farmer's house. The house of Browning and his beast was dark and silent. The wind kept slapping into our backs and ushering us toward the house that we no longer had the option of going around.

"This is stupid. This is so stupid," Matty kept saying.

"She said she's trying to find the deer," I said. Any time any of us said anything, there was a distinct feeling that the calm in our voices was entirely manufactured.

She glared at me. "Call her. Again." Then she added, more softly, "Please."

"Her phone's *dead*," I said, sounding more abrasive than I'd meant to. I tried to tell myself that if Lump was calm enough to write out a secret code, then she had to be all right.

"Shit, this is so *stupid*," Matty said.

"I thought she was your Cabin Guardian," Faisal said.

"Not tonight. I got Nara to do it since Lump wanted to spend the night in the infirmary," she said, before breathing out through her teeth and trying to get a better view of the house.

"Because of her ear?" I asked, trying to retrace Lump's hypothetical steps.

"We have to go. Fuck," she said. She blinked hard and shook her head. "What? Sorry, no, not because of her ear. She said she wasn't feeling good and wanted to spend the night making deer posters. She got the all-clear from Test. Cabin's empty anyway since Shelly's doing the rec-center camp-in tonight for the girls. I think we got played by a child."

There was an edge in her voice, there was worry, and the feeling was working its way deeper and deeper into me too.

"What do you guys think?" Michael asked, staring out across the lawn. "This has got that distinct 'it's a trap' kind of feel to it. Matty, go offer Browning a reach-around. Distract him."

She looked at him and nobody said anything.

Faisal cleared his throat.

"I'm just kidding," Michael said. "Don't do that. Faisal, go give Browning a reach-around," he said, trying to recover.

"We need to go. Right fucking now," Matty said, more to herself than us.

"So what's the plan, then?" Michael asked.

"We show that mean motherfucker what's what," Faisal said, raising his eyebrows up and down. "We cut across his property. We have to, right?"

"Doesn't have lights between his house and the barn," Matty said. "Which we know because Faisal destroyed them last year," she said, forcing humor into the conversation, like she didn't want us to know how scared Lump had her.

"I'm sorry I wasn't watching where I was sprinting when I was being shot at," Faisal said, sounding the same way.

There was a black path running through the heart of the

farmer's property, between the barn and the house, where a small utility pole drooped lazy, pathetic wires. "What do you think, Moses?"

And like that, the decision was mine. A decision with an outcome that I could concretely influence. No in-between, no two sides of a story, just a simple choice:

Run wildly into the night or walk quietly through it.

I crouched by the fence and looked across the field. In a dead sprint, it wouldn't take long for us to get across. Less than a minute. My heart was beating against my chest like it was trying to remind me that the decision was real and actual and dangerous and that there was a literal, loaded gun that might be pointed at us. Whether it was the cheap-beer-flavored confidence or seeing Matty stand up against her past, I looked at them and I said: "We run."

Matty frowned and said, "We run."

"Fuck yeah, we do," Faisal said.

"Ready?" Matty asked as she tightened down the straps on her enormous belly.

We looked back and forth among each other.

"Wait," I said, throwing my hands out, making Faisal give a false start.

"What?" Matty whispered, looking around to see if I'd seen or heard something.

"I'll go first," I said, because Lump needed help. The snowflakes were coming down in heavy clumps and my alcohol-thinned blood was making my body shake and I expected the cold slithering feeling in my guts to flare up, but it didn't; the feelings that told me to shut up and mind my own business were so faint and far away that I could almost manage to ignore them. "Sneak through—see if he set up landmines or something. I'll signal the all-clear and get a head start back."

Matty nodded for a second like she was going to agree with me, then said, "Fuck that, we're all going."

We moved as fast as we could and we moved quiet and the plowed, frozen dirt didn't catch our feet or twist our ankles and, goddammit, we were untouchable.

I tried to stay on the rough grooves of the plowed field but it was impossible to stay completely straight running in the cold dark. Every time my foot slipped and rolled into the uneven lines I expected to hear my ankle snap and an unhinged shriek steam-whistling out of my mouth followed by a monster clawing its way out of the house followed by the sound of me being eaten alive by a dog. But every time my foot slipped, my momentum carried me on; the small white-gray sheets of ice would crack under my shoes and, instead of shattering beneath me and letting me fall, turn into traction. I ran and the broken ice carried me.

We slowed to a creep as we got to the dim corridor running through the farmer's property.

I took a deep breath.

As I slid past the frosted-over glass door, I saw Browning in his chair, asleep with his back to the huge windows. He'd fallen asleep watching an old home movie. It was a woman and a child at a park, laughing and playing, stuck forever in a moment more important to the viewer than the people who were actually living it.

We were almost through Browning's dark yard when I thought of Charlie. About just how much I didn't want to be sixty years old and still staring into the past.

I wanted to be more like Matty.

The nighttime clouds were scattershot and glowed silvery blue and the stars were trying to come through. I could still taste the jungle juice in the back of my mouth and coating my teeth, making my face feel hot and buzzy, like my eyes were swimming in gasoline. I almost leaned into Browning's truck for support before realizing that it would probably set off the alarm. Instead I crouched, and let my stomach roll over on itself.

When the feeling passed, I howled, silent, for all the living ghosts.

I howled for them all.

The stars didn't shine any brighter but they didn't disappear. And while it looked like they were frozen in place—while everything looked frozen forever in place—they were moving.[23] Every second I stared at them, their light got hundreds of thousands of miles closer, as though if I stared for long enough they'd stop being stars and start being suns or galaxies or planets and all the abstraction would fall away and everything would make perfect, undeniable sense.

But they didn't become any clearer and maybe that was okay.

I stood. I moved into the moonlight, away from the farmhouse.

"Okay, Lump. We're coming and you're not going to get caught by Test," I said, huffing into the wind. "Then we're going to find our deer."

The yellow glow of the house washed over us and we moved low, stealth-running along the edge of light, past the rusted

---

23 Moving like all things are moving—whole complex, intricate, unique galaxies that are barreling through the cold expanse and giving the impression of static when they are anything but stationary.

Chevy, over the chew toys, along the row of burn barrels, by the empty chicken coop.

I snapped my head back and stared at the chew toys and swatted at Faisal's back. I pointed at the toys. We stopped and stared at the industrial-strength rubber chew ring. The corner of the barn was chewed up and down for almost four feet and the giant piles of shit were unquestionably outside of the animal pen next to the cattle barn.

"Those are new," he said.

The growl that came from under the steps of the house sounded like the night sky was ripping apart. Like the rusty hinges on the gates of hell. Like a giant fucking dog trained to eat teenagers. I looked for glowing red eyes staring out of the dark but there was only that sound.

"Are you shitting me . . ." Michael said.

"Matty," Faisal said, "do you still have your knife? We might have to knife-fight a dog."

"I don't want to knife-fight a dog!" she said.

The beast emerged. The animal that came out from the porch steps was less dog and more bear. At some point in its ancient, hateful life it had been a bloodhound but had since chosen to forgo empathy and kindness in the name of slobbering violence.

"Looks like Farmer Browning owns a big dog," Michael said.

"That's not a dog, that's a horse," Faisal said.

Michael took a slow breath and knelt down. He pulled a half-eaten bag of Fritos out of his coat. "Besides, what's the line from *Lethal Weapon 3*? 'Boldness, be my friend'?"

"No, you already said the line from *Lethal Weapon 3*."

"Mike. What are you doing?" Matty asked through gritted teeth.

"Well. We can't knife-fight a dog. Porcupines, okay, but not dogs. I think I should try and make friends with him."

"Make friends?" Matty said.

"Yeah. Now, don't run; he'll only chase you down and kill you."

"Stop quoting *Lethal Weapon*," Faisal hissed.

Michael got on all fours and held the bag of snacks in his mouth and made whining noises over the Fritos. The dog took three very swift, low, and utterly silent strides toward him, its murderous eyes void of sympathy. Michael made more whining noises and started tossing small, crumbly handfuls of Fritos at the dog. The snacks bounced off the unflinching animal's snout and ears.

"Who'sagoodboy?" he said, putting his ass up and hands flat on the ground. "Or, girl. Who'sagoodgirl?"

The hound's lips pulled back and we saw every one of its dingy yellow teeth. Behind the dog, in his own world, the farmer was still asleep in front of the TV.

Michael rolled over and bent his arms and legs like a submissive dog, still whining and tossing Fritos at the enormous bloodhound. The dog let loose a single nuclear blast of a bark and the television screen inside paused almost immediately, sending static bars through the woman and the child.

"Ah, fuck," Michael said, sounding like he'd honestly thought his plan would work.

The dog lunged at him and the outline of the farmer's head was gone from the now-rocking armchair. Faisal pulled him up just as the animal filled the space he'd been occupying. "Run run run," they both started yelling.

The dog leapt up and tackled Michael to the ground, tearing

at his coat pocket until the other snacks burst out like a zebra getting gutted on a National Geographic special. Faisal pulled him back up, leaving behind the dog, which was whipping a handful of Slimjims back and forth. The back door of the farm burst open and the farmer did, in fact, have a shotgun clenched in his hands.

A very stupid part of me thought about waving my hands and telling him to aim for me since, little did he know, I was bulletproof.

A blast of orange-yellow sparks licked out of the gun that the farmer had pointed at the sky and because it had nothing to echo off of, the shot shredded the night around us. The dog bounded after us until the slack on its leash ran abruptly out. It snapped back and let loose a volley of deep, ass-puckering howls as we made for the tree line.

We put whole worlds between us and the farm before we stopped. Matty punched Michael in the heart and said, "What were you thinking!" and then started laughing because, despite its best efforts, the beast couldn't stop us. The beast had, in fact, been nearly tamed.

"Had to try," Michael said, smiling and trying to catch his breath.

There was blood in our faces; we'd stared the hound down and come out alive.

I straightened my back, pulling my hands off my knees, and looked toward the distant farmhouse. "For what it's worth," I said, "that was a Mossberg, not a Browning." They looked at me and for a half second I thought I'd said something stupid or lame or overly factual. Like they knew my whole story and what happens to my friends.

"Fucking Farmer Mossberg," Michael said.

And then they laughed.

We laughed and I couldn't tell if I was hot from running or cold from sweating, but I knew that I didn't care because this time, when the hounds came running, we moved together.

But as we headed into the woods toward camp, our laughs died out quicker than they had at the start of the night.

"See?" Michael said. "Nobody even had to go try to seduce the lonely farmer."

Faisal put his hand over his face and muttered, "Dude. God damn it."

Matty started shaking her head, looking down the road and anywhere but Michael.

"What, no. Wait," Michael said. "I'm kidding. Are we not laughing about this yet?"

"No, Mike, we aren't laughing about this yet," Matty said, still looking well down the road.

"Guys!" Faisal stage-whispered. "*Not* the time. *Not* the place. *Talk about this later.*"

But I knew something they didn't: they were already talking about it. They were miles into the conversation, miles ahead of other people who never brought anything into the light and who spent years bottling up steam and pressure.

The trick would be to keep talking before one of them got shot.

# THIRTY-SIX:
# HELLO, DARKNESS

THE CAMP WAS DARK except for the entrance, which was lit by a single dingy bulb bolted to a utility pole. As we ran under the pole it flickered out. Nobody stopped to question Matty's godlike powers and nobody made any more jokes.

We cleared the gravel lot, flanked the welcome center, crossed the fields, and followed the path to the nurse station because none of us quite believed that she'd try to pull something this big—I must have missed her the first time, and she was here, safe, where she belonged. But of course it was empty.

"Maybe she showed up and they sent her back to the cabin. If that's what happened, then she probably didn't know about the camp-in tonight," Michael said in a voice so calm and reasonable that Matty wouldn't look at him. Like she wanted to tell him that calm was not what this situation called for. "Probably found it empty and decided to sneak out. She'll be fine. She's just being us," he said, extending his hand. "I bet you an actual, real-life billion dollars that she's back and in bed though." She didn't shake his hand.

"Okay," Matty said as we got to the cabin. We stood in the bright circle cast down by the cabin's front light. "I'll be right back."

She eased the door open and slid into the dark. Our eyes all went off in different directions. Michael spit a wad of phlegm into the snow.

"So this sucks," Faisal said after nobody volunteered anything else to say.

"I think if we can survive your grievous, arrow-related injuries, we can survive a child sneaking out. I mean, we used to sneak out," Michael said, eventually looking up at his friend. Rallying in the face of uncertainty.

"We do sneak out. We are snuck-out right now," Faisal said back.

When Michael responded, you could tell he couldn't get away from the situation. He wanted to joke and keep making light of things, but there was a weight to everything that kept pulling his attention to the trees. "Yeah, but when we were in fifth grade . . ."

". . . all we wanted to do was break into the mess hall," Faisal said, steering the conversation toward something we could handle. None of us seemed quite able to look the situation in the eye, to think honestly about the seriousness of the situation should Matty come out empty-handed.

"It sounds like you were having the exact same experience then as you are now," I said. "Were you breaking into the mess hall for snacks because you smoked weed on top of the rope wall?" I could hear Charlie saying, *Give them something else to pay attention to,* even though I was right there with them, watching that creeping uncertainty close in around us.

"Of course not. That's ridiculous," Michael said, trying to smile.

"Preposterous," Faisal agreed in an impossibly comfortable tone.

"We convinced our Camp Buddy, Aaron Jenners, to sniff a ton of glue so he'd pass out, and then we broke into the mess hall because we'd heard that was where they kept the confiscation box," Michael said pointing at Faisal.

"It was supposed to be the El Dorado of porno mags and Jolt and cigarettes. A pornucopia."

"What'd you find?"

"We couldn't get in," Faisal said. "We thought about knocking out a window and making it look like a bear broke in. Like we'd trash the kitchen and Mike'd shit on the floor but secretly it was a thin cover for our caffeine porno heist." He changed topics without breaking stride. "I've gotta pee again."

"Why are you always peeing?" Michael asked him.

"You know when you blow up a rubber glove and the finger inflates?" Faisal asked.

"Don't say what I think you're going to say," Michael said.

"That's how bad I've gotta pee. It's in the tube. It's just," he flicked his finger out. "Straight out, full of pee."

"All five of them," I said, because it was easier than thinking about Lump being actively gone.

None of us laughed. Not really. We laughed the way we thought we were supposed to, as if laughing and joking could keep the ice from groaning and cracking beneath us.

Matty swung out of the cabin, her pregnant belly gone, cutting our quiet laughter off.

"She's not there. I checked everywhere."

"She's still *out*?" Michael said, not trying to pretend that everything was fine.

"It's almost two in the morning. Jesus. This is bad," she said, finally looking at us. She held up a handful of papers. "I found this on her bed—which, by the way, had a bunch of pillows under the blanket like a goddamn prison break."

I took the handful of papers. The first was a new poster—one with the word *DRAFT* written across the front in bold red letters. It was a *FOUND* poster with a caption that read:

*Attention everyone! Good news: I have saved the day.*

After that, a few torn-out pages from a puzzle book that dealt with code-breaking, followed by a few drawings of airplanes and one self-portrait of a small child with an aviator hat. I passed the papers around and tried to take a deep breath.[24]

"Come on," I said, heading toward the rec center. The zipper on my coat had started to come down and night cold made the thin, scratchy fabric of the referee shirt feel frozen against my body. Like the vertical bars on the shirt were cold, solid steel.

Nobody really said anything.

We checked the rec center and when Matty came out a few minutes later, nobody needed to ask if she'd found her. Her face said it all.

"Did you talk to the other girls?" I asked. "See if they talked to her?"

---

24 Breathing deeply affects the hypothalamus, which connects to your nervous system, which helps regulate your heartbeat. Breathe in, breathe out. Breathe in, breathe out.

"They all just groaned and said they hadn't seen her and then went back to sleep."

"You said that her last text was all numbers? Like a code?" Faisal asked, holding the sheet up.

"Yeah. Except it's not the same code from the papers on her bed. She either kept the page with this code on it or made up her own. What about the *FOUND* poster?"

"What about it?" Michael said.

"Why would she make it before she found the deer?"

"Because she's a hyperconfident little troublemaker who is trying to ruin all of us," Matty said.

"We should check the barn anyway."

"We have to check it *all*," Matty said, talking faster than usual. Her breath kept coming out in heavy clouds from her nose. "It's getting late and it's getting cold." She shook her head. "We have to look everywhere." She pulled in deep breaths and let them out slowly. Deeply in, deeply out.

# THIRTY-SEVEN: COIN TOSS

AFTER WE CHECKED AND RECHECKED all the cabins, we headed into the black woods toward the lake that would be no problem for an adult to swim across and even less of a problem for a lost child to drown in.

The exhaustion was starting to set in. None of us talked if we didn't have to. We looked where we had to look, which was anywhere except each other.

The first place we came to was the rope wall.

Nothing.

We kept moving and nobody said anything for a couple of minutes until we got to the archery range. We did our best to not talk about the weird itching that we were all feeling in the backs of our guts. That distant, nagging, dreadfully slow sense that somewhere, at some point, a joke had stopped being a joke.

The archery range was devoid of all children, but the bull's-eye targets were still set up against the hay bales. While they were discussing where we should look next, I ran my hand along the rough burlap edge of one of the targets.

Michael hugged Matty from behind and said, "We're not going to find her because we're going to be out here looking everywhere and freezing our collective tits off while she sneaks back to her cabin. She's probably back there now. Matty, it's going to be all right."

She was holding his coat sleeve between her thumb and forefinger but she was looking off into the night, not smiling or saying anything back.

I was thinking about pressure and how it ends up defining a relationship when I looked over at Faisal who was craning his head down to the target next to him. Whatever he was reading was written at hero-child level in small hero-child handwriting. I pushed off the target I was leaning on and dropped next to him.

It said:

*6225 59 7315 56 2211 55 91226 32226*

And it was glowing green.

"You think she wrote it?" he asked.

It was the same type of numerical grouping as the text I'd gotten.

"Yeah. It was her. That's my marker."

I took my phone out and brought up the text she'd sent. "Look at the 55. Look how the rest of them are grouped together. They're similar."

*"Dude."*

*"Yeah."*

"She wrote another one?" Michael asked. They crowded around us to read it. "What does it say?"

"Lump!" Matty whisper-called.

We waited but the only response we got was nighttime camp ambiance and Matty saying "shitshitshit" under her breath.

"I don't know," I said, even though I felt like I *should* know—knowing how to think through something, how to figure it all out, that's what I was always good at. And even though I'd only known them a couple of days, I could tell they thought so as well. For some stupid goddamn reason they had that look in their eyes like I was the hero who knew what should be done or what the hidden message was because I was supposed to be smart and the more I looked at it and the more I didn't understand what she was trying to say, the more I wanted to say, "We aren't even friends! Why did you have to start treating me like one of your friends?" but instead I just stared at the string of numbers that might have been able to tell us exactly where she was while that itching, scratching feeling in the pit of my stomach worked its way higher through my back like it was slithering around the rungs of my spine, clawing its way up and up and up.

We headed for the icy maintenance roads that would wind us around the small lake.

"If you could invent anything, what would it be?" Michael asked, using his second wind to try to make light of the situation.

As much as I appreciated the idea in theory, I appreciated it more when Matty said, "Not right now, Mike," without looking at him.

He persisted. "Because me, I would invent a media player that had a shuffle kind of function. Like you would play a movie and it would shuffle around a hundred different endings and a hundred different outcomes for each character. It would revolutionize movies."

"Lump!" Matty called into the woods.

Every twenty or thirty feet we would pass a clearing where we could see tiny frozen ponds. You could tell that they were only a few inches deep by the sticks poking out of them but something about them made my stomach bunch up.[25]

"Because what's the worst part of any horror movie?" Michael went on. "Or action movie. Really, just about any movie. Any time you see James Bond getting lowered into a tank of sharks, you know he's going to get out of it somehow. Any time Bruce Willis is trapped and surrounded by terrorists, all you have to do is think about how far into the movie you are. Oh, I've still got forty-five minutes left? There is absolutely nothing for me to worry about."

"Mike, shut up," Matty said, holding a hand out and facing the dark line of trees. Something in the woods cracked. It sounded like the thin white ice on the small ponds cracking underfoot.

Their tension was familiar territory for me. It had usually been Charlie who I'd gotten mad at, until he made enough jokes that we'd both moved on. Nothing was ever really brought out into the open. Not enough.

Michael was chewing on the inside of his lip. "Moses, you try. She probably thinks she's in trouble." And for a second it all made sense; of course we couldn't find her. She was hiding. She

---

25 The little frozen ponds reminded me that it's the little ones that freeze first.

was a kid out after lights-out and now the adults were looking for her.

And I tried to make it sound like I believed that when I said, "Lump?" into the dark. "Lump, it's us. It's Moses. Come on, it's okay, come out. You're not in trouble."

For a few moments, while our bodies pumped gallons of adrenaline, we stopped being cold. Our veins gushed neon.

"Lump?" I said again.

There was this feeling like we were standing in front of a jury—like there was some huge, cosmic coin flip happening just past our line of sight. Heads: Lump comes out of the dark, pushing branches out of her way, dirty and cold and frustrated that we stopped her from finding Harriet Tubman the deer. Or, better: she comes out of the tree line leading the small, lost animal.

Tails: nothing.

Tails: we wait and wait and eventually we silently decide that whatever we heard was just the wind or the woods or some animal we couldn't see and that we have to keep moving. Keep looking. Keep ignoring the terrible suspicion that nothing is right.

The coin landed. We moved on.

# THIRTY-EIGHT: END TIMES

"MIKE. STOP." MATTY'S shoulders were hunched up when she said it, each word fully contained in an exhaled breath.

"I'm just saying," he said, smiling a Charlie smile. "That's not a kid-shaped hole. That's more like a baby-shaped hole."

We'd been working our way down the maintenance roads and talking about the lake that had a rim of ice when Matty saw a hole and started breathing fast and talking about how we had to call for help. She glared at him but he kept going, kept trying to salvage it by making more jokes. Jokes that none of us could laugh at. "Like if a baby was out here because it was drunk and decided it wanted to catch the reflection of the moon so it broke the ice with a big rock and then fell in."

"You aren't funny. You're being an asshole. Stop being an unfunny asshole." She said the words I'd thought over and over for years before.

Faisal and I tried to make ourselves invisible.

"Jesus Christ, Matty, it's *fine*. She'll be okay."

"Don't fucking talk down to me."

It was like watching old Hill–Baltimore home videos.

Faisal and I hung back while they walked and argued. I took my phone out of my pocket and clicked it on, hoping there would be another message or a missed call, but there was nothing. I hit "call."

"Trying her again?"

"Yeah."

After a few seconds, I hung up. The breathing exercises didn't help. The fucking clues she'd left behind didn't help. Nothing helped. There was no trump card to play that would just put an end to her being gone.

"Nothing?"

"Voicemail."

"She probably turned her phone off to conserve battery. That seems like a Lump thing to do."

I pictured her phone smashed to pieces in the road, where she'd dropped it when she got hit by a mulch truck. I pictured her phone at the bottom of a freezing lake. Chewed to pieces by things with claws and needle-sharp teeth. I pictured her phone stripped of its SIM card and battery, burning in a stranger's basement incinerator.

I called again just because, and once again heard her mother's recorded voice. Faisal pushed his hands into his pockets and shook some change around. The sky was black and the stars were white and the intermittent clouds were silver gray.

Faisal and I started poking around in the surrounding clearing, checking for anything that might pass as a clue.

"They've been fighting a lot lately," Faisal said, looking off over the lake. "Maybe not more than usual, but more . . . loudly."

I grunted in a way that I hoped conveyed, "Hm, what's going

on with them?" After a moment, I added actual words. "Has the Dalton stuff come up before?"

"No. It very specifically never did." He bent over, quick, and grabbed a candy wrapper. He slowed down as he stood back up and realized how old it was. He held it out to me anyway, without much enthusiasm. "This probably isn't a clue."

"Probably not, no."

He wedged the trash in his back pocket like he planned to get rid of it later.

"But he knew they dated, right?" I asked, steering us back to Dalton.

"Yeah, but—" He paused like he wasn't sure he was supposed to tell me any more. "Dalton's one of the biggest pieces of shit I've ever seen Matty hang around with. Guy's a manipulative little douchebag. And eventually Matty left his douchey little drug-dealing ass behind and got with Mike, who's a fucking sweetheart that never pressured her into anything. But when the night finally did come, Mike got real nervous since it was his first time and Matty didn't want him to feel bad or anxious so she said it was her first time too."

"How do you know all this?" It didn't seem right hearing this story from a third party, even if the third party was Faisal.

"Third-wheel privileges. Like I said, I'm a load-bearing friend. Which, so, hey: fourth-wheel privileges, huh? Got ourselves a proper structure," he said. Paused. "Just so you know, either one of them would tell you any of this stuff. Especially now."

"Why do you say that?"

"You looked uncomfortable," he said, scooting some leaves around, looking for any sign of Lump.

"Ah." I thought, for a second, about how to phrase my next question. "What abou—"

"He never asked. It's not hard to fake losing your virginity to another virgin. And, as far as I know, they just never really talked about it. She just kind of became the myth, you know?"

"I've only known you guys for a couple of days, but is this the kind of thing that would set them off? They don't seem like the public-fighting type."

He laughed a small humorless laugh under his breath. I looked at him and said, "What?"

"Relationship drama," he said, shrugging. "That's what we're talking about right now. While a kid is—"

"Yeah."

"I guess it's that or go crazy, right? Anyway. This whole shit between Matty and Mike wouldn't have been the kind of thing to set them off—even if he did have to find out from Dalton. Dalton was just a stupid, dead-eyed catalyst. Matty sent out her application to Northwestern a few weeks ago and, of course, Mike waited until last month to even start thinking about the idea of applying to college. Which isn't a huge deal because there's still time to apply, but he decided to apply to Northwestern too. Thing is, nobody ever really expected Mike to do the whole hyper-competitive college thing. He's great and I love him but he spent the first three years of high school being professionally good at dodging work and responsibility. Years of bullshit and he has one talk with the guidance counselor who tells him he should apply, and he does. Gets all kinds of fired up about it."

The more we talked about Michael, the more of Charlie I saw in him.

"She's mad because he's getting his shit together? That doesn't sound like Matty," I said, like I knew something—anything—about her. The words were like a litmus test for the conversation. To find out if it was bullshit small talk or something more real and more human. He'd answer like we were acquaintances or like we were friends.

I could see Charlie's face whenever the topic of college came up. Like it was a topic that made his mouth go dry. After all, who was I to want to leave our hometown?

Faisal squinted one eye shut and shrugged, dipping his head a little like he was weighing his response. "No, not really. That's not it. I mean, you'd expect her to be a little pissed about how she's spent four years crushing all of her classes, legitimately earning her way, making early enrollment deadlines, *and*"—he hesitated for half a breath, almost course-correcting away from it before choosing to say—"it was the school her mom went to." For a second, he looked me in the eyes to see if that registered. It did. "Then to have Mike decide on a random Tuesday afternoon a few weeks before the deadline—it just got to her, you know?"

The fight before us kept sending up fragments like mortar shells that we couldn't help but overhear. Words like "honesty" and "love" and "hurt" burst outward and upward like bombs hurled up into the dark.

"Does that mean you're going to Northwestern too?"

"Fuck no," he said, laughing a little.

"Really?"

"I mean, maybe someday. My parents would love it, but I'm doing Community before I do anything else." He said it easily. He said it like there was nothing to be scared of. Like it was okay to stay close to home. "What about you? Harvard? Princeton? Yale? Big . . . Science School One?"

"Honestly, I have no fucking idea."[26] The fucked-up part of me wanted to smile and laugh—a deep and real smile over an honest laugh—because I really did have no fucking clue. In the midst of Charlie's fallout, the idea of Duke had been a life preserver. It had been a tangible Somewhere Else I could be that would put the rest of my life behind me.

But now I was in the woods, hundreds of miles from Chicago or my family or Charlie, and it was all still right behind me all of the time. Why would Duke be any different?

"I know that feeling. But you know, honestly, fuck it. Things'll work out. Or, I guess, they won't. Hundred years from now, we'll be dead and we'll have made all the choices we were going to make."

My phone went off in my pocket and I had it out before it finished its first vibration. It didn't go off again because it was just a text from my dad using binary telling me that he loved me too.

When I shook my head and muttered, "Fuck," Faisal said, "Not her, then?" I could tell by the look on his face that his heart had started beating as hard as mine when the phone buzzed.

"No. Just my dad."

After a few seconds of silence, he said, "Anyway, Mikey getting his shit lined up to apply: that's not it. I know you just met us and all, so this probably doesn't mean a lot, but she almost cried, she was so proud of him. *Matty Gable* almost cried. So no, that wasn't it. It was because nobody—not even Mikey— expected Mikey to do college. They had this sort of proverbial cliff they were heading toward once school ended and college

---

26 And for once, I wasn't lying.

started. It was this urgent, pathetic romance that was going to end in an explosion of hormones and shitty poetry but the cliff kind of just disappeared."

They were trying to be polite by not arguing in front of us, but the night was quiet except for the light wind that carried the majority of their fight toward us.

"Remember when the world was going to end in 2012?" he asked me.

"Because of the bullshit with the Mayan calendar?"

"Yeah. It's kind of like that."

"A fake end of the world."

"No, I mean suddenly it's like New Years 2013. How productive were you in 2012?"

"How productive as opposed to other, less apocalyptic, years?"

"Right."

"Probably a little more productive than usual. Depending on what qualifies as productive."

"Everyone—at least as far as I can tell—felt a lot more, what? Urgent, I guess? About things. Like even though it only took five minutes' worth of Googling to know that nothing anywhere ever said the world was going to end at the stroke of midnight, everyone felt like they had to get it all done before the literal end of the world.

"They wanted to think the world was going to end. Even though most people had to know, somewhere, on some basic level, that the world wasn't going anywhere, Hollywood still made movies about it. Writers wrote novels about it." He started ticking off examples on his fingers. "TV shows, blogs, shirts, Facebook groups, everyone. Everyone got in on the end of the world." He swiped his hand in front of him like he was ushering the past by. He cleared his throat and spit a wad at the freezing lake. "People went nuts for it."

He smiled a little. "They lost their apocalypse, I think," he said, nodding toward Matty and Michael. "Without the world coming down around them, they had to face some things about themselves."

This was the apocalyptic fallout that Charlie and I hadn't had. After everything, when the sky fell, we never got the day after. We just ended. They'd found out that they had to really and honestly start being around each other. Like all the people who woke up the morning after their night-long, end-of-the-world, orgy riots to find that the sun was still there and there were still nothing but commercials on the radio and who had to start honestly dealing with who they'd found out they were.

"I guess you add that to the thing with Dalton, and now . . ." He shrugged at the situation around us. "They don't know what to do." He took a breath and cracked his neck. "So, what do you think?"[27]

"I think we should keep moving."

"Yeah," he said, before cupping his hands around his mouth and calling out to them. They walked over without saying anything else as though nothing was wrong and we hadn't heard them yelling at each other. "We need to keep moving."

---

27 I think not every relationship gets a proper apocalypse. That you have to keep an eye on your past. That you can run and run and run but if you look away from that motherfucker, it'll sneak up and whisper in your ear that it's always right there behind you. That there's merit in stopping and turning and letting your past come screaming into your open arms. That honestly and authentically being around others is maybe the hardest thing in the world.

# THIRTY-NINE:
# SLOW-MOVING LIGHT

TEST HAD THE CORDLESS PHONE dug into the side of his head. He didn't stop glaring at us. Faisal started to stand up with his hands out, ready to say something, but Test pointed at him and said, "Shut up. Sit down." His attention returned to the phone. It was 5:08 in the morning.

We had checked around the ice-rimmed lake. We'd checked the barn. We'd looped back through the camp.

Matty's hands were clamped in her lap and she wouldn't look at any of us. Even after Michael had given up trying to make her feel better, Faisal had tried to tell her that it was going to be okay. They didn't recognize the look on her face like I did though. The one that said, "We are immeasurably fucked."

Test plucked his glasses off with his free hand and rubbed the bridge of his nose, and spoke into the phone. "Elaine. Hi." His eyes were closed behind his pinched fingers. "No, not really. I need you to get the faculty together. Quietly." He turned his back to us. The hair he still had stuck up in the back like a crown and the front collar of his white undershirt, beneath his Camp Jaye'k zip-up, had drool marks that were only just now drying.

We'd checked by the utility sheds. We'd checked by the main roads. We'd looked in the boys' cabins; Michael and Faisal had both quietly gone through their own individual child-armies and gotten groggy answers that no one had seen Lump.

The TV in Test's office was decades old. It had the thick plastic dials that gave you fewer than ten preset options, and someone at some point had dropped it because there was a starburst smattering of cracks across the middle of the screen.

We'd checked Lump's bed again, hoping to find her fast asleep.

Outside the tiny office window there'd been snow falling in heavy sheets. The same snow that had covered any footprints we'd hoped to find when we'd circled the camp three times and realized we needed help because things were not okay. At just after five in the morning we'd knocked on Test's door.

The snow had turned into a wet drizzle.

Faisal reached over and swatted at Michael's arm and pointed at a picture on the wall. A vacationing Test stared back from the *Dad of the Year* frame posing with a daughter who looked hauntingly like her father.

"What a horrible co-winkie-dink," Michael said, trying to smile.

"This isn't funny," Matty said. "Lump is missing." She checked to see if Test was listening. "She is actually *missing* and *it is our fault.*"

My guts squirted sour. The ten-year-old in me wanted to believe that it was over and that things would be okay since we'd gotten an adult, but just because we asked for help didn't mean that the situation was over or that Lump was okay.

"If there's any kid I'm not worried about, it's Lump," Faisal said, his eyes straight ahead. "Trevor, sure. Bryce, yeah. Kid would, God willing, get eaten by dogs. She needs to be found, but she's okay. We'll find her."

"I said shut up. All of you," Test said, the mouthpiece of the phone pulled away from his face. "Sorry. Camp Buddies. I don't think it's anything like that. At least I hope it—no, not like that . . . right. But she's MIA. Yeah. Yep. Good, all right, thanks." He hung up the phone and stared at us. He leaned against his desk where the clues from Lump's bed were spread out like you'd see in an old detective movie.

The *DRAFT* posters she'd made, the mockups of the deer, the codebook with the missing pages, and the pictures she'd drawn of a hero-child in an aviator hat. All the clues that we had, that weren't pointing us where we needed to be pointed.

We stared back.

He kept staring.

"Shut up," he said to me. He had seen my lips starting to move. "Elaine is getting the faculty and the Buddies together and we're going to find her. And while she's getting a *search party* together, I need some questions answered. Do I need to ask the very obvious questions?"

Matty took a deep breath and looked Test in the eye, but Michael cut her off.

"She snuck out after lights-out," Michael said. Matty turned her head, slow, and looked at him with eyes that were all whites. Eyes that said, "She was in my cabin, I didn't ask you to fucking answer for me." Michael nodded at her, then at Test like it was common knowledge. Faisal ran his hand down his jaw, clicked it back and forth before blinking once, hard. "I mean, I assume it was lights-out. I talked to you on the phone a few minutes before you went to bed and everything was fine."

Test turned to her. "Let me get this straight. She left the infirmary after lights-out," he said, nodding condescendingly at us. "Then she came back to the cabin, found it *empty,* then went off into the night."

"The cabin was empty because Shelly had the girls in the rec center," Matty said.

He rubbed his eyes. "How'd you know she was missing, Ms. Gable? Room full of snoring kids, how'd you have her pegged as missing?"

"She called me," I said. "I missed her calls and now her phone's dead so I woke them up." I pointed somewhere between the three of them. "Because they know the camp, and they know the kids."

"And why are all four of you sitting here?" he said to me, still rubbing his eyes with his thumb and finger.

"She called us—"

"I'm asking *him,* Bachman."

"Because I—*we* couldn't find her." I said, looking at the others.

Test dropped his hand and moved his head to catch my eye. "You couldn't find her."

"Right, and s—"

"—I'm not finished. You couldn't find her and now she's missing. She's out in the freezing rain because you four chose to spend valuable time trying to save your own asses."

Michael started to ask how we were trying to save our own asses when Test cut him off.

"Stop. No more shit. You were out after LO."

"We were just trying to find her," I said.

"What was that, Mr. Hill?"

"I sai—"

"I know what you said. All of you: get out of my office. The horn goes off at seven—that means we're going to have a lot more kids to keep track of. Keep looking for her. When we find her, we sound the alarm—whistles, calls, whatever it takes to get everybody together. We reconvene at the rec hall at noon. Go, now."

On the wall next to the old TV there was an old framed print of an even older Norman Rockwell painting where a kid in a huge, sagging uniform was saluting some flag or figure behind the viewer. The left half of the painting was yellowish white from years of sun damage, and it was like the kid in the picture couldn't see the encroaching off-white that was slowly obliterating everything behind him, so he just kept saluting.

# FORTY: MY FIRST NOTHING

THERE'S A MOMENT THAT does stand out to me from my life After Charlie.

It's July. The school year was rough; the crowded hallways were easier than ever to walk through, since the people parted around me like waves.

People I'm supposed to have been friends with—even in passing—looked through me or over me or past me. People who I wanted to scream at: "I was there when you tried to bring your dog back from the dead," or "My cousin had a huge crush on you."

I was a ghost.

Summer doesn't seem like it's going to be much better. For the first few weeks, I just sleep or go online or watch movies.

Come mid-July, I'm so fed up looking at my computer screen or the back of my eyelids or the TV that I get up and go for a drive without knowing where I'm going. Freddie's been fixed so I tell myself I need to test it out, and at first I just drive around Guthrie, but I hate the sight of town too, and the cops all know me and in a small town it's hard to avoid any landmarks, let alone the one you almost burned down.

So I head north to the city. I hug Lakeshore Drive with the gigantic buildings on my left and the massive, endless blue on my right.

And eventually I'm in Evanston.

And eventually I'm on 94.

I don't remember when I turned the radio off, but I realize I'm driving with nothing but the ambient sounds of the car. And for a little while, nothing sounds like gunshots.

# FORTY-ONE:
# SEARCH PARTY

WE SEARCHED.
   And we searched.
   And we searched.
   And we searched.
   And we searched.
   And we searched.
   And we searched.
   And we searched.
   And we searched.
   And we searched.
   And we searched.

# FORTY-TWO: 12:08

EVENTUALLY LUMP WAS MISSING for long enough that we made our way back to the rec hall. Each time I blinked I dreamed of Lump running through the freezing night surrounded by hungry animals with frothing mouths.

At 12:05 I swallowed three No-Snooze pills and, at 12:08, two shapes moved past the window by the door. They'd whisked through my peripheral vision and were standing behind the door like they were discussing some pre-entrance plan. I blinked, and when the door opened Lump came rushing through, exhausted and cold and freshly bandaged but wildly alive and frantically needing to tell her adventure story, but then I blinked again and it was just Test outlined in the doorway against the cold afternoon wind.

He had her muddy, dripping aviator hat.

# FORTY-THREE: SPIRALING ROUND . . .

THE FOUR OF US LEANED against the railing facing Test. The Maybe-Dickwad/-Hole and the other Buddy were inside presiding over the kids, who could tell something was wrong. We hunched against the wind Test had been out in for hours—his legs and face were red with windburn, but he took his gloves off and unzipped his coat when he talked to us.

Faisal stood between Matty and Michael, and I stood at the end.

"We found it in a tree on the north side of the grounds," Test said when Matty asked where they found the hat. "It was ten, fifteen feet up a pine."

"She was climbing," I said. "She was probably climbing to get a better view."

"A better view of what?" Michael said.

I shook my head. Leaning on the railing, I could almost see through the trees to the road where the lights ran in both directions. The clouds in the otherwise exceptionally clear sky were scattered enough that they threw down circles of darkness that sailed across the snow-covered gravel parking lot, and in every one of the shadow scenes I saw Lump. The light she moved in was moonlight: not the yellow sunlight, but pale moonlight that only existed in the spotlight circles piercing down through the day. It made sense to me that a half dozen Lumps were running around and playing and cartwheeling and rolling around with baby deer and leaning against the pillars of daytime moonshine because I was more asleep than not. The only response that made sense to me was to say, "She found us."

"Moses?" the Lumps all said.

"—ses?"

I blinked and the cloud shadows were empty. "Sorry?"

"Pay attention," Test said. Somewhere far away through the trees, something was making a wailing noise.

"Did you call the police?" Faisal asked.

"I called the Department of Natural Resources first," he said loftily. "DNR's got stations scattered for a hundred miles around here. Put an APD[28] out on her."

"What about her parents?" Matty asked, not realizing how much that family already had to deal with on an everyday basis.

The awful fucking wind kept assaulting us, blowing into, under, and through our clothes. All of us except Test hugged ourselves warm. The distant wailing noise picked up and it sounded like a trapped animal.

"They're a couple hours away on account of thinking they had a vacation on their hands, but they're on their way," he said. But he was barely talking to us. The wind was too cold for this

---

28 He meant APB. Which he didn't do—he asked for help. A camp director clearly can't issue a legitimate all-points bulletin.

time of year, even the daylight hours felt all too frozen and life-less. "When was the last time any of you slept?"

Nobody answered.

"You've been up all night and I need you all to be rested. We could have a long night in front of us." He took the cordless phone he was carrying around out of his cargo pocket, pinched the bridge of his nose for moment, and dialed 911. He angled the phone away from his mouth and said, "Sleep, food, then back to it, okay? I need you guys t— Yes. Hi," he said, bringing the phone back to his mouth.

We headed for the cabins while Test began explaining to the dispatcher that there was a child missing and when his voice died mid-sentence, we all turned and looked at him.

"Beg pardon?" The deep crease between his eyes went deeper. "What do you mean someone already called? Who called?"

The wailing animal came barreling toward the camp's drive-way.

Just beyond our sight line and the parking lot, swooping lights blasted through the snowy, late autumnal trees—all of the scarlet and lemon leaves weighed down under swaths of white—and turned the snow red and blue. The wailing sirens followed as two squad cars, a fire truck, and an ambulance came roaring down the small, winding driveway.

"Holy Christ," Test said, cramming the phone into his pocket.

We ran toward the front of the building right as the first police car came to a slippery, snowy stop in front of us. Two officers spilled out, each with a hand on their belt, the driver saying something into her shoulder-mounted radio.

"Who called you?" Test said.

I looked at Test like he was a tired, bedraggled woodsperson in shorts who had just yelled semi-accusingly at the cops for showing up exactly when we needed them. The officer looked at him the same way.

"We got a distress call from a child. *Sir,* please step back," the immense police officer said to Test, who couldn't figure out what to say to whom or where to stand. "She told us the name of the camp and that she was lost before the call cut."

The other vehicles came roaring down the path and packed themselves tightly around us.

"Wait," I said. "*She* said that? 'She' like Lump? Lump called?"

"She's *okay,*" Matty said to us while Test talked to the officers. "She's *still okay.*"

The officer didn't take her gloved hand off her holster when she spoke. "Dispatch got a distress call from a young girl," she said. "Like I said, her phone died before she could tell us anything other than the name of the camp." You could tell she was used to talking to panicked-looking people in the middle of the woods.

"But you traced it, right?" I said. "You traced the call here so you know where she is?"[29]

"To the camp, yes."

"What else did she say?" Test asked. "Did she describe where she was, if she was hurt, if there were houses around?"

They bounced back and forth, sharing non-information while the EMTs drank coffee out of thermoses and talked with the other first responders, all of us alternating between vibrating with nervous adrenaline and settling into static because nobody knew

---

29 Which, of course, they had, because they were there, and which was a stupid question because GPS accuracy is still shit when it comes to emergencies.

the extent of the situation and maybe, just maybe, if Lump had called 911 not that long ago, we could find her soon.

Test suggested bloodhounds; the cop ignored him and spoke into her shoulder-mounted radio. "Dispatch, we have a 7002, possible 1001, requesting additional units."

The tinny, crackly voice on the other side of the radio responded that they understood and would be sending more cars.

"So what do we do? Do we do an Amber Alert?" Michael asked.

The officers had relaxed out of their initial Full Alert Mode that cops are always in when they first show up.[30]

"No, that's not how that works. Not if she's just lost. If she's lost then we find her. But we need to rule out other options."

"What other options?" Test said. "One of my kids is missing and she needs to be found." He talked with his hands, speaking with his fingers splayed out like he was chastising a child, which the officer didn't appreciate. "No, tell me. What other options are we considering?"

But he knew the other options. He knew them the same as we all knew them, and if my guts hadn't already been frozen through, they would have turned to water when the officer answered him:

"We have to rule out the possibility that someone took her." I pictured all the Lumps in the radiant nighttime sunlight, smiling and playing until twisted, gnarled hands reached out of the dark and whisked them away, one at a time, into the woods.

"We don't have time to consider that," Test said, not trying to hide the tired anger in his voice.

---

30 The kind of Full Alert Mode they use when bowling alleys are on fire.

"I need you to step over here and speak with me," she said to Test. The officer looked over at her partner and nodded; the partner said something into his radio before turning to the EMTs. They all started moving.

Test and the officer talked about the possibility of abduction. They talked about the locals and the Buddies and the off chance that someone had stolen her away in the middle of the night, and after a while, the officer was convinced.

"We can assign Buddies to watch the campers this evening. A slumber party in the rec hall," Test said. "I'll get flashlights and whistles either way—get them to the rest of the faculty." He power-walked to his office.

"We split up," I said before anybody could ask what they thought we should do. "This isn't a horror movie and there isn't a killer on the loose, so a bunch of teenagers splitting up at camp in the woods to cover more ground is the best option."

"Attractive teenagers too," Faisal said, the humor in his voice reflecting the new energy we were all feeling.

"Just to be safe: no showering, no drugs, no skinny dipping, and no sex," Michael said. He pointed at Matty. "Consider yourself cut off," he said. "You too," he said, pointing at Faisal.

"You're not my type," Faisal said.

"Bullshit I'm not."

There was a trace of electricity in their voices that hadn't been there since the night before. Something alive and resonating and reverberating, something coming back from the darkness.

Like volts to the heart.

Matty said, "We've got this," as I thought it.

The tree line around us was a mix of mostly old pines and small birch trees with peeling bark, and if you looked high enough you couldn't keep track of where one tree's branches ended and the other's began.

Michael went to squeeze Matty's hand but she flinched back just noticeably enough that Faisal and I had to pretend we didn't see anything. Michael smiled and nodded just as discreetly and said, "She's okay, Matty. We'll find her."

She was almost smiling when her eyes went sharp as she saw Test jogging up behind us.

"All right, let's do this," he said, tossing small LED flashlights to each of us. He had more in a Meijer bag, which we knew because one of them was on and, when he moved, the bag would twist around like a searchlight hidden in a thin fog. It was just after one in the afternoon, but sun wasn't going to last. I didn't want to think about what those flashlights implied or that we might not find her until we really needed them. "I'll round up the others. You all: *go*."

We went.

I checked to make sure my flashlight worked, and after we agreed on our separate directions, we ran. In front of the rec hall there was an audience of monsters. All along the railing running the length of the building were the pumpkins we'd carved. I shot past them all; one at a time the monstrous faces beamed at me; the city-crushing giants wrecked cities despite me; and the audience of silent, purgatory-stricken faces smiled or snarled or glared or rolled their eyes, and at the end there was one soul made of an infinite winding loop that circled up into the stalk. Whether it was my momentum or the velocity of October, the last pumpkin spun on its axis so the wavy line blurred into one perfect continuous spiral like there was infinity waiting for the poor monsters too.

The plan was dispersal. The plan was to explode out and rain down numbers and safety on the only lost child we knew. Through the big windows of the rec hall, Test was tossing flashlights to Buddies and gesturing toward the wilderness. Through another window the remaining Buddies were setting up pillow forts and tents and lanterns for a makeshift camping adventure.

I ran for the petting zoo. I knew she would've started at the broken fence where the deer escaped. Everyone else was sticking to the roads and the paths and looking around the lake and they were all in a light different than my own. But I had to start from the beginning; I had to start where she would have started, in case we missed something.

My light was the barn light. The one that shone down on the broken fence where only a stupid kid with a hero complex would go. So I went.

I told myself to think like a kid.

Think like a hero child.

What would Charlie do?

I ran.

For hours and days and years I ran. I moved between trees and over frozen puddles and cold branches and around the voices calling her name; I moved with the wind; I moved always forward. All of the spots we'd already checked were checked again and again because now we knew she was close.[31] The other voices ricocheting around the afternoon knew it too. The voices were fueled; they were unshakable beacons.

I sprinted down the trail toward the barn before bursting into

---

31 We knew she was close because she had to be. That was the only acceptable truth: she was close; she would be found.

the clearing where it sat against the tall, frozen grass. The barn was exactly how we'd left it but it was completely changed, just like everything else. Like the world was broadcasting through a high-definition filter of potential. Everything was radiant. Everything was a clue. All because of that one EKG beep—the one nobody is ever sure they hear. The one that cuts through all the noise in the world.

"Lump?" I yelled. I pressed my ear against the barn doors and listened. Inches away, the other baby deer were curled up warm and safe, surrounded by a cast of chickens, goats, and at least two teacup pigs. I pounded on the wooden door, rattling it against its old hinges.

One of the animals—probably one of the pigs—let out a startled crying sound and started making noises. I called her name again. I closed my eyes and tried to shut out all of my senses except for hearing. I waited to hear her say something back; I waited to hear her shush the animals; I waited to hear the metal *click* of the door's lock being thrown open.

The only thing I could hear were the sounds of the search party off in the woods. I kept moving.

I cut through the snow.

I barreled through the cold.

Unlike Prufrock, I affected.

At some point it rained. The only time I stopped was when I checked my phone to see if anyone else had called with any new information and to catch my uncatchable breath. There were no messages, so I called her.

Voicemail.

I moved.

By five in the evening, the sun was beginning to sink behind the western trees while voices echoed across the woods, calling out to the missing child. The night sky was clawing its way up as the day disappeared.

October twentieth was unstoppable; the save had to be in the day, whatever was left of it.

She had to be found before the sun sank and declared her missing. Because survival rates plummet when more time passes. Getting to her before the sun disappeared meant defying the headlines that would read, "Local Girl Missing For Second Day."

I told myself to think. To focus. To step back from it all to see the bigger picture. The last shreds of daylight were all but gone; the freezing rain had stopped but had settled into a glass coat over the world.

"Fuck you, asshole," I said to myself. "Fuck you, think. Think."

I thought of the rope wall; I ran.

The deeper I went, the darker the sky turned. The stars faded in a billion at a time and the world went further into pitch oil, stampeding through the remnants of the day. I chased the light and couldn't stop the color bleeding from the sky.

The fence around the rope wall rattled in the crisp evening air because I kept rattling it and cursing at it. It was locked because we had made sure we locked it and it was covered in barbed wire to keep less resourceful youths than ourselves out.

I flung my coat over a section of the brownish barbed wire. Without my coat but still wearing a hoodie, a long-sleeved thermal undershirt, and a referee T-shirt, as well as a hat and gloves, the air still felt like a frozen hurricane hitting every inch of my body.

At the top I could see the world, but it was getting too dark.

Lights were beginning to show up: light from the cabins click-ing on, light from the dingy yellow utility bulbs, a lazy green light swooping in slow circles above the trees, flashlights through the pines, stars struggling against the night.

I focused on the laser dot in the center of my mind. The swirl-ing nexus of a whirlpool. The cherry ember of a Winchester cigarette against an infinite blackness. I opened my eyes.

"Holy shit," I said and looked above the trees at the dim, swooping light. The dead light from the airfield that hadn't worked in ages. The one right next to the windsock Lump had seen that was still snapping back and forth.

I ran.

# FORTY-FOUR:
# ELEPHANT SHAPES

IT'S LATE SPRING AND WE'RE sitting on Freddie the 2002 Mercury in the immense parking lot at O'Hare waiting for Grandma to land, and from the middle of the sky to the horizon the blue is mottled with planes.

Charlie's on his third cigarette of the hour.

"You ever think about what makes your heart beat?" he asks me out of nowhere, out of the cloud of nicotine smoke he's bathed in. I'm reclined against the hard, smooth glass of the windshield and Charlie is laid out across the roof, cigarette pointed to the sky, resting between his fingers. "Like there's something that keeps it going. And," he says, rolling to his side to face me, making the roof of the car pop, "you had a first heartbeat. Think about that: you had a *first* heartbeat. Like there was a time before your heart ever beat, and then—" He swipes his hand, sending a thin line of smoke spiraling up to the planes.

"So does everybody," I say. "A first heartbeat."

"Exactly. And it's fucking wild. All of these people landing in all these planes, all of them had a first heartbeat and all of them'll have a last."

And I'm thinking the same thing, except I was imaging the planes in the distance as flying away instead of getting closer. Every once in a while, if we don't say anything for long enough, Charlie asks about beating hearts. He's done it before and he'll do it again because there's still a year before we burn down a bowling alley.

I want to ask him why he thinks the planes are landing instead of flying away but I don't because it's always been easier for him to ask weird, oblique questions than it is for me. And I think, if we had never seen the car beneath us or anything like it and we were blind, it would feel different to both of us. If asked, Blind Charlie would say that the car was a hollow sheet that led to a downward slope. And if Blind Moses was asked, he'd say it was all hard skyward incline. Beneath both of them, though, "Sympathy for the Devil" by the Stones is playing.

It's one of the first times I notice that Charlie and I have truly inherent fundamental differences. All these years and it never occurred to me just how differently we see things.

How we'll always see things differently.

Even after we'd blown up at each other, I'd never thought that we were really, truly different people.

After all, we were each other's other half.

# FORTY-FIVE: . . . AND AROUND

IT WAS FARTHER TO THE airstrip than it seemed, and there was no clear path. Each time it felt like I was headed straight for the green light I found myself turned around and trying to reorient myself. The sun couldn't reach all the way through the trees, but it wanted to.

The airfield looked like an abandoned airfield because it was one. I came through the trees by an old, blasted-out logger road that dumped out to a landing strip littered with tires and mangled pieces of metal that looked like they were dripping with tetanus. I could see straight through what was left of the small hangar, and at the far end of the property there was a small pillbox guard station with a sixty-foot tower climbing from its roof. On top of the tower there was the swooping green light.

I cupped my hands around my mouth and yelled her name. When she didn't answer I tried calling her real name.

"Allison!"

Her real name echoed back to me.

"Sorry I called you Allison," I said. Then, "Lump?"

More nothing. Just ghosts of sound. I jogged down the dilapidated airstrip, checking around the piles of tires for anything that might help. I checked the hangar.

"Lump!" I called. My voice banged off the rusty walls. Aside from the stacks of old newspapers and burnt-out oil drums, the hangar was gutted. Out of the corner of my eye, I could see the hangar as only Lump would see it: filled with streamers and golden light, one mighty plane fueled to travel around the world.

My breath burned in my chest and my legs shook like cowards as I ran to the guardhouse. I pulled my phone out to check for messages, but it was dead.

I tried the big, locked door before pressing my hands against the squat building's glass and peering in. At first I didn't see anything, just a closet and an old control panel in front of an equally old calendar that showed a woman poking her head out from behind a mostly transparent shower curtain. And then I saw it.

"Fuck."

I ran to the other side of the building. There was a hole in the wall where something forever ago had punched through. On the inside, though, there were fresh candy wrappers laid atop a *FOUND* poster.

I shoved my shoulder against the hole and tried to squeeze through, but it was impossible for anybody other than a child.

While the guardhouse wasn't huge, there was a smaller door inside of it that was closed.

"Lump?" I called while I circled back to the front and started banging on the glass. "Are you in there? Lump?"

I went quiet and moved my ear to the glass. There were corners under the control panel I couldn't see, and there had to be something behind the door.

"Lump, if you're in there: don't move. I'm breaking the glass. I'm coming, okay?"

I pried a rock the size of a volleyball from the frozen ground.

"Okay, Lump," I said with the boulder cradled against my stomach. I swayed my arms and torso back and forth and gathered window-destroying momentum. "Here . . . it . . . comes," I said and underhanded the huge rock at the dirty glass.

The rock hung in the air. It floated in lazy thousand-frames-per-second slow motion until it hit the glass and obliterated it. I let one sharp puff of air go and climbed through. I didn't hear my feet crunching over the broken glass and I didn't feel my palms cut on the window frame because I was trying to look everywhere at once and I kept picturing worse scenarios:

We'd missed the hole where she'd fallen into the lake.

She was wandering farther and farther into the woods, away from us and warmth and safety, with winter screaming closer every minute.

She had found the bears she wasn't afraid of.

Someone had found her, and this someone had taken her.[32]

I looked under the control panel; I opened the small door and of course she wasn't there because it was just a broom closet filled with mouse shit and cigarette butts; I looked at the calendar for clues. I blinked hard and the poster was still on the ground. It didn't disappear or shimmer away like a dream trying to be remembered.

There was another code written on the paper. Another expanse of seemingly random numbers.

---

[32] I focused on her finding a bear. I focused on the bear roaring at all the things that a child like Lump was too naïve to be afraid of. The bear was protecting her until we found her.

*711 627 4310 913 915 519 3626*

Below the code it looked like she'd written a note to herself. It said, "Up down equal. How many X."

And when I shook the candy wrappers off to read it better, the goddamn poster still didn't disappear like a bad dream because I was awake and there was blood on the picture of the deer. Just a few smudged fingerprints, but unambiguously blood all the same.

I felt carved out. It was that empty sensation in your gut that reaches out and makes your palms and fingertips cold and feels like maybe you forgot to put all the bones in your feet. It was cold outside of me and it was cold inside; early-evening, Midwest-October cold, and the trees were bare, inky shadows against a pink, billowing sky that was just a painting in front all of the unlimited space full of dead stars. I was cold. I was hot. I was all there and I was not there at all.

The numbers refused to make themselves understood.

I couldn't stop my breath speeding up and the childishly impotent frustration that shuts you up because if you talk your words are going to come out cracked and staggered because you're too busy trying not to cry or scream.[33]

There was a metal control box on the wall. The rusty lever sticking out of it, ending in a faded red rubber tip, had been pushed up. The only part of the lever that wasn't rusty was a small semicircle at that bottom that was a clear, unvarnished silver. My hand pulled the lever down and, outside, the lazy green

---

33 Panic is one of only a handful of innate human emotions.

light clicked off. My hand pushed it back up and the light came back to life.

I unlocked the door and stepped out. Everything felt disconnected and upside down and heavy. My legs decided that I needed to sit down.

"She's probably dead. Or she's about to be," Charlie said, sitting next to me. He took a pull from his cigarette before offering it to me.

I waved it away.

"We have to talk, Charlie. About me and you."

"I know," he said, looking off into the middle distance the way I always imagined he would when we had this talk.

"We weren't good together. Something broke between us and it never got fixed."

"I know," he said again, lacking the devastating rebuttal I was always certain he'd have.

"I hated you so much of the time. As much as I loved you, I hated you too."

Charlie nodded and took a deep drag on his cigarette.

"We were toxic. You were reckless. I was always the one left to pick up whatever mess you made. I was always the one left standing because you were always so confident that I'd get back up. Pull some stupid, dangerous shit: let Moses deal with it. It's okay, he's family and he's bulletproof."

He raised his hand. "Can I say something?"

I smiled, even though I was terrified of what he'd say. "Yeah."

"We're going to have this conversation for a long time. But first: I have good news. Give me your hands," he said, placing the cigarette in his mouth.

"I don't have time for this, Charlie."

"Would you just give me your hands?" he said around the Winchester like I was being an unreasonable asshole.

I held my hands out, palms down, and he shook his head, puffing air out of the corner of his lip, and said, "Other way."

"I have to find her, man."

He nodded and smiled with the corner of his lips and blood started trickling down his forehead. It started as a single bead that lolled down his brow, around the concave of his eye, and worked its way around the groove of his mouth, and when it dripped off his head it fell on my gloves. He took my hands. The blood kept flowing until it covered his face like a mask.

Everything but his eyes; they were clear, and when mine connected with his, he said, "Then go find her," right as he dug his thumbs into my bleeding palms.

I sucked air into my mouth and swung my hands in front of my face, spattering blood onto my cheeks. My gloves were soaked through with red and there were still tiny slivers of shattered glass sticking out of the dark fabric.

I would need stitches across my palms and wrists, and I knew they'd heal to look like brackets.

The sun was fifteen minutes lower in the sky than I'd remembered it being. In the non-wind I could hear the faraway voices of the search party calling out for her; the only other noise was the hum from the green light spinning around a hundred feet above me.

I pulled my gloves off and looked at my raw hands and after two deep breaths I made fists as tight as I could. It was like grabbing two live wires: white pain exploded outward like the universe being Big-Banged and after the red blur faded around my vision everything went unfathomably vibrant.

"*Think*, you fucking asshole."

Nothing but the faraway voices and the hum of the light spinning around. Faraway voices and green light. Nothing else. Nothing but green light bouncing off the snow and faraway voices looking for Lump, who wandered off to save a hurt and scared baby deer named Harriet Tubman.

I went to dig my fingers into my palms again but stopped.

"No fucking way," I said, digging the code sheet out of my pocket. "You fucking idiot, no way." I pulled her last scribble out, the one that said "Up down equal. How many X." It wasn't a note. I read the first code. The first number in the sequence told you whether to count up, down, or stay equal—zero to four meant down, five meant equal, six to nine meant up. The second number was how many, whether up or down. The last was where to start. It was just a stupid roundabout number to letter cypher.

*112 518 447 9826 55 3119 421*
*A R C H E R Y*

I read the next one, the one we'd found at the archery range:

*6225 59 7315 56 2211 11318 91226 32226*
*A I R F I E L D*

Under each of the coded numbers on the *FOUND* poster, I wrote the corresponding letter.

B
I
G
N
E
S
T

I stood up fast enough to make my head swim and ran back into the guardhouse, skittering to a crouching stop in front of the hole. Off in the distance, sitting at the top of the tree line, there was a huge brown-and-black nest.

Below it, halfway between me and the trees, there was a strange puddle of light. I blinked and the box was behind me; I blinked and I was at the strange puddle of light that wasn't light at all but a dirty, discarded *LOST* poster.

A hundred yards away there was an orange square stuck to a low pine branch, just visible in the fading light.

As I ran, so did the nighttime wind; it picked up and numbed my hands and face. I shoved the *FOUND* poster in my pocket and looked for the next one.

I yelled her name and I swear, for just a second, the world listened. The wind went quiet and I could almost see the words swelling and pushing through the forest, demanding to be heard and felt but, more than that, demanding color into the bleak expanse.

The next one was sticking out of a log, lower than the rest. I followed its trajectory.

"Lump!" I said.

"Lump!" I said.

"Lump!

"Where are you?

"Please.

"Please, Lump, where are you?"

I looked and I looked and I looked and I was afraid to move too far in any direction because moving meant risking the already thin and fading cosmic radio signal. Moving meant risking the footing in the avalanche; the grip on the orange ring while the ship plummets under the cold water.

I closed my eyes and turned my head to the side and I focused on hearing everything in the world because she had to be in that everything somewhere.

The wind rattling the trees; my breath coming out hot and sharp; my heart; the dead leaves under my feet; crying.

A whimper; soft and young and a million miles away, but a living whimper.

"Lump?"

The sound ignited my feet and I ran into the wind, following the noise.

"Lump!"

The wind answered and I shook my head like it would shut the world up. I listened. And I listened. And I heard it.

I moved.

The slice of color stuck in the low branches of the tree made it seem like part of the sunset had caught itself on the tree's outstretched fingers. The neon-pink piece of paper with the drawing of the deer flapped against the breeze. This one was *FOUND*.

"Lump! Where are you? Lump! It's okay, I'm here!"

I grabbed the flyer and the adrenaline turned my eyes into

radar, into sonar, into infrared, X-ray. I demanded the color flyers into my vision. I told the stars that were hiding themselves away behind the pinks and reds and golds that I needed the color here. Here. Not there.

Twenty yards away, half in the dirty snow and torn up, was the next one. One of the original *LOST* flyers.

It was covered in mud but the orange color on it blasted defiantly out from the ground. The crying was louder, closer, and it sounded sick.

"Lump!"

And I knew.

I knew where she was.

Thirty feet away I could see an incline that went up six or seven feet and was covered by a felled spruce that made for a makeshift shelter and I knew she was in it because there was no other cover for a hundred yards and I could hear her. I dodged around the crater left by the ripped-up base of the tree and slid down.

She was curled up atop the spiral center of a muddy galaxy of bruise-colored *LOST* and *FOUND* flyers. I locked my eyes on hers. I couldn't see her coat anywhere and her ears were whitish blue because her hat was somewhere else altogether.

"Lump," I said, edging in under the branches. "Where's your coat?" Her right hand was wrapped snug around her body midhug, but the other one was stretched palm-out. Her Amelia Earhart shirt was muddy and torn but you could still see the image of the famous pilot waving to an unseen crowd.

Her eyes didn't follow mine as I inched closer.

"Lump? *Lump?*" My coat kept snagging on the branches of the tree. Every time I tried to reach in and grab her hand, my coat would catch and I'd be pulled back. "Fuck—I mean—sorry—come *on*," I said pulling my jacket off. "It's okay, Lump, I'm here. I'm right here."

I started talking under my breath so she couldn't hear me: "Please, fucking god*dam*mit, please be okay.

"I'm coming, Lump. Hey, listen: say something, okay?"

I couldn't get my stupid goddamn coat off because my hands didn't want to work the way I needed them to. When I finally had ripped my coat off to the waist, I heard the crying again.

It was the single sweetest sound I have ever heard.

I threw myself into the tangle of sharp branches, wedging through the ones thin enough to wedge through and trailing my coat behind me.

Her color was off—blue in all the places you expect someone to be blue when they're supposed to be pink—but the crying was there, just past the veil of green pine.

She cried again and I was made of light and air and hope; I was the white knight, the survivor climbing from the wreck to save the other passengers.

But her lips were wrong.

The cry lingered, tapering off into an almost buzzing sound, and her lips didn't move to the sound. Like her audio was off.

"Lump?" I said.

I broke through and as she filled my vision I saw her coat. It was next to her, not on her shoulders or her arms or on her back, but next to her wrapped around the crying deer with a twisted, bloody leg. The deer made a braying noise and nuzzled closer to the girl, licking at the Band-Aids on her cheek and ear.

"Lump? You didn't give your—"

Her eyes were glass.

Her lips were purple blue.

"No. *No. Fucking* no—what were you thinking?" I said, pulling her toward me and throwing my coat over her. Her shoulders were sharp even under my puffy coat, but I rubbed my hands up and down and up and down like I was trying to start a fire.

I felt for a pulse.

"Lump: listen to me: come on now."

I pulled my coat back and laid my hands across her chest, pumping them up and down. I listened for breath.

Chest compressions.

Listening.

Chest compressions.

Listening.

I pinched her nose and tilted her head back to open her airway and breathed my air into her lungs to keep oxygenated blood flowing into her brain and vital organs. I compressed her chest less than two inches because of her age and at a rate of one hundred compressions per minute.

Again.

And again.

You repeat.

You repeat.

Then you start yelling. Yelling for someone to *please for Christ's sake please help* because you found her.

And you don't think anyone hears you.

And the baby deer bleats against her because you're screaming for help.

And you sit back because if you keep pressing her chest plate down you know you'll crush it.

And you stare at her.

You don't cry.

You don't notice the rip in your shirt and scrapes beneath it.

You don't feel anything because everything is mute. You try to say something but the only thing you hear is the clicking in your mouth that has run out of saliva.

Someone behind you is yelling that they found you. That they're here.

And, save for the single-tone whistle of wind through the trees, everything goes very quiet.

# FORTY-SIX: CHARLIE

BUDDHA EXPANDS, AND BURSTS, and the officer fires a round into Charlie's head and I watch the black-red dot appear above his eye and because I'm just a little bit behind him I feel pieces that belong inside of him land on me and I wipe my face with one hand because it's a reflex but even as I'm doing it I think, *Please don't shoot me too I just need to clear my eyes.* And then Charlie's turning but it's only because time feels like it's gone slow and really he's just falling but for a second he's framed by the fire and the lights and I think he's going to say something to me that makes everything make sense like it's all just an elaborate Charlie joke and the police officer is in on it and the people at the bowling alley are in on it and everybody in the world except me is in on it but then the officer starts breaking down because even he knows that what just happened was the last thing in the world that was supposed to happen but he manages to radio in for backup before screaming at me to get back down with a voice that is all cracks and rubble and I don't know what to do or what to say because already Charlie's blood is starting to get cold on my face like it's going to freeze in place like a mask like a shroud like a scarlet reminder like half my face is going to be a sheet of blood for the rest of my many many many years because I know I'm going to have a long life starting in this exact moment like I'm watching the violent birth of my new life as someone who was there when his cousin and best friend got shot in the brain and I'm always going to be that person and there's no way I could ever not be that person because how can you possibly hope to change after something like that something where everything changes something where everything you know is just gone and you were directly involved and you know that you are going to have to look his parents in the eyes and tell them what happened and how they might tell you that they forgive you but the fact is that from that moment on and for every moment to come this is you forever and ever and it will follow you and it will drag you down and you will see it in all of your corners until you are old and gone.

# FORTY-SEVEN: WAVES

WHEN SHE DIDN'T WAKE UP, I walked away.

I walked toward her cabin because my feet took me in that direction and it seemed as good a place to go as any.

I knocked on the cabin door even though I knew there was no one inside, and then I knocked again. There was no one: no Matty waiting in the cabin, no straggler campers hiding in the shadows. No one was going to answer the door—especially not Lump—so I opened it myself.

There were no games planned, no itinerary that involved running through the fields and learning about ecosystems or making hand-dipped candles or learning archery. The students, all but one, would eat and go home. I didn't go all the way in. I didn't need to. Instead, I edged in just far enough to feel the warmth of the cabin.

"Thank you, Lump," I said.[34]

Because I *was* thankful. In a stupid, sad way I was so thank-

---

34 Because I couldn't think of anything else to say. I should have said sorry too, over and over and over.

ful to her because somehow she'd reset my scales. Because somehow, even though she was just a little kid who hadn't been afraid of the things she should have been afraid of, she helped me remember that my heart is a muscle and not a machine since machines don't hurt the way mine did.

Machines are numb, and this was the furthest thing from numb.

I nodded to her ghost that I knew would follow me until I died and went to close the door but stopped because her shoes were still by the door. They were the shoes she had worn during the inside activities, not the boots she'd worn when she'd run off into the woods to save Harriet Tubman. They were in a small, straight line with the right shoe resting atop the left.

And I was thankful. But when I saw her shoes resting like they were waiting for her feet, resting like lonely frozen waves, my knees folded and I squatted and cried into my hands.

# FORTY-EIGHT: ANIMALS

SOMEONE SPRINTED PAST THE cabin.

Then someone else.

I looked up because why the fuck were people running? What was there to be that energetic about when a kid was dead? I dragged my hands along my cheeks and poked my head out of the door, ready to grab the next sprinty fucker I saw and yell in their face.

And I went to; I saw the perfectly coiffed tour guide running toward me and I went to grab him but he grabbed my sleeve and started pulling me with him, and he said, "She woke up."

And I started crying again.

# FORTY-NINE: FUCK THAT . . .

THE EMT WAS LOADING her into the ambulance and even though it was cold his sleeves were rolled up and he was sweating. I overheard somebody say that she'd been dead for three minutes.

The side of her face was purple and red from where she'd laid her head down and her one eye looked like glass, but her chest had resumed its rise and fall. For three minutes and maybe a little longer, I knew what it was like to be Charlie. I knew how he felt.

And for the first time in a long time, Charlie made a little sense to me.

# FIFTY: . . . AND THIS TOO

AS THINGS STARTED TO SETTLE down, as Test talked to the people who needed to be talked to, I dream-walked toward the back of the silently flashing ambulance. They'd bandaged my hands when she'd stabilized, when everything in the world felt like it was stabilizing.

Allison, who everyone called Lump because she was clumsy and who was trying to take her name back, was less than ten feet away from me, breathing in air that allowed her brain to fire off magnificent signals to her heart which pumped blood and kept pumping blood and kept her living and being Allison or Lump or whatever name she could ever want.

She was sedated and she was hurting, but she was stabilizing.

She had wandered into the cold and found her deer, and when she couldn't find her way home, I'd found her.

Fuck anyone who said otherwise.

Fuck the people who'd insisted that Charlie and I were hateful or lost.

She was alive and I was part of that.

I tried to figure out which song would fit. Which song would start playing in the movie as I walked toward the back of the vehicle.

And of course it was always going to be "Sweet Child o' Mine." The EMTs were talking with the police and talking over a clipboard a thousand miles away and I could hear Guns 'n' Roses's opening chords ripping into the sky as I reached out with bandaged hands, grabbed the vertical handle next to the ambulance doors, and hoisted myself up.

Lump was somewhere in a fog of semiconsciousness, wrapped up to her shoulders in a big blue blanket. The kind of blanket that all ambulances and hospitals seem to have an infinite number of; the kind of blanket my family was all too familiar with.

She was pale and an entire side of her face was thick with gauze and her hair was slicked back, but goddammit she was alive. The tubes running out of her arm, the beeping machines, they were all proof.

And she turned her head.

And her eye started to clear.

And she saw that it was me.

And her face crumpled. Even through the thick ambulance door, I could hear her crying and struggling against the machinery.

"Lump?" I said stupidly, because at first I thought she was just happy to see me, but the more she struggled and cried the more it became crystal fucking clear that she was a lot of things, none of which were happy.

It was a dawning, rolling anger that bloomed out from every inch of her.

My stomach dropped to my feet as I stood there on the bumper looking at her thrashing and crying, then screaming when the IV tore loose from her arm.

The EMTs didn't say anything as they pulled me backward off the vehicle, causing me to spin out and land on my ass. In the moment that the doors were opened and the EMTs were clambering in, I heard the nuance in her sobs and it was only six slurred and hard-fought syllables:

". . . supposed to be my friend . . ." over and over and more and more distant as one of the EMTs administered a sedative.

And I thought of the messages I missed. The clues she'd left that I hadn't figured out. The long, miserable hours she'd spent thinking she was going to die. And I realized she blamed me; I was the friend who wasn't there when she needed me to be.

Then the door was closed.

And I saw one of them climb into the driver's seat.

And then they left.

# FIFTY-ONE: FALLOUT

"CAN YOU HEAR ME?"

I think Test set a cup of coffee in front of me. He must have, because we were sitting in his office and there was a cup of coffee in front of me.

"I'm sorry?"

"I said: are you all right?"

Nothing felt real. Everything in the world was beautiful and right and everything in the world was teeth and claws. I picked up the cup of coffee with hands covered in bandages.

The TV in the room was on but it was silent, playing a tape off an old VCR. Even though the volume was turned all the way down we could hear the sound of the tape making a quiet hissing noise. Boris Karloff was in a silent, flaming windmill and the townspeople were waving their torches and pitchforks at him. The flames would take him in a few minutes and everyone in the town was unified in their hunt for the terrible monster. Just like Charlie wanted.

"Yes."

"Good," he said. He removed his glasses and pinched the bridge of his nose.

There were no sirens and no alarms, just the silent, spinning light of the ambulance somewhere miles away.

Test kept rolling her hat over in his hands. Under the telescopes of his glasses, his eyes were red and puffy.

"Did you call her parents yet?" I said. Part of me was convinced I was dreaming, that I found her and she never woke up. But then I'd catch myself and realize I wasn't dreaming, but I couldn't shake the fucked-up feeling that things were still wrong.

She was alive; she would stay alive.

So why didn't things feel okay?

He nodded. "Twice. Once right after the police showed up and again when she woke up. They'll be here soon. She's being taken to Bannister and her parents'll be here within the hour to get her things."

"You ever have to make that kind of phone call before?" I wanted to tell him that I've been there when that phone call, that radio call, is made. I know how hard it is.

"No."

Neither one of us said anything for what felt like a very long time.

"So what now?"

She was supposed to have been found, muddy and scared but otherwise whole. In the movies, this was where we were supposed to be celebrating. But she was still terrified and it still felt like I'd let someone down who was counting on me.

I would have taken on every bastard in the world wearing a

WARMTH shirt over the look of hurt on that kid's face when she saw me.

"Now?" He tossed the hat on the table and a thin cloud of dust puffed up into the shaft of lamplight angling in through the hall, a shaft made of dust and particles and time-eaten dead things. A shaft of light only visible because of decay. "Now we eat. Then we tell the kids."

The first emergency vehicle to leave was the fire truck. They'd left early when there weren't any fires they could see or fight. Then one of the cop cars left because there was no one to arrest.

The ambulance was the last to go.

After we'd all come spilling out of the woods in a frenzy of lights and shouting, the EMTs had taken her out of my arms. When they took her, her cold, stiff boots scraped against my hands and sent a bolt of pain rattling through my body like she was insisting I pay attention. And eventually they loaded her into the ambulance and bandaged my shredded-up hands. And eventually, after bandaging my hands, after she saw me, the ambulance drove away. It sank silent into the dusk, where, after a while, it got hard to distinguish the branches from the vehicle from the western sky because the last of the sun was so bright it made everything into a single brilliant mass.

I said, "She was my responsibility." I wanted him to say it.

The actors playing the townspeople were so convincingly livid that it seemed even though they knew Boris Karloff would leave the set, remove the makeup, and walk into normal, human life, some part of their minds had chosen to forget it. Like everyone was so desperate to be human and to be together that they were willing to burn the actor to death.

And I thought, *I get it.*

I get what Charlie was going for. Even if he could be a bastard, he knew the power of tragedy.

"She was a lot of people's responsibility," he said sharply. Like there was room enough for both of us in that tiny office.

I said, "When are her parents coming?" and the words sounded like Charlie.

"They'll be here. Soon. Sooner rather than later."

"But when, exactly?" I asked. I wanted to plan accordingly. Even though she was alive, her parents still deserved a shot at me. If the look on that kid's face told me anything, it was that the pain was only just starting.

"Listen, Moses, you know we aren't going to keep the kids here any longer than we have to. We're already in the process of calling parents and telling them their kids are coming home a few days early and why. They'll be on the road first thing in the morning. But I want *you* in a cab tonight. The sooner the better."

It was the opposite of getting punched in the stomach. It was like he reached through the fog and pulled my guts forward with both hands. I smiled at him with all the teeth I could muster.

"I just think I should talk to them."

He stared into the still-swirling column of dusty lamplight before shaking his head. Then he turned his head toward me and said, "I'm giving you one chance to shut up."

"What?"

"We had a camper almost die today. Sorry, no, we *had* a camper die today. And by the grace of something a hell of a lot holier than luck, she woke back up. What do you want me to say here, son?"

I couldn't look him in his giant, bifocaled, magnified eyes

when I said, "I want you to tell me when her parents will be here."

"No."

"Why not?" I said, somewhere between laughing and crying.

I focused on her parents, on how if I could just talk to them and tell them that I was responsible for their daughter, they would have somewhere to focus all of their hurt. They wouldn't blame their kid for running out into the night, they'd fight the asshole who was supposed to keep her safe and be her friend.

"Because I know what you think and it doesn't matter. Not right now, not in what this situation is."

"Please."

"Here's what happened: she asked to spend the night in the infirmary, likely knowing full well that her cabin would be empty when she asked to be excused. That, or she came back and found it empty. Either way, an opportunity presented itself and she took it. Do you know why Lump took the opportunity to leave?"

"I don—"

"Because she was an eight-year-old doing what eight-year-olds do. She wasn't thinking about who was in charge," he said. For a moment, he just looked at me. "And then you knew she was out there. Right outside of these walls, and you spent hours looking for her. Instead of asking for help and talking to us. And now you're going to try to make this about you and your little guilt complex. So what? I'm going to ask you again: what do you want?" He breathed out slow and hard through his nose. "Do you really think we didn't do our homework on you? I have final say in who comes in from your program, which means I read everything I could on you. Not just the big flashy headlines, but every little offhanded mention that showed up online. I heard your side of it, and I know what happened with your cousin, and I'm not going to let you try to steer this mess today. End of story."

Just focus on her parents.

Just focus on using the pain for something else.

My pulse was hammering in my temples.

"We snuck out." I waited for his face to drop and the rage to wash over him but the anger—the pure, white fury—never came. And neither did the forgiveness. "Did you hear me? We snuck *out*. Out of the camp. We left when it was our responsibility to stay."

I recognized the look that washed over his face. It was a fighting look. The one that always happened right before the judgment call. But there was something different too. Something I didn't recognize.

"Why are you looking at me like that?" I finally managed.

"Because I'm disappointed in you."

I racked the words "I don't care if you're disappointed in me" from the language center of my brain; without thinking, I breathed enough air into my lungs to load them into my mouth; and when I went to pull the trigger on them, I couldn't.

I wanted to say, "Who asked you to be disappointed? I didn't ask you to give a shit about me."

I itched at my chest, right over my heart, half expecting to find the Superman shirt I was always going to grow into.

He went on. "I'm disappointed that you are going to make this about you. Like that little pity monster in your guts needs anything more to jerk off to."

I didn't mean to say "Wow," but I did anyway.

"Do you really think you and your friends are the first to have snuck out of camp? Now you're going to sit here, right in front of me, and try to make this about you?"

"Don't justify what we did."

"I'm not justifying anything." He said it like I was being a stubborn asshole.

"She trusted me and tried to tell me and now—did you see her face? She's hurt. Bad," I said. I sounded like Charlie Baltimore. "If I can just talk to her parents, I can help."

"That's why I want you in that cab. I had a feeling you were planning something stupid."

I was too busy trying not to throw up or disappear to say anything back.

More than just not recognizing the look he gave me, I didn't recognize whatever it was that I was feeling. It was anger, but I didn't know what it was directed at; it was hurt, but I didn't know where the pain started or ended or ebbed or flowed; it was a feeling like being lost; like falling; like wanting to cry and not remembering how to.

I turned the volume up in my head as loud as it would go.

*FOCUS ON HER PARENTS.*

*FOCUS ON THE HURT.*

"Do you understand what I'm saying?"

I shrugged because I couldn't get words to come out of my chest.

"Stop feeling sorry for yourself; this isn't about you."

"I— What?" Of all of the things I was used to hearing from adults and judges and preachers, "Stop feeling sorry for yourself" ranked at the bottom.

I blinked at him and said, "Um."

He got up and poured himself a cup of coffee and, as he went to sit back down, he turned the TV off before flames reached the monster. He sat on the edge of the big desk and didn't put any sugar or cream into his coffee.

"Where was I?" he asked. "Right. When this is over, I'm going to write you an honest report and show it to anyone who asks: that you're stubborn, that you think you're above the rules, that you aren't a team player, that you'd rather fart around than be a productive Buddy, and, if they ask for something off the record, I'll tell them that you're a condescending little pecker-head. And that will be the entirety of my report."

Please just focus on their hurt.

Fuck, please.

For Christ's sake.

I wanted the TV back on with the black-and-white monsters. I tried to ask him to put it back on but nothing came out. Just silence. Eventually I cleared my throat and tried again. "Her parents are going to want to see me."

The dark TV showed our reflections on the convex screen because even when the lights were out and the power was cut and all the world was dark, there was still movement in the blackness.

"Why?" he said.

"Because I found her. Because I was on Lump Detail. Because I was her friend. Because she tried to get me to find the—"

"They're going to want a lot of things and they're going to want to talk to a lot of people and eventually they might want to talk to you. But that doesn't happen today."

"She called me. Before she called nine-one-one, she called me." I didn't look him in the eye when I said it.

"You were her friend and she was in trouble," he said, answering. "Why would she have called anyone else?"

Every time he tried to turn me away from her parents, every time he kept me from making the situation about myself, I felt like I was made of smoke. Like there wasn't anything holding me together except a thin outline that somehow looked like me and sounded like me but was really just a shape waiting to dissipate into nothing. Like a dead bug just holding shape and waiting to dissolve into the light.

What would Charlie do?

What would Charlie have me do?

He sat on the edge of the desk and his hairy, bare knee kept bumping into me. I saw him lean forward and place a hand on my shoulder. But his hand didn't go through me. It didn't swim through the smoke of me and send me twirling into spirals that would break apart around the low hanging lights. His stupid, awkward hand and his weird, uncomfortable knee that was exposed by his weird, uncomfortable shorts, if nothing else, insisted that I was solid.

"Moses, you have to leave. You understand that, right? Please understand that."

"What am I supposed to do?" I said, and before he could answer I said, "Where am I supposed to go?"

"You'll go to the police station to help them understand what happened. It will just so happen to time out that you'll miss her parents. They can come here and talk to me."

He looked at me. *At* me, not through me. He could see me. "Moses, I can't tell you that everything is okay and that there isn't going to be a storm riding in on this. I don't know who her parents are going to hold responsible. Me, for one; probably Matty; probably you; probably all of us. That's just how this works: they choose who to blame and how to deal with it. It's not up to me and it's sure as hell not up to you. I'll be sure to ask one of the lawyers that will be descending here in the next few weeks. I wish this had a different ending. I do. But you can't fix this. There isn't some magic set of words that makes this better. You stepping in front of the train doesn't help anyone." He paused like he was deciding on how to say his piece. "Except for yourself. And not in some enlightened, I-need-to-take-care-of-me kind of way. You self-destructing in front of that girl's parents only helps you."

I made myself think about Charlie. I pictured his head snapping back not-quite-immediately after the officer pulled the trigger on his service weapon. I thought about how he never told me his plans or let me in but how everyone in town rallied around the pain we caused.

But I thought about Lump too. I couldn't help it. About how everything was different now.

About how, unlike Matty and Michael and the rest of the world, Lump was my promised end-of-the-world delivered for all the days thereafter. She was the famine that starved all of my hate and guilt. The flames that showed me that I was flammable.

How every time Test told me to shut up, the pain in my chest flared up and made me look into its depths.

The more I focused on Charlie, the more this strange other pain flared up. This alien feeling that I never experienced after Charlie.

This was grief—true, honest grief—and this was the opposite of mechanical. Where I felt anesthetized and robotic over Charlie—where it seemed like there had to be something broken inside of me because I never cried over him—with Lump, I felt it all.

The human need to just hurt.

The need to hurt for someone other than myself.

I felt myself stand up to leave. The cup of black coffee was still steaming and Test was still there, ready to talk or listen, but I felt myself moving toward the door. I realized that, even though the desk lamp was on directly over it, the Mexican jumping bean hadn't moved once throughout our entire conversation.

As I left his office, I heard him say not to go far, that he was calling a cab for me.

# FIFTY-TWO: WE, THE ANIMAL FOUR

I WALKED THROUGH THE DOOR, under the "Nakwatuk" sign. All we could do was wait.

The camp felt different—like every single person there had the same thought process going on. Like everyone was part of the same shitty dream. When Matty looked up and saw me, the same sort of delayed, faraway recognition from the bus fell over her face. "Moses," she said. She was sitting on the stage; her face was puffy and Michael was holding her hand. Faisal walked out of the kitchen holding Styrofoam cups of coffee for them and his eyes were pink.

"Hi, guys."

The cold wind outside ushered me in. Matty strode over to me, her gleaming eyes pinned to the floor, pulling Michael with her, and hugged me. Faisal set the coffees down and came over.

"Hey, man." He didn't ask if I was okay or how I was doing. "Water's still hot in there; you want some coffee?"

I nodded and went into the depths of the kitchen to make a drink.

All of the rest of the campers had been rounded up and

brought to the cafeteria, where the adults would explain to them what had happened. They'd told us that the Buddies would be brought in later but that, in the interim, they wanted to minimize the overwhelming nature of the situation. We waited in the rec hall.

The four of us were sitting on the stage with our backs against the dirty curtain backdrop. My phone was plugged in next to me in case the cab company called, sucking in life from the current behind the wall.

"She didn't have her coat on. Lump, I mean. It was wrapped around the deer. Deer's fine."

"She gave her coat to the deer?" Matty asked.

I answered her the only way I knew how: "They were burrowed up in this nook under a tree. Hypothermia'll do that. It's called paradoxical undressing. When hypothermia starts to set in, a lot of people get confused and start taking layers off. Either because of the hypothalamus failing or because after the muscles get exhausted they relax and release bursts of blood into all the extremities. The person thinks they're overheating. But, then again, it was Lump. Maybe she's just the kind of kid that would give her coat to a fawn. And hiding in the nook, that's terminal burrowing. Sometimes it's called hide-and-die syndrome." I told myself to stop short of listing statistics for exposure deaths.

Michael squeezed Matty against his side and started chewing on the inside of his cheek. Faisal stared into his coffee.

"Do you know why I thought you recognized me?" I asked Matty. She leaned forward and looked past the wedge of curtain that had climbed up between us.

My hands were shaking and my pupils were huge.

"What?"

"On the bus. I thought you recognized me from somewhere else."

"Oh."

"Do you guys remember about a year ago when a couple of kids back home burned down a bowling alley?"

They looked at each other. They were tired and they were hurting but I needed them to listen just a few minutes longer. I needed my friends to listen.

"Okay. Do you remember when a couple of kids burned down a bowling alley with a bunch of gods on top of it?"

Something clicked with Michael. He pointed, bobbing his finger up and down in thought. "Yeah, I remember something about that. Happened a few suburbs south of the city. Something about burning nativity scenes or Mohammed or Buddha. Something. I remember my aunt being pissed about it."

"Mine too," Faisal said, staring into his coffee while the memories articulated themselves in his head. "Yeah, my aunt and uncle called the house and said that they were burning Jesus over in Guthrie."

"It wasn't just any Jesus," I said. "It was Rock 'n' Roll Jesus. Bought on special order. We stole him from a prie . . . sorry, *minister's* yard."

"That was you?" Michael asked.

"And my cousin, Charlie. They televised the whole courtroom drama on and off for about six months after. They called it a hate crime at first."

"Shit," Matty said. "I do remember something about that. But I never watched the courtroom stuff. I don't remember hearing about your cousin though."

"Yeah—yeah yeah yeah, there *were* two, I remember that," Michael said, still scanning his archived memories. "But the other one got shot. He died— Shit, sorry. I didn't mean—"

"He didn't die," I said.

"Wait, no, I remember watching some of the coverage when I was in the waiting room. When I was getting stitches," Faisal said to his friends, as if to verify the story. "There was the cop that . . . did it. And was giving his testimony. I remember him saying that he 'pulled his service revolver and fired a single shot, hitting the suspect in the head.'"

"Why do you remember that?" Michael asked him.

"Because it was fucked up. I remember thinking how fucked up it was that this guy shot an unarmed kid in the *head*. I kept watching and waiting for them to say the kid had a weapon or something but they never did. He didn't die?"

"You didn't see him in court because he was still at St. Anne's." I raked my hand through my hair. "That was before they moved him to Golden Hills. A long-term care facility. He's in a coma."

It didn't take long for the news to get bored with our story. By the time the facts had come out they'd lost their shine and luster and people'd stopped watching. They didn't want to watch my Aunt Mar cry about her son. People were a lot less interested in seeing Charlie laid up in a hospital bed with half of his hair shaved off and a ragged, zipper-shaped line of thick stitches along the side of his head. Not after the facts came out. Not after they stopped calling it a hate crime.

They especially didn't want to watch after it came out that it was a prank.

It's not that I didn't try to make them see us. They just wouldn't. And they didn't see a lot of things and they certainly never saw his eyes. I know because I tried to get them to film it and show it, but they didn't want to and neither did Aunt Mar. I just wanted one shot—one shot that showed the scar and the tubes and Charlie's eyes that you could only see if you pulled his eyelids up. His right eye is a milked-over, foggy placeholder; an eye not of a storm but in it. But his other eye, his left eye, is still so goddamn clear like it sees miles further than any other eye in the world.

I took another searing mouthful of the beverage. For a campground out in the middle of Nowheresville, Michigan, they had good coffee and blisteringly intense hot sauce.

"I didn't know the whole thing was supposed to burn. Charlie did. Charlie set it up. We had different ideas about what it meant to bring people together."

"Your cousin tried to burn a bowling alley down?"

"No. Not the bowling alley. That part was an accident, I think."

"And you didn't know?" Michael asked.

I felt that familiar twisting in my guts. The feeling that was equal parts hurt pride and fruitless, pathetic anger. "No, I didn't know. He even asked me if it smelled funny when we were on the roof that night. Wanted to see if I could smell the lighter fluid he was spraying on the pallets. Other than that, though, I think it was an accident. This is more of a community service situation for me than a team-building weekend."

"That's fucked up," Faisal said. "Why didn't he tell you?" he asked, knowing my story and asking about Charlie instead of saying he would pray for me.

"Because that was how he was. That was how we were."

"But the Jesus thing, that was on purpose?" Matty asked.

I answered the question I had the answer to: "It wasn't just Jesus. It was Jesus, Buddha, Vishnu, Lou Reed, and a Pakistani flag. Everyone always thinks it was just Jesus."

"Wait," Matty said. "If it was an accident and he was the one who rigged it, why are you here?" She asked the question I always thought she would, and instead of venom, there was only honest curiosity.

"I was still trespassing and I was the one driving the car. Test made it pretty clear that they wouldn't have let me around kids if I was a felon."

"The cop shouldn't have shot him," Matty said, angry *for* me.

"Officer Alan Powell," I said. Faisal snapped a look at me like he recognized the name. I cleared my throat. "I don't think he meant to. Charlie stood up when he was supposed to be on the ground."

"That's bullshit. That's what they always say."

"Nah, he did. He had his gun on me. And, honestly, I'm pretty sure he was about to shoot me. So Charlie stood up. I think he was just scared. I think the situation got way worse than he'd planned it to."

"He still shouldn't have shot him," Matty said.

It was hard not to smile when I said the outlandish sentence: "We were standing in front of a bowling alley engulfed in flames with a bunch of religious idols melting behind us to Guns 'n' Roses," but the words still came out shaky. "And the guy that shot him . . . he's ruined."

"They fired him?" Michael said.

"No, not at all. The department was very supportive. Lots of other officers saying, 'You did what you had to do' and 'It was an impossible choice.'"

"Wait. What was his name again?"

"Alan Powell."

"Al Powell? Like R—"

"Like in *Die Hard*. Trust me, Charlie'd laugh too. Not that this Officer Powell looked anything like Reginald VelJohnson."

"I mean, hey, a coma's not so bad, right?" Michael said. Matty bored holes through him with her look. "I mean, considering the—" He swallowed. "Sorry."

"It's not that kind of coma," I said. "He's a three on the Glasgow scale—he's not going to wake up, and eventually his parents'll have to make a decision about life support."

"I'm really sorry," Michael said.

And I said, "I'm not." And I said, "The worst part of it was when they told me that he wasn't going to wake up, there was a part of me that felt numb and there was part of me that was happy." And I said the word again, from the deep hot center of my chest: "Happy. How fucked up is that? Part of me was happy. And ever since, I haven't been sure I'm a human being with a beating heart because how could I be happy that my cousin was never going to wake up?" The words flew out of me like scattered black birds against a brilliant sky. "That's what fucked me up the most. But this? Lump? This hurts so much."

Whether it was the drink or the honesty or the night catching up to me or the new ghosts I'd be carrying with me, I felt my drums beating and I knew they weren't mechanical. In the middle of my chest, the muscle kept hammering away, loud and constant and human.

Like maybe the machine wasn't a machine at all.

Like maybe the mechanism to hurt and feel wasn't broken and never was.

Another sip and the door opened. Test stepped in. Despite the cold weather and his huge coat, he was still wearing shorts.

"Anyway. Matty: you asked about my life story. That's it—that's the one." I stood up as Test got closer.

"Moses," he said as he walked over to us.

We're always in the aftermath of the storm. We're always staggering from one disaster to the next. And at the same time, we are the storms in other people's lives. We are the disasters that lay waste to cities and anticipated apocalypses.

But we are also so much more.

I used to think that happy endings were just prologues for tragedy; that if you kept your eyes open for long enough, you'd see the tapered line where the shining moment ended and the grimy, black downfall began. And it's true: happy endings always precede tragedy.

But tragedy inevitably precedes hope. That's just gravity. The same way the fall always follows the float. What comes up will inevitably come down; the big secret is that what falls will always rise again. It's all a spiral.

Charlie ended my life when I was eight, but he started it too. Someday, I will be new again. I'll be new until I'm not.

And then I'll fall.

And I'll rise.

Then fall.

Then rise again.

Faisal's face contorted when the crosswind wafted over my cup. "What the hell are you drinking?"

"Home recipe. Nothing you'd want to drink. I'll see you guys. Let's meet up in the city when we're all back."

They nodded back at me like that was the most obvious thing in the world.

I stepped out into the lamp-lit night. A world that kept on existing beyond every angle of your pain's perimeter.

"Taxi's GPS was acting up—they called asking for last-minute directions. They'll be here in fifteen," Test said. "Might be a good time to get your bags."

# FIFTY-THREE: EVULSION

"MOSES!" MICHAEL SAID, calling from behind me while jogging. He caught up and smiled one of those sad funeral-smiles. One of those everything-is-fucked kind of smiles. "Where're you going?"

"Barn."

"Oh," he said. He was keeping up with me even though I hadn't invited him to come along. But I was hoping he would. I was banking on it.

"You all right?" he asked.

"Yeah."

"You're lying."

"Yep."

We were quiet for a stretch. The moon was bright enough that we could see how the trees around us were covered in names carved into their wood. The names were from always: ones that, according to their dates, were only carved a few months ago, right next to the ones that had long since turned into the trees' scar tissues. There were enough names carved into enough trees that, statistically, many of them were long since dead.

I didn't say anything because I was looking at the trees that were living testaments to the dead and that got so dense and complete that, as far as I could tell, they had to go on forever. And because I knew that the more I didn't say, the harder he'd insist on trying to help.

I told myself to think of Charlie. Even if I hated him sometimes, he wasn't always wrong. I could grieve for Lump's pain like a real, live person, but I could be like Charlie when I needed to be.

I just had to hold it together for a few minutes longer.

"That's okay. Not being all right," Michael said. He was keeping pace even though I was walking fast and with my hands shoved in my pockets and answering with single-syllable words. "So hey, Moses . . ." he said.

He stopped and expected me to stop too.

We were deep enough in the woods that nobody could hear us, but not so deep that we were lost. We were somewhere between the children and the adults and the winding gravel was dusted with snow.

Some of the names carved into the trees were higher up than others. They were high enough that when the trees were in full color or filled with green leaves or red buds they'd be invisible. It was only when the trees died for the season—when the leaves all fell away and the wood went gray and all the color dissipated—that the birds packing the branches and the nests tucked safely away in the highest parts of the ancient trees became visible. I stopped and turned toward him.

"How're you and Matty doing?"

"We broke up," he said, the way you'd expect someone to report on the weather. Like he was a machine. They were finally dealing with their apocalypse. "She's on the fence about it, but we broke up." He pulled a pack of cigarettes out of his coat pocket and shook one out.

"You smoke?" I said.

"I'm mourning my relationship," Michael said over his cigarette and behind his cupped hand. He took a long pull, burning a quarter of the goddamn thing down in one go. He held the cloud in behind puffed cheeks for a few seconds, nodding. And then bent at the knees and coughed until he almost threw up.

"When did you have time to buy cigarettes to start this new habit?" I felt like Test. I felt like a parent. I felt like Charlie.

"I bought them off a kid." He sounded like he expected me to laugh or give him a high five.

"One of the Buddies sold you a pack of Pall Malls?"

"No. One of Bryce's shit-ass little friends."

"What are you doing?" I asked him. Except I knew. I was all too familiar with playing the asshole. More than that, I was familiar with other people doing it too.

"Jesus, this is awful." He spit a thick wad of phlegm into the gravel.

"What are you doing?" I asked again.

"Fucking up. I should have bought menthols," he said, coughing.

"Menthols aren't the reason you're fucking up."

He brought the cigarette to his lips again. "I know." And he said it like me. Like someone who thought the best course of action was to give the hungry crowd exactly what they wanted. He'd be the asshole he assumed Matty thought he was. The worst parts of Moses Hill and Charlie Baltimore mixed together.

What I didn't say:

"Remember I told you about the guy that shot Charlie? Powell? And how wrecked he was by what happened? During his deposition he told everyone how he put his gun to his head every night since the night we'd burned the bowling alley and all the gods down. He'd press the gun into his forehead, right above his eyebrow—which he thought was metaphorically resonant because it's where he shot my cousin, who was also supposedly my other half. He said he tried to pull the trigger for three months and that he wanted the same dice roll he gave Charlie: coma, brain death, or miracle. He turned in his resignation papers after he pulled the trigger and found that the safety was on even though he swears he turned it off. My point is, the life he'd had before was gone and, in its place, he found something new. But that something new had a price tag."

What I did say:

"You take another drag of that and I'm going to kick your ass." He smiled at me but I kept staring at him; he cupped one hand and tried to start a game of Rock, Paper, Scissors. "I'm not kidding. There's no bluff clause or joke here; if you put that fucking thing in your mouth I'm punching your goddamn teeth out of your head."

The smile faded and his face changed. Sometimes people burn bridges because, after all, at least a burning bridge makes light for everyone else.

"It isn't up to you," he said, snatching the Pall Mall out of his mouth and pointing at me with the two fingers holding the cigarette.

"This is though."

"What *I do* isn't up to you. *That* choice isn't yours," he said, and placed the cigarette back between his lips.

My nerves still echoed with Evulsion. Powell had paid the price for his something-new, and so had I. Sometimes the world needs to be given something to come back from. Give them a fight they can win and they'll be warriors. Give them the end of the world and they'll make love. Give them the brink and they'll fight it.

I head-butted him through the cigarette.

No one in the history of head butts expects the head butt.

He reeled back and grabbed the side of his face like someone had just extinguished a lit cigarette with a flying head butt to his face. I launched myself forward again, going for the tackle.

In my head, Charlie was telling me to make sure Michael's trajectory was headed in the right direction. To keep him from paying the price for his new, battered life.

I'm not sure what happened next because I was staring up at the sky, the wind knocked clean out of me.

*"The fuck is wrong with you?"* he asked me. He had me straddled with my arms held down with his knees. Even after everything, part of me expected his hands to go to my throat; to match his handprints to where Charlie's brother had almost crushed my windpipe. He swiped an arm across his face and left a smeared line of blood up his sleeve. His eyes were wide; his eyes were open.

My head was swimming, but I started laughing because I hadn't expected him to be that fast and because he still hadn't done anything other than defend himself. I could taste the blood on my teeth. My breath kept hitching and I choked on the air but that made me laugh harder.

I was Moses. I was Charlie. I was both halves evolved into someone new. The best parts of Moses Hill and Charlie Baltimore mixed together.

Hopefully.

"You're crazy. You're actually crazy," he said, pulling his hands back.

Get them mad and they'll realize how much they care. Give them something they can triumph over. Give them a transformation they don't even realize is happening.

"Hey," I said, cutting the laughter off. "She can do better than you. You don't deserve her." I smiled. I relaxed. I didn't struggle.

Give them a choice where the only possible outcome is a life made better: go left, become the beautiful, human animal; go right, be the gleaming hero. Rig the game. Stack the deck. Make them pay attention.

He leaned into my face and didn't say anything for a moment. He pulled me closer by my jacket. He would hit me and Matty would leave him behind because she'd see Dalton in him; neither one of them would know he was baited into it and she'd leave and his heart would break but someday, a lifetime from now, I knew he'd find a version of himself built from the flaming wreck.

Or he'd unclench his fists. He'd let the blood drip from his face and fall wherever it was going to fall and let me be the villain. He'd walk away, not weak for bleeding but stronger because of it. Every drop of unavenged blood would bring him closer to the person he thought he should be.

He didn't growl anything or threaten me. There were no warnings. He just looked at me with his sad, hurt eyes before clearing his throat and spitting a wad of red out away from us. He pushed me back down, using the momentum to stand up.

As he walked away, I said, "Good choice," under my breath. The entire pack of Pall Malls was spread out on the path. Inside, just down the walkway and past the big doors and down the hall, the campers were hearing about Lump.

I sat up on my elbows and let my head clear. When the world

slowed down, I reached over and picked one of the loose Pall Malls off the ground and stuck it in between my lips, staring down its barrel. I lay back.

Right as I plucked the cigarette out of my mouth and flicked it, unlit, into the woods Michael crashed out of the door and back down the path. I could hear him storming up to me for fifty yards before he said, "What the *fuck* is wrong with you?" He kicked a tidal wave of gravel at me. "It's not about *you,* asshole. We're your *friends.*"

I wanted to tell him that that's exactly why it was about me because forgiving others is a skill, but forgiving yourself is an art. Especially when no one knows you need forgiving.

"Mike: that kid got fucked up because of me, okay? She was my responsibility." I said it as plainly as I could because I still felt like it was true.

"Get over yourself," he said. "Bad things happen, you fucking douchebag. That's *it.* You're not the only one bad things happen to, or is Lump not enough goddamn proof of that?"

I dug a piece of gravel out of the back of my head. I lay back and closed my eyes, picturing him going back to his friends covered in blood. Going back to Matty with a blood-spattered face. When I opened my eyes he was gone. I didn't know how much time I had before my phone buzzed in my pocket with a call from the taxi company, but it wouldn't be long. I also didn't know how much time I had before her parents arrived.


Harriet Tubman was asleep in the warm barn. She was cuddled up on top of the other deer and she had a series of bright green Band-Aids holding a thick swath of bandage to her leg. She was alive. She was safe. Her world was, at least for the immediate time being, apocalypse-proof.

I was sitting on the steps in front of the rec center waiting with my bags and thinking about what Test had said. About how her parents had already been through enough and how they didn't need me stepping in front of their unfolding disaster.

The ceramic Buddy was covered in water-logged, melting snow that covered his sign to the point where it was unreadable.

If I'd still been hallucinating, I would have seen Charlie on one side of me and Lump on the other. I was between living ghosts.

I imagined them fighting over me and I could almost hear them but I was too awake or too tired to make out what they were saying. So I imagined it: I imagined Charlie telling her that she was being a child on account of her being a child and Lump telling him that she was *eight and three quarters* and that the way to save the world isn't to make it hurt more, plus he wasn't even a real ghost because he was still technically alive. To which Charlie obviously rolled his eyes and muttered about her being a fucking hypocrite.

If I laughed at Imaginary Lump and Imaginary Charlie calling each other fake ghosts, I knew I'd break apart, so instead I just smile-frowned and let my eyes get hot and wet.

I imagined Charlie leaning over and saying something about how this kid could fuck right off, since what did she know? I wanted to look over at Lump and see what she thought but I couldn't because she wasn't there because she was wrecked in an ambulance, about to start her new and different life. Instead, I kept my head rested on my arms and imagined her not saying much of anything to Charlie which was somehow even worse than hearing her side of the imaginary argument.

It was like she was getting further and further away. Like the imaginary Lump wanted to yell something at me but couldn't. Like she wanted to tell me to just get in the taxi and leave.

"I don't know what to do," I said.

I looked to my left to see if Charlie was there but he wasn't either because he was in a hospital bed a million miles away with tubes running out of his all-but-dead body.

I kept my eyes on the tree line because there were no ghosts and no judges and no Test to tell me what to do. All I had to do was deal with whatever car came first: if the taxi came, get in, drive away, let them suffer in peace because maybe it wasn't all my fault and we're all entitled to grieve and hurt how we each need to; if her parents showed up first, open my arms, look them in the eye, and say I did it—that it was my fault and I was their daughter's friend, and let them focus all of their pain into one perfect, defined focal point. While they were searching for some kind of meaning in all the broken pieces, I'd tell them to get a blood sample from me because I'd been drinking—that, even if it didn't show up, there were plenty of witnesses who could attest to the fact that I had been drunk off my ass. To look at my texts that I'd missed. To look at my criminal record. And they'd listen to it all.

I just had to listen to Charlie one last time. Be selfish, one last time, and make up for how wrong things went at the bowling alley.

It was just a matter of waiting because the ghosts were gone. It was just me and my luggage.

I pulled my phone out and brought up my contacts.

I cleared my throat.

And I hit Call.

Three rings later, my mother said, "Hey, Super Boy!" and I felt my face and nose tingling and my throat catching and the hot pressure in my chest and when I didn't say anything back fast enough she said, "Moses? Are you okay, what's going on?"

"Mom?" I didn't try to keep my voice even.

"Yeah, sweetie, I'm here."

"Mom, I'm really not okay right now and I just need to talk to you and Dad."

Ten minutes later, the door behind me opened. I didn't look back to see who it was but as soon as I saw the bare knees sit next to me, I knew. Test sat down. I knew he'd be gone soon so I told my parents I'd call them back when I knew we could talk for as long as we needed to.

"Taxi called. They're pulling around the bend now. You ready?"

"Don't really have a choice."

"Sure you do. Just have to make it and live with it."

"Where are her parents?"

"Close."

I heard it before I saw it. Whichever car it was, it was louder than the late night Midwest wilderness. Test didn't know which one it was either, because he looked like he was figuring out whether or not I needed to be restrained.

The lamplight glinted off the cab's windshield. Nathan the groundskeeper was keeping his schedule because the dirty little streetlights around the camp's driveways were already on and humming. Test stood up and brushed his hands off on his shorts.

He waved to the big, clunky cab and walked over to it as it pulled up. He spoke to the driver for a second while I got my bags together.

Before I piled in, Test nodded at me—not like a dealmaker but like someone who, for some reason, had decided to give a shit about me. I set my duffel bag on the seat next to me. The cab was a minivan with a King's Ride decal on the side and the driver was a forty-something woman drinking a Big Gulp that smelled like Mountain Dew. She was poking around on the GPS, getting it back to the home screen. She leaned over and breathed deep through her nose.

"You smell like a campfire; I love that smell." The smell was in my jacket and in my hair. It was woven through every inch of me. When I die, I will smell like campfires and northern pines and winter come early. "Got any requests, hon?"[35]

"Requests?" I asked.

She held the old-school iPod up. "Makes the ride better for everyone, I think," she said, and winked at me. "So?"

I thought about it for a second, looked at her, and said, "How much classic rock do you have on there?"

Her face lit up and she moved her shoulders back and forth,

---

35 I've got requests, Charlie. I want to apologize because you never tried to hurt anybody. I've always had requests. And now I'm going to start doing something about them. I do love you. And I miss what we should have been. What do I request? I don't have to request that you and Lump stay with me because I'll carry you both forever. My request is a beginning that has already been granted. My request is to learn from my ghosts: to do something I'm nowhere near 99.999 percent sure will work because sometimes risking the fall is worth it. My request is myself.

mom-dancing in the driver's seat. "Honey, I've got it all. Creedence to Zeppelin, the Stones to Motown."

I started to imagine asking Charlie which song we should listen to, but it was Lump I saw sitting next to me. Lump, who was proud of me for getting into the cab instead of talking to her parents. Even if she hated me. Even if she never wanted to see me again.

"Skynyrd?"

"Got Skynyrd."

"'Tuesday's Gone.'"

And Lump smiled.

"You got it." As she shuffled through the iPod, she asked, "So what's the plan?"[36]

I gave her the police station's address and she hit play on her iPod.

We started moving, crunching over the snow and the rocks, warm in the music, and as we made our way up the drive I saw them.

The dinged-up 2007 Honda Odyssey puttering down the driveway was the most terrifying thing I'd have ever hoped to see. It was the fire crawling toward the prison-cell powder keg. It was the sixth desperate pull of the trigger. The eyes under the bed that remind you that there are monsters worth fighting.

Along the driveway, Charlie stood looking at me; he was thin, and he was wearing his hospital gown, and one of his eyes was cold and dead, and he pointed at them.

We pulled to the side of the narrow driveway to let them pass.

---

36 The plan is to know certain truths that I was too fucked up to see before, like: I can hurt too; I can miss people in my own way; I can care about things deeply; I am not a machine or a superhero or a miracle and that is exactly how it should be.

When they parked, I saw the stickers on the back windshield: a father stick figure holding a briefcase, a mother stick figure in a dress, and, next to the dog sticker, a little girl sticker.

The man who climbed from the driver's seat, at over six feet, couldn't have weighed more than one hundred and thirty pounds. Her father's hair was so thin that the light cut clean through it and gave him ghost hair, just like she'd said. He moved like there was cancer in his bones despite it being in his organs and his eyes were swollen, but he stood with cartoonishly good posture.

Every move Lump's mom made was brisk and urgent—every adjustment to her hair and shirt, every shuffling of her purse—like every second she was jolting awake and finding herself staring over the edge of her own endless abyss.

We started moving again.

Everything started moving again.

"Goodbye, Charlie," I said, under my breath.

She put the van in gear as we pulled up to the stop sign at the front of the drive. The CB radio fixed to her dashboard beeped, loud, but she didn't seem to hear it because she was looking back at me.

I watched Lump's parents disappear safely into the building. They'd have somewhere to put their hate, and if that somewhere was me, that would be okay. They could hate me because Lump was alive, and her name was Allison, and the world would come to know it. I could live with that.

Under the camp's welcome sign, just outside of the van, the muddy, graffiti-covered light above the camp's entrance flickered out.

# ACKNOWLEDGMENTS

Thanks, Mom, for the endless love and patience (even when I was nine and drove the car across the bank's parking lot while you ran inside, especially since I was definitely still young enough to get kidnapped). You're a saint, and always have been.

Thanks, Dad, for all the character building (car window, car battery . . .) but never being afraid to kiss us goodnight or tell us "I love you."

Thank you, Jess, for always being the big brother I need, and never being anything less than my biggest advocate in every aspect.

Thank you, Karen Olson, for being my first reader, my best friend, and my excitement translator.

Thanks, Seb, for being my other first reader and for putting eyes on "Charlie" (as well as everything else) from its earliest stages. Drinks are on me, bud.

Thanks for being as weird as me, Eric—I would have ended up being a boring asshole if it weren't for you. I'm glad we didn't blow up the neighborhood after digging up that gas pipe in my backyard when we were kids.

Thanks, Emilia, for sitting across from me at a steakhouse in Michigan forever ago and telling me that this was something I could actually do. To say nothing of taking my author photos and putting up with me since high school.

Thanks, Jillian, for knowing I was a writer before I did.

Thanks, Paul, for the deer and for being a creative sounding board since I was like ten years old.

Thank you, Thisbe Nissen and T. Geronimo Johnson, for being such pillars of empathy and creativity. Thanks, Scott Bade, for the same.

Thank you, Jennifer Kocis and Steve Chisnell, for showing me how to care about reading widely and writing creatively.

Thank you, Susan Paley, and Emily Dumas, and Dean Hauk—there are people in the world who would have never become readers without you. You're real-life superheroes.

Thanks to my family, for being so relentlessly supportive and for never asking why I didn't go to school for something else. Thanks for the endless supply of love and stories. Grandma and Nana, you kept us from sinking: thank you.

Thanks to Molly Ker Hawn, for saving me from working at the US Post Office by sending me an email in the frozen heart of winter telling me you wanted to talk. Bonnie-Sue was right about you: you're half editor, half lawyer, half superhero, and all badass (she was right about the mama moose thing, too). I don't think you'll ever really know how much good you do in this world.

On that note: thanks, Bonnie-Sue Hitchcock, for being a voice of support since day one.

Thank you, Sarah Dotts Barley, for taking a chance on me and for never telling me there were too many swear words or that any of the jokes were too dark. Moreover, thank you for bringing me into the Flatiron family—I can't imagine a better home for Moses and his friends.

Thanks, Noa Wheeler, for reading Moses's story early on and helping get it into the shape it needed to be in.

Thank you, Anna Leuchtenberger and Melanie Sanders, copy editors extraordinaire—I don't know how you do what you do (or how you do it so well), but writers like me would be lost without you.

Thanks, Bo Barley, for making sure the JAMA network doesn't come after me with torches and pitchforks (and for explaining tension pneumothorax in terms I could understand[1]); thanks, Natalie, for the help with Ambu bags.

Thanks, Keith Hayes, for the cover I never would have in a million years been able to design. It's perfect, and everything I never would have thought to make.

And finally, when I was seven or eight years old, a grizzled, well-read, tattooed, punk-rocking Lumberjack of Death from Detroit let me blast him point blank in the face with a baseball—just to show me it only stings for a minute. Thank you, Jimmy Doom, for teaching me to never be afraid of the pitch.

---

1. Namely, Mark Wahlberg getting shot in *Three Kings*.